All The
Crooked
Saints

Also by

MAGGIE STIEFVATER

The Raven Boys
The Dream Thieves
Blue Lily, Lily Blue
The Raven King

The Scorpio Races

Shiver
Linger
Forever
Sinner

Lament: The Faerie Queen's Deception
Ballad: A Gathering of Faerie

ALL THE CROOKED SAINTS

MAGGIE STIEFVATER

SCHOLASTIC PRESS · NEW YORK

All rights reserved. Published by Scholastic Press, an imprint of Scholastic Inc., *Publishers since 1920*, SCHOLASTIC, SCHOLASTIC PRESS, and associated logos are trademarks and/or registered trademarks of Scholastic Inc.

The publisher does not have any control over and does not assume any responsibility for author or third-party websites or their content.

Library of Congress Cataloging-in-Publication Data available

ISBN 978-0-545-93080-2

10 9 8 7 6 5 4 3 2 1   17 18 19 20 21

Printed in the U.S.A.   23
First edition, October 2017

The text type was set in Centaur MT
Book design by Chris Stengel

For David,
finally

COLORADO, 1962

I

You can hear a miracle a long way after dark.

Miracles are very like radio waves in this way. Not many people realize that the ordinary radio wave and the extraordinary miracle have much in common. Left to their own devices, radio waves would not be audible for much more than forty or fifty miles. They travel on perfectly straight paths from their broadcast source, and because the Earth is round, it does not take them long to part ways with the ground and head out to the stars. Wouldn't we all, if we had the chance? What a shame that both miracles and radio waves are invisible, because it would be quite a sight: ribbons of marvel and sound stretching out straight and true from all over the world.

But not all radio waves and miracles escape unheard. Some bounce off the ceiling of the ionosphere, where helpful free electrons oscillate in joyful harmony with them before thrusting them back to Earth at new angles. In this way a signal can leap from Rosarito or Nogales, knock its head on the ionosphere, and find itself in Houston or Denver, stronger than ever. And if it is broadcast after sundown? Many things in this life work better without the sun's meddlesome attention, and this process is one of them. At night, radio waves and miracles can caper up and down so many times over that in some unpredictable cases, they eventually reach transmitters and saints thousands of miles away from their sources. In this way a small miracle in tiny Bicho Raro might be heard all the way in Philadelphia, or vice versa. Is this science? Religion? It is difficult even for scientists and saints to tell the difference between the two. Perhaps it doesn't matter. When you cultivate invisible seeds, you can't expect everyone to agree on the shape of your invisible crops. It is wiser to simply acknowledge that they grow well together.

On the night this story begins, both a saint and a scientist were listening to miracles.

It was dark, true-dark in the way it gets in the desert, and the three Soria cousins had gathered in the back of a box truck. Above them, the bigger stars had been pushing the smaller stars out of their heavenly home in a pretty little shower for about an hour. The sky beneath was pure black all the way down to the greasewood and rabbitbrush that filled the valley.

It was mostly quiet, except for the radio and the miracles.

The truck was parked in a vast stretch of scrub several miles from the nearest town. It wasn't really anything to look at, just a faded red 1958 Dodge moving truck with a somewhat optimistic expression. One taillight was fractured. The right front tire was ever so slightly flatter than the left. There was a stain on the passenger seat that would always smell like cherry Coke. A little wooden alebrije that was part skunk and part coyote was strung up on the rearview mirror. The truck had Michigan plates, although this was not Michigan.

The radio was playing. Not the one in the cab—the one in the cargo area, a teal-blue Motorola unit taken from Antonia Soria's kitchen counter. It was playing the Soria cousins' station. Not the one they liked to listen to—the one they had created. The box truck was their broadcast studio on wheels.

They, their. Really, it was Beatriz Soria's truck, and Beatriz Soria's radio station. This is every Soria's story, but it is hers more than anyone else's. Although it wasn't her voice playing over the AM radio waves, it was her complicated and wiry heart powering them. Other people have smiles and tears to show how they feel; enigmatic Beatriz Soria had a box truck full of transmitters in the Colorado desert. If she cut herself, wherever she was, the speakers in the box truck bled.

". . . if you're tired of singin' only to swingin'," the DJ promised, "you'll find us after the sun goes down but before the sun comes up."

This voice belonged to the youngest of the cousins, Joaquin. He was sixteen years old, took himself very seriously, and preferred that you did as well. He was suave and clean-shaven, with headphones pressed against a single ear to avoid spoiling his hair, which he had oiled into an Elvis pompadour of considerable height. Two flashlights illuminated him like golden, premature spotlights, leaving everything else in purple and blue and black. He wore the same shirt he had been wearing for two months: a short-sleeved red Hawaiian-print number with the collar popped.

He had seen a shirt worn similarly in the single film he had managed to see in 1961 and had vowed to re-create the look for himself. A garden of soda bottles filled with water grew by his feet. He had a phobia of dehydration, and to combat it, he always carried enough water to moisten him for days.

After dark, he did not go by the name Joaquin Soria. In the mobile station that roamed the high alpine desert, he called himself Diablo Diablo. It was a DJ name that would have scandalized both his mother and grandmother had they known, which was the point. Truth be told, it scandalized Joaquin himself a little. He enjoyed the thrill of danger each time he said it, superstitiously believing that if he whispered a third *Diablo* after the name, the devil might actually appear.

Here was a thing Joaquin Soria wanted: to be famous. Here was a thing he feared: dying alone in the parched dust outside Bicho Raro.

". . . some more of that dancing and dreaming," Diablo Diablo's voice continued, "the hottest sounds of '62, from Del Norte to Blanca and from Villa Grove to Antonito, the music that'll save your soul."

The other two cousins in the truck, Beatriz and Daniel, raised their eyebrows. This claim of covering the entire San Luis Valley was certainly fraudulent, but Joaquin's interests tended more toward things that would be nice if they were true rather than things that actually were true. No, the station did not cover the valley, but what a kind place the world would be if it could.

Daniel shifted position. The cousins were knee to knee in the back of the truck, and because of this cramped proximity, Daniel's long foot couldn't help but unsettle one of Joaquin's water bottles. The metal cap burst across the floor, skittering on its rim as if pursued. The wires on the floor shrank back from the water. Disaster whispered briefly. Then Joaquin snatched up the bottle and shook it at Daniel.

"Don't break the truck," he said. "It's new."

It was not new, but it was new to being a radio station. Before the truck had been pressed into its current role, it had been used by Ana Maria Soria's brother's wife's sister's family to transport the Alonso brothers from painting jobs to bars. The truck had grown weary of this tedium and had broken down, and since the Alonso brothers preferred painting and drinking to lifting the truck's spirits, it had been left to grow weeds. In fact, during this time, it had collected enough moisture for a crop of swamp timothy and sedges to grow fast and thick over its roof and hood, completely transforming the truck into a wetland in the middle of the desert. Animals came from miles to live in this oasis—first a beaver, then twelve leopard frogs with their creaking-rocking-chair calls, then thirty cutthroat trout so eager for a new home that they walked to the truck across the valley. The final blow came when four dozen sandhill cranes arrived— as tall as men and twice as noisy. The chaos of this swamp kept everyone awake, every hour of every day.

Beatriz had been tasked with driving the animals away.

That was when she had discovered the truck beneath it all. Her slow restoration of the truck had evicted the animals so gradually that the new marsh hardly noticed it was being asked to leave, and soon most of the Soria family did not remember that it had even been there. Even the truck seemed to have been mostly forgotten. Though the wooden planks of the floor were still stained with rust-red circles from paint cans, the only reminder of its time as an ecosystem was an egg Beatriz had found under the gas pedal. It was enormous, hand-sized, mottled like the moon and light as air. She'd made a gauzy hairnet hammock for it and hung it in the back of the truck for luck. Now it swung to and fro over Korean War transmitters, third-hand tape decks, broken turntables and scavenged tubes, resistors and capacitors.

Diablo Diablo (*Diablo!*) crooned, "Next we're gonna spin a pretty little number by the Drifters. This is 'Save the Last Dance for Me' . . . but *we're* not done dancing, so stay tuned."

Joaquin did not, in fact, spin a pretty little number by the Drifters, though it did begin to play from one of the tape decks. The entire broadcast had been pretaped in case the station had to take off in a hurry. The Federal Communications Commission took a dim view of America's youth establishing unlicensed radio stations in their free time, particularly as America's youth seemed to have terrible taste in music and a hankering for revolution. Fines and jail time waited for offenders.

"Do you think they might be tracking us?" Joaquin asked

hopefully. He did not want to be pursued by the government, but he wanted to be heard, and he longed so badly for the second that he felt it was his duty to assume the first was inevitable.

Beatriz had been sitting by the transmitter, fingers hovered vaguely over it, rapt in her own imagination. When she realized that both Joaquin and Daniel were waiting for her to answer, she said, "Not if the range hasn't improved."

Beatriz was the second-oldest cousin. Where Joaquin was noisy and colorful, Beatriz was serene and eerie. She was eighteen years old, a hippie Madonna with dark hair parted evenly on either side of her face, a nose shaped like a J, and a small, enigmatic mouth that men would probably describe as a rosebud but Beatriz would describe as "my mouth." She had nine fingers, as she had cut one of them off by accident when she was twelve, but she didn't much mind—it was only a pinkie, and on her right hand (she was left-handed). At the very least, it had been an interesting experience, and anyway, it wasn't as if she could take it back now.

Joaquin was in the box-truck station for the glory of it, but Beatriz's involvement was entirely for intellectual gratification. The restoration of the truck and construction of the radio had both been puzzles, and she enjoyed puzzles. She *understood* puzzles. When she was three, she had devised a retractable, secret bridge from her bedroom window to the horse paddock that allowed her to cross barefoot in the middle of the night without being stabbed by the goat's head burrs that plagued the area. When she was seven, she had devised a cross between a mobile and a puppetry set so she could lie in bed and make the Soria family dolls dance for her. When she was nine, she had begun developing a secret language with her father, Francisco Soria, and they were still perfecting it now, years later. In its written form, it was constructed entirely from strings of numbers; its spoken form was sung in notes that corresponded to the mathematical formula of the desired sentiment.

Here was a thing Beatriz wanted: to devote time to understanding how a butterfly was similar to a galaxy. Here was a thing she feared: being asked to do anything else.

"Do you think Mama or Nana are listening?" Joaquin (Diablo Diablo!) persisted. He did not want his mother or grandmother to discover his alternate identity, but he longed for them to hear Diablo Diablo and whisper to each other that this pirate DJ sounded both handsome and like Joaquin.

"Not if the range hasn't improved," Beatriz repeated.

It was a question she had already posed to herself. The signal of their first broadcast had reached only a few hundred meters, despite the large TV antenna she had added to the system. Now her mind ran along each place the signal might be escaping before it got to the antenna.

Joaquin looked surly. "You don't have to say it like that."

Beatriz did not feel bad. She hadn't said it like anything. She'd just said it. Sometimes that was not enough, however. Back home at Bicho Raro, they sometimes called her la chica sin sentimientos. Beatriz did not mind being called a girl without feelings. The statement seemed true enough to her. "Anyway, how could they? We took the radio."

They all peered at the transistor radio pilfered from Antonia Soria's kitchen counter.

"Small steps, Joaquin," Daniel advised. "Even a small voice is still a voice."

This was the third and oldest cousin in the truck. His given name was Daniel Lupe Soria and he was nineteen and his parents had both been dead for longer than he had been alive. On every knuckle but his thumbs he had an eye tattoo, so that he had eight of them, like a spider, and he was built a little like a spider, with long limbs and prominent joints and light body. His hair was smooth and straight, down to his shoulders. He was the Saint of Bicho Raro, and he was very good at it. Beatriz and Joaquin loved him very much, and he loved them as well.

Although he knew of Beatriz and Joaquin's radio project, he had not previously accompanied them, as he was usually very busy with the matter of miracles. As the Saint, the coming and going of miracles occupied most of his thoughts and actions, a task he took great pleasure in and greater responsibility for. But tonight he grappled with a matter of personal importance, and he wanted to spend time with his cousins to remind himself of all the reasons to practice caution.

Here was a thing he wanted: to help someone he was not allowed to help. Here was a thing he feared: that he would ruin his entire family because of this private desire.

"Even a small voice is still small," Joaquin countered crossly.

"One day you will have become famous as Diablo Diablo and *we* will be the pilgrims, going to see you in Los Angeles," Daniel said.

"Or at least in Durango," Beatriz revised.

Joaquin preferred imagining a future in Los Angeles to a future in Durango, but he didn't protest further. Their faith was enough for now.

In some families, *cousin* doesn't mean anything, but that wasn't true for this generation of the Sorias. Even as the relationships between the older Sorias rubbed sand into pearls, these three Soria cousins remained inseparable. Joaquin was fanciful, but in this truck, they enjoyed his outsized ambition. Beatriz was remote, but in this truck, Daniel and Joaquin did not need anything more from her than what she easily gave. And everyone loved the Saint of Bicho Raro, but in this truck, Daniel was able to be simply human.

"Here. I'll check the range now," Beatriz said. "Hand me the radio."

"Hand it yourself," Joaquin replied. But Beatriz merely sat quietly until he passed it to her. There was no point trying to wait out Beatriz.

"I'll come with you," Daniel said quickly.

Back in Bicho Raro, there was a pair of twin goats named Fea and Moco who had been born under notable circumstances. It is common for goats to have twins and sometimes even triplets, so it was not notable that Fea and Moco were twins. What was unusual was that Moco was born first and then Fea's mother decided that she did not have the energy or interest in giving birth a second time in the same night. So although Fea would have been just as happy being born minutes after her twin, she remained in her mother's womb for months while her mother worked up the motivation to birth again. Finally, Fea was born. Her additional time in the womb, away from the sun, had turned her coat jet-black. Although to the outside eye, Fea and Moco appeared to be merely siblings or even unrelated, the two of them remained as close as twins, always attentive and fond of each other's presence.

This was the way it was with Beatriz and Daniel. As close as Joaquin and Beatriz and Daniel were, Beatriz and Daniel were closer still. They were both quiet on the inside and outside, and they both had a hungry curiosity for what made the world work. But there was also the closeness created by the miracles. All of the Sorias were gifted with the ability to perform miracles, but into every generation, there were born a few who were more suited to the task than others: They were stranger or holier than other people, depending upon whom you asked. Daniel and Beatriz were the most saintly at the moment, and as Beatriz wanted desperately to not be the Saint, and Daniel wanted little else, balance was achieved.

Outside the truck, the cold desert sky pushed up and out and away, a story without ending. Beatriz shivered; her mother, Antonia, said she had the heart of a lizard—and it was true that she had a reptile's preference for the claustrophobia of heat.

Although Beatriz had a flashlight tied up in the hem of her skirt, she didn't retrieve it. She was not remotely worried about the FCC, but she nonetheless did not want to call attention to their location. She had a strong feeling, in the way a Soria does sometimes, that there were miracles afoot, and she had been told, in the way all Sorias are told, that there were consequences for interfering with miracles.

So they walked in the near-dark. The light of the partial moon was quite sufficient to pick out the silhouettes of spiky bayonet and spindly manzanita and raggedy creosote bushes. Juniper released a damp, warm smell and Russian thistle tugged at Beatriz's skirt. Far-off light from Alamosa browned the horizon, looking natural from this far away, like a premature sunrise. From the radio, Diablo Diablo said look, said wait, said listen, here's a single you're not going to believe, a hot little number that hasn't gotten enough play from the big guys.

Inside Beatriz Soria's mind, thoughts turned busily, as they always did. As she and Daniel moved through the dark, she thought about the casual ingenuity of the portable radio they carried, and also about a time when people had imagined the night air was full of nothing, and also about the expression *dead air*. And now she thought instead about how really she was pushing through a crowded atomic city of invisible chemicals, microorganisms, and waves, the last of them detectable only because she held this magic box capable of receiving them and spitting them back out for her mortal ears. She leaned into these invisible radio signals as she would a heavy wind, and with one hand she snatched at the air as if she might feel them. This was an impulse that she often had, to touch the invisible. She had learned after years of childhood correction to reserve it for moments when no one else was watching. (Daniel did not count as someone else in this regard.)

But she felt only the slow creep of an approaching miracle. The radio's signal had begun to fray; another station was gulping a syllable here and there.

"Beatriz?" asked Daniel. His voice sounded a little hollow, a cup with no water in it, a sky without stars. "Do you think consequences are meaningful if we haven't seen them for ourselves?"

Sometimes, when a question is about a secret, people will ask a different but related question, hoping to get an answer that will work for both questions. Beatriz realized at once that this was what Daniel was doing now. She did not know what to do about the fact of his having secrets, but she answered as best as she could. "I think an untested consequence is a hypothesis."

"Do you think I've been a good saint?"

This was still not really the question in his mind, and in any case, no one who had spent even a minute in Bicho Raro would have possibly spoken against Daniel Lupe Soria's devotion. "You are a better one than I would be."

"You could be a fine saint."

"The evidence doesn't agree with you."

"Where is your science?" Daniel asked. "One piece of evidence is not science." His tone was lighter now, but Beatriz was not comforted. He was not ordinarily troubled, and she could not forget the sound of it in his voice.

Beatriz turned the radio slightly to reduce the crackling. "Some experiments only require one result for proof. Or at least to prove it's not responsible to perform them a second time."

Loudening static hung between the two cousins, and eventually, Daniel said, "Did you ever think that maybe we're doing it wrong? All of us?"

This, finally, was a real question instead of a hidden one, although it was not *the* real question. But it was too big a puzzle to be answered in only one night.

Further conversation was interrupted by a shudder in the shrub before them. It twitched and shivered again, and then a shadow roared out of it.

Neither Beatriz nor Daniel flinched. This was because they were Sorias. In their family, if you were going to leap at every shadow that suddenly appeared, you needed to plan on some fine calf muscles.

The roar resolved into a great, hushing thud of wings, and the shadow resolved into an enormous bird in flight. It flapped close enough that Beatriz's hair moved against her cheek: an owl.

Beatriz knew many things about owls. Owls have enormous and powerful eyes, but these remarkable eyeballs are fixed in place by bony protuberances called sclerotic rings. This is why owls must move their heads in all directions in lieu of flicking their eyes from side to side. Several owl species have asymmetrical ears, which allows them to accurately pinpoint the origin of a sound. Many people do not realize that, in addition to possessing powerful vision and hearing, owls are very attracted to miracles, though the mechanism that draws the birds to them is poorly understood.

Daniel leaned close to turn off the radio. The quiet hurried around them.

On the other side of where the owl had appeared, distant headlights came into view. In a place like this, you could go all night without seeing another vehicle, and so it was with interest that Beatriz watched the two tiny lights travel from right to left. It was far too distant to hear, but she knew the sound of tires on the gravel so well that her ears pretended they caught it. She lifted her hand to see if she could feel the sound with her fingers.

Daniel closed his eyes. His mouth moved. He was praying.

"Headlights! Are you two stupid?" Joaquin had grown bored waiting for them to report and now called to them from the open back of the truck. "*Headlights!* Why didn't you say right away?! The FCC!"

Beatriz closed her fingers and lowered her hand. She said, "They aren't headed this way."

"How can you know?!"

"They're going to . . ."

She lifted a vague hand and allowed that gesture to serve as the rest of the sentence.

Joaquin sprang back inside to rip wires from the battery, then leaped back out and began to tear up ground wires with a great and fearful energy. But Beatriz was right, as she often was. The headlights continued on their distant path without pause, illuminating motionless antelope and clumps of grass. The vehicle was headed unerringly toward Bicho Raro. It was hunting not for a radio signal but for a miracle.

Daniel opened his eyes. He said, "I need to get there before they do."

There would be no miracle without a saint.

2

There were two people in the vehicle driving toward Bicho Raro that night: Pete Wyatt and Tony DiRisio. Pete and Tony had run into each other in western Kansas many long hours before. Not literally, but nearly. Pete had been hitchhiking alongside endless prairie, slow-motion counting the mile markers out loud four or five times an hour, when a big owl flew right overhead, making him jump a few inches. A second later, a car skidded into the space Pete had just been occupying. Tony had rolled down the window, peered through the cloud of dust and gravel, and demanded, "What's my name?" When Pete had confessed that he didn't know, Tony's expression had cleared. "You'll have to drive," Tony said, unbuckling his seat belt, "because I'm too high."

This was how Pete, a kid who had driven his father's sedan only a few dozen times since getting his license, found himself piloting an aggressively unattractive Mercury station wagon painted an overdone egg-yolk yellow. Tony DiRisio liked large cars. When he'd visited the Philadelphia car dealership to purchase it, he had brought only a tape measure and his checkbook.

He felt there was a permanence to a car that was over seventeen feet long and covered with wood paneling.

Tony himself was handsome as a cigarette. Currently, he wore a white suit and dark sideburns. Both had appeared stylish at one point, but by the time Pete met him, they were rumpled. He had been driving the Mercury for five days and driving himself for longer. He was only thirty-four, but he had lived all of those years twice, once as Tony DiRisio and once as Tony Triumph. After surviving a childhood too boring to repeat in polite company, he'd become a DJ at an easy listening station too boring to play in polite company. Over the past few years, he had transformed himself and the station into a household fixture by the expedient of bringing random housewives into the station to play their pick of the hour. He became a hunted man; Philadelphia women now sought him in grocery aisles and on neighborhood sidewalks, hoping to catch his eye. The local rag ran pieces analyzing the type of woman he was likely to invite: what they'd been wearing when discovered (shoes without heels, mostly), how they had worn their hair (often in rollers), and how old they'd been (usually over fifty). The headline mused, "Does Tony Triumph Want His Mother?"

Here was a thing he wanted: to stop having dreams of being laughed at by tiny birds with very long legs. Here was a thing he feared: people watching him while he ate.

He also missed his mother.

Pete Wyatt didn't know any of this about Tony. He was not an easy listening fan and had never been east of the Mississippi anyway. He was only a few weeks out of high school, a clean-cut fellow with dull brown hair and bright brown eyes and reasonably tidy fingernails. Although he was more than a decade younger than Tony, he had been born old, already a good rock to build a church from the moment he first rolled out of his mother.

He was one of those folks who couldn't avoid helping. At twelve, he'd organized a canned food drive and set a world record for the most pounds of creamed corn ever donated to the poor. At fifteen, struck by the unspoken misery of being a friendless child, he had saved up enough money to give every first grader in his old school a baby chick. A miscommunication with the newspaper covering the story had resulted in three Indiana poultry farms doubling and then tripling and then quadrupling the donations. Two thousand chicks had arrived in Pete's hometown, one for every student in his school system, plus three extra. He'd trained those three to do tricks for old folks' homes.

Pete had intended to join the military after high school, an army man like his father, but doctors had found a hole in his heart. So the day after he graduated, he'd packed up his shame into a duffle and started hitching from Oklahoma to Colorado.

Here was a thing Pete wanted: to start a business that made him feel as good as two thousand baby chickens. Here was a thing he feared: that this strange feeling in his heart—this palpably growing emptiness—would eventually kill him.

Colorado is a long way from most places. This meant the drive would've been long in any circumstance, but it seemed even longer because Pete and Tony, like a lot of people who were destined to be friends, couldn't stand each other.

"Sir," Pete said, rolling down his window several hours after taking the wheel, "do you think you could give that a rest?"

Tony smoked in the Mercury's passenger seat as the dusty afternoon followed the car. Pete had been looking for road signs to let him know how far they had to go; there were none.

"Kid," Tony said, "do you think you could get that stick out of your ass?"

"If the point of me driving all these miles was 'cause you were too high, and I've been coughing on your smoke for ten hours, I don't—I guess I don't see what the point is, then."

Some people find the effects of marijuana calming. Some people find it calms them, but they're offended by its usage. Still others are not offended but find it makes them anxious. And then some are both offended and anxious. Pete belonged to this final group.

"You always this pedantic? Why don't you turn on the radio?"

There was no knob. Pete said, "I can't. The dial's missing."

With satisfaction, Tony replied, "Damn right it is, because I threw it out the window in Ohio. I didn't want to listen to its whining and I don't want to listen to yours, either. Why don't you just point those lost-puppy eyes of yours right out the window and stare at God's country for a while."

This advice was mixed. If Pete had had something to distract him from the changing landscape, he might not have been as hard-struck by it. As it was, after Tony had concluded his smoking and nodded off to sleep, there was only Pete and the great outdoors. Over the course of the day, the landscape ran alongside the car, shifting from plains to hills to mountains to bigger mountains, and then, suddenly, became desert.

The kind of desert that is located in that corner of Colorado is a hard one. It is not the painted rocks and elegant cactus pillars one finds farther southwest, nor is it the secretive pine-furred mountains and valleys of the rest of Colorado. It is barren scrub and yellow dust, and blue-tinged, sharp-teethed mountains in the distance that want to have nothing to do with you.

Pete fell deeply in love with it.

This strange cold desert does not care if you live or die in it, but he fell for it anyway. He had not known before then that a place could feel so raw and so close to the surface. His weak heart felt the danger but could not resist.

He fell in love so fiercely that the desert itself noticed. The desert was accustomed to the casual love affairs of strangers passing through, so it cruelly tested his affection by raising a dust storm. Grit buffeted the vehicle, creeping in through the edges of the windows and drifting in the corners of the dashboard. Pete had to stop to remove tumbleweed and branches from the Mercury's grill and to shake sand from his boots, but his love remained intact. Unconvinced, the desert then encouraged the sun's full power to beat down upon Pete and Tony. The heat in the car climbed from double digits to triple digits. The dash cracked in the sunlight, and the steering wheel grew hot as molten iron under Pete's hands. But as sweat rolled into his collar, and his mouth dried out, Pete was still enamored. Then, as the afternoon got old, the jaded desert conjured what little rain it could manage from the sky just north of the Mercury. That rain rolled into a flash flood that dragged sloppy mud across the highway, and in the thin evening light, the desert let the temperature drop suddenly below freezing. The mud froze and thawed and then changed its mind and froze again. All this indecision heaved open a crack in the asphalt, which the Mercury fell into.

Tony woke with a start. "What happened here?"

"Weather," replied Pete.

"I like weather like I like my news," Tony said. "Happening to someone else."

Pete opened the door with some difficulty; the car was at an unnatural angle. "You steer."

He climbed out to push and Tony put his shoes back on before slithering into the driver's seat. The desert watched as Pete strained to free the Mercury from the gap in the road, heaving one shoulder against the rear bumper. The spinning tires sprayed a moist, cold layer of golden dirt onto Pete's legs.

"Are you even pushing, kid?" Tony called out.

"I am, sir."

"Are you sure you're not pulling?"

"We can switch places," Pete offered.

"There's a helluva gap between *can* and *should*," Tony said, "and I'm not eager to close it."

Finally, the Mercury broke free. Pete's eyes followed not the vehicle as it trundled forward but instead the varied and complicated horizon of the desert. The very last of the sun played over it and every stalk of grass dripped with honeyed light. His back ached and his arms were pebbled with goose bumps, but as he savored the view and sucked in big, juniper-scented breaths, he was still besotted.

The desert, which was not given to sympathy or sentiment, was nonetheless moved, and for the first time in a long time, it loved someone back.

It was not until several hours later, after night had fallen, that Pete worked up the nerve to ask Tony where he was headed. Before, it hadn't really mattered; it had been obvious they were both going to be sharing the same path for a while, since they had met up in the part of Kansas that went away only if you kept going west.

"Colorado," said Tony.

"We're in Colorado."

"Near Alamosa."

"We're near Alamosa."

"Bicho Raro," said Tony.

Pete looked at him hard enough that the Mercury swerved as well. "Bicho Raro?"

"Did I stutter, kid?"

"It's just . . . that's where I'm going, too."

Tony shrugged with only his dense black eyebrows and looked out the window at only the dense black night.

"What?" Pete said. "You don't think that's a coincidence?"

"A coincidence that you don't want to get out and walk in the middle of the desert? Yeah, it's a miracle, son."

Because Pete was an honest soul, it took him a long minute to process Tony's meaning. "Look, sir, I've got the letter from my aunt right in my shirt pocket. You can see it for yourself—I'm heading to Bicho Raro."

He fumbled it out of his pocket as the Mercury swerved again.

Tony took a gander. "This is probably your math homework."

It turned out that the sweat of several days of walking by the highway had smeared the last letter Aunt Josefa had written Pete. Tony didn't really care either way, but to Pete, the implication that he was anything but truthful, that he was a *freeloader*, was well-nigh unbearable.

"I'm going there for a summer job. My aunt visited there a few years ago. She lives up near Fort Collins now, but back then, she was in a, well—I don't know why I would tell you this, but she was in a real bad place and says they helped her out of it. She wrote me and told me they have a box truck I could have as my own, and they're willing to let me work off the price of it with hard labor."

Tony blew more smoke. "What the hell do you want with a box truck?"

"I'm going to start a moving company." As Pete said it, he caught a flash of the logo in his imagination: WYATT MOVING, with a friendly-looking blue ox straining against a yoke.

"You youths get such funny idears these days."

"It's a fine idea."

"A moving company's what you want out of life?"

"It's a fine idea," Pete repeated. He gripped the wheel and drove in silence for several minutes. The road was arrow straight and the sky was dream-black and every landmark was the same post with barbed wire nailed into it. He could not see the desert, but he knew it was out there still. He could feel that hole in his heart pretty acutely. "Why are *you* going to Bicho Raro, then?"

Here was the truth: Every morning before working up the nerve to go into WZIZ for another fun! fresh! friendly! broadcast, Tony drove across Philadelphia to Juniata and idled near the park there, where he could be surrounded by people who he was certain had no idea who he was. Many folks find this an unpleasant sensation, but for Tony, who felt he lived life under a microscope, it was a relief. For a few minutes he was Tony DiRisio and not Tony Triumph. Then he put the car in drive and went to work.

One morning several weeks before, a woman had knocked on his window. It was raining outside, and she had a grocery bag over her hair to preserve her curls. She was about fifty. She was the sort of lady Tony would usually ask to be on his show, but she was no eager housewife. Instead, she told him that her family had talked about it and they'd decided he needed to find the Soria family. Tony could see that they were all standing several yards behind her, having sent her as head of household to do the reporting. They knew who he was, she said, and they didn't like to see him like this. The Sorias were no longer in Mexico, so he wouldn't even need to worry about crossing the border. He just needed to start driving his car west and listen for the sound of a miracle in his heart. The Sorias would give him the change he needed.

Tony had told the woman that he was fine. Shaking her head, she had given him a handkerchief and patted his cheek before departing. Tony's eyes had been dry, but when he'd turned the handkerchief over, written upon it in felt pen were the words *Bicho Raro, Colorado.*

What Tony asked Pete now was, "You superstitious, kid?"

"I'm a Christian," Pete said dutifully.

Tony laughed. "I knew a guy who used to tell all kinds of hair-raising stories about staying out here in this valley. Said there was always strange lights—flying saucers, maybe. Said there were mothmen and skinwalkers and all kinds of critters out here walking at night. Pterodactyls."

"Trucks."

"You're absolutely no fun."

"No, there." Pete pointed. "Doesn't that look like a truck parked over there?"

Although Pete didn't know it, he was pointing at the very box truck that he had come all this way to earn, the box truck that was currently holding the Soria cousins, including the one he was going to fall in love with. As he squinted to see more, the rear door of the truck closed and the light went out. In the resulting blackness, Pete wasn't sure he'd seen anything at all.

"Lizardmen," Tony said. "Probably."

But Tony had glimpsed something as well. Not outside of himself but, rather, inside. A curious tug. He remembered suddenly what the woman had said about listening for miracles. Only *listening* wasn't exactly what he was doing right now. He didn't *hear* anything. He wasn't intercepting a sound or a song. His ears weren't doing any work. It was a mysterious part of him that he had not used before this night and would never use again after.

Tony said, "I think we're almost there."

3

Bicho Raro was a place of strange miracles.

When the Mercury scuffed into the compound, dust bloomed and died around the bumper as it lurched to a stop. The egg-colored station wagon sat among an odd collection of cabins and tents and barns and houses and sagging barns circled close to one another, dead cars run adrift in barbed wire, and rusting appliances sinking into the banks of the feeble water share. Most of it faded into invisibility in the night. A sole porch light shone from one of the houses; shadows darted and fluttered around it, looking like moths or birds. They were not moths or birds.

Before the Sorias, Bicho Raro had been barely anything at all, just the elbow end of a massive cattle ranch that had more in the way of fields and less in the way of cattle. This was before the Sorias had left Mexico, before the Revolution, back when they'd been called Los Santos de Abejones. When they'd been Los Santos de Abejones, hundreds of pilgrims had come to them for blessings and healings, camping outside tiny Abejones for miles, right up into the mountains. Merchants had sold prayer cards and charms on the road to those who waited. Legends had crept out of the town, carried on horseback and tucked in people's satchels and written into ballads played in bars late at night. Amazing transformations and terrifying deeds—it did not seem to matter if the stories were good or bad. As long as they were interesting, they drew a crowd. The impassioned crowd had christened babies after Los Santos and had raised armies in their name. The Mexican government at the time hadn't thought much of this, and they'd told the Sorias they could either stop performing miracles or start praying for one to save them. The Sorias had turned to the Church for support, but the Catholic Church at the time hadn't thought much of the dark miracles and had also told them they could either stop performing miracles or start praying for one to save them.

But the Sorias were born to be saints.

They'd marched out of Mexico under the cover of darkness and had kept walking until they'd found another mountain-edged place quiet enough to let miracles be heard.

That was the story of Bicho Raro.

"This is it, kid," Tony said, and climbed out of the Mercury with some of his usual swagger restored. There is a certain confidence to coming to the end of a two-thousand-mile road trip, however uncertain the next beginning might be.

Pete remained behind the wheel, his window rolled down. He was reticent for two reasons. For starters, his experience in Oklahoma had told him that places like this were often populated by unleashed dogs, and although he was not properly afraid of dogs, he had been bitten by one as a younger child and had since preferred to avoid situations where large mammals ran directly at him. And also, he saw now that Bicho Raro was not a proper town, as he'd thought it would be. There would be no motor inn where he could stay the night, and no easily accessible telephone with which to contact his aunt.

"You're gonna have to get out of that car eventually," Tony told him. "I thought this was where you were headed. *Both going to the same place*, you said! *Believe me, my aunt told me to keep walking until I found a Mercury*, you said! *You callin' me a liar, sir?* This is the place!"

That was when the dogs burst out.

Sometimes, when dogs emerge at farms, people come out afterward with reassuring statements about how the dogs' barks are worse than their bites, how they look savage but are kittens at heart. *Wouldn't hurt a fly. Members of the family, really.* Visitors are comforted by the knowledge, then, that these dogs are kept mostly for their alarm purposes, and to frighten away large predators.

No one would say that about the dogs at Bicho Raro. There were six of them, and although they were littermates, they were six different colors and sizes and shapes, all of them ugly. There were meant to be twelve of them, but these six were so bad-tempered that in the womb, they'd eaten the other six. They were so bad-tempered that when they'd been born, their mother had lost patience with them and abandoned them under a parade float in Farmington. There, a tenderhearted long-haul trucker had scooped them into a box to raise them to weaning age. They were so bad-tempered that he took up drinking before leaving them in a ditch near Pagosa Springs. A pack of coyotes tried to eat them there, but the puppies learned how to walk and then run and turned on the coyotes, chasing them nearly all the way to Bicho Raro.

That was when Antonia Soria, Beatriz's mother, had found them and taken them home. They were still bad-tempered, but so was she, and they loved her.

Tony stood his ground for a hot minute. Pete rolled up his window. Antonia Soria's six dogs snarled and circled, their hackles up and their teeth bared. They hadn't killed a man yet, but the *yet* was displayed prominently in their expressions.

This was how Tony came to be on the roof of the Mercury when the lights of Bicho Raro began to flicker on. Now that the lights were coming on, it was obvious that there were owls everywhere. There were horned owls and elf owls, long-eared owls and short-eared owls. Barn owls with their ghostly ladies' faces, and screech owls with their shaggy frowns. Dark-eyed barred owls and spotted owls. Stygian owls with eyes that turned red in lights at night—these owls weren't originally from Colorado, but like the Soria family, they had come from Oaxaca to Bicho Raro and decided to stay.

The dogs were trying to get on the hood of the car to reach Tony; Pete activated the windshield wiper spray to repel them.

"You're a real war hero," Tony snarled. One of the dogs ate his left shoe.

"I could just drive us out of here," Pete said. "You could hold on."

"Boy, don't even *think* about turning that key."

"Are you sure this is it?" Pete asked.

"Damn *pelicans*," Tony said. The promise of a miracle was rolling off him thick now, and the owls were swirling down low over the top of the Mercury. From Tony's vantage point on the roof, he could see a row of small elf owls sitting on the roof of one of the metal-sided garages. They had big eyes and long legs, and although they were not laughing at him, it was close enough for Tony's skin to crawl.

From the safety of the driver's seat, Pete looked for signs of human life. He found himself looking at someone who was looking back.

A girl stood watching him from the porch of a small cabin. She wore a beautiful wedding dress and a very sad face. Her dark hair was pulled back into a smooth bun at the base of her neck. Her dress was wet, and so was her skin. This was because, despite the porch roof, it was raining on her. Rain originated from nowhere and spattered on her hair and face and shoulders and clothing, then ran off the stairs and formed a fast-running rivulet into the brush. Every part of her dress was covered with monarch butterflies, their orange-and-black stained-glass wings likewise soaked. They clung to her, unable to do anything but slowly move their wings or climb across the fabric. Butterflies are fragile fliers and cannot fly in the rain, or even in the dew. Too much water makes their wings too heavy to fly.

This was Marisita Lopez, one of the pilgrims. It had stormed around her ever since she had experienced her first miracle, and now rain constantly poured on her head and out of her eyes. It was not as beatific as one might imagine to live under continuous precipitation in a desert. The ground, instead of enjoying the sudden influx of moisture, was ill-prepared to accept it. The water pooled and ran away, striking down seedlings in its path. Floods, not flowers, followed in Marisita's wake.

Here was a thing she wanted: to taste vanilla without crying. Here was a thing she feared: that the prettiest thing about her was her exterior.

Pete didn't know it to look at her, but she had been preparing to make a terrible decision directly before they'd arrived. Now she could not act until the night had quieted again.

Rolling down his window, he called, "Can you help us?"

But Marisita, absorbed in her own dark night, withdrew into the building behind her.

He called again, "Is there *anyone* out there?"

There were. There were aunts and uncles and grandmothers and cousins and babies, but none of them wanted to welcome the pilgrims. It was not that they wanted to refuse these newcomers a miracle; it was simply that every bed was already full. Bicho Raro was brimming with pilgrims who couldn't move on. And since the Sorias could not offer a room, there was only the miracle to attend to. Daniel would handle it, and the rest of them wouldn't have to leave their warm homes or risk any contact with the pilgrims.

At that moment, however, Daniel was creeping back to the

Shrine while Beatriz and Joaquin remained in the truck with the radio, trying to time their own return in such a way that it would not raise questions.

Because of this, Tony and Pete might have spent quite a long time on top of and inside the Mercury, if not for the fortuitous arrival of another vehicle.

The rescuers were Judith, Beatriz's older sister, and Judith's new husband, Eduardo Costa, coming down from Colorado Springs. Eduardo was driving his brand-new Chevy stepside pickup truck. The general agreement was that Eduardo loved the truck more than Judith, but at least he took good care of both. The two of them—three, if you counted Judith—had not been anticipated in Bicho Raro until the next day but had decided to take advantage of the cool temperatures to make the drive after sundown.

Judith used to be the most beautiful woman in Bicho Raro, but then she'd moved, and now she was the most beautiful woman in Colorado Springs. She was so beautiful that people would stop her on the street and thank her. She had gone to school to learn how to make her blue-black hair do whatever she wanted it to do, and now she made other women's hair do what she wanted it to do in a small hairdresser shop where she worked with several other women. Her lips were the same rosebud as her younger sister Beatriz's, only Judith painted hers a bloody red that set off her flawless brown skin and gleaming dark hair. She had been wearing artificial eyelashes in the womb and when they had fallen off in the birth canal, she had lost no time in replacing them. Where Beatriz took after their father, Francisco, Judith was more like volatile Antonia.

Here was a thing she wanted: to have two gold teeth where no one could see them but she would know they were there. Here was a thing she feared: having to fill out forms before medical appointments of any kind.

Eduardo was the most handsome of the Costas, which was saying a lot, but he was not so handsome that people would stop him on the street to thank him. The Costas were cowboys and bred quarter horses for the rodeo. The Costas and their horses were all fast and charming, and could turn on a dime faster than you could say *¿Qué onda?* They were also very good at what they did, and neither the Costas nor their horses would ever kick a child. Eduardo wore clothing even fancier than his wife's— bright red cowboy shirts to match her lips and tight black pants to match her hair and blocky fleece-collared leather coats to emphasize her shapeliness.

Here was a thing he wanted: for singers to pause in their singing to laugh during a verse. Here was a thing he feared: cats lying on his face and smothering him while he slept.

Judith and Eduardo took stock of the scene as they pulled into the compound. The enormous wood-covered Mercury, the Italian American perched on top of it, the square silhouette of Pete inside, the slobber of dogs drawing picturesque arcs across the diorama.

"Ed, do you recognize that car?" Judith asked.

Eduardo removed his cigarette to say, "It's last year's Mercury Colony Park in sunburst yellow."

Judith said, "I meant, do you recognize the man on top of it?"

"Then you should have said, 'Do you recognize the man on top of it?'"

"Do you recognize the man on top of it?"

Eduardo framed Tony DiRisio with his headlights as he approached—Tony shielded his eyes—and peered closely. "No, but I like that suit."

One of the dogs had just gotten ahold of the left sleeve of the aforementioned white suit, and Tony, accepting discretion as the better part of valor, allowed the dog to have the entire coat rather than his left arm.

"It's just like Mama to leave them out here," Judith said angrily.

"I bet she's making one of those flowers."

"Don't talk about her," Judith said, even though she had been about to say the same thing herself.

The Chevy nosed up beside the Mercury. It was just high enough that Eduardo Costa and Tony DiRisio were now eye to eye. Eduardo honked his horn to startle one of the dogs off the hood of the Mercury. Then he removed the cigarette from his lips and gave it to Tony.

"Hola, traveler," Eduardo said.

Judith patted her hair and leaned into the conversation. "Are you here for a miracle?"

Tony sucked the cigarette, then flicked it at one of the dogs. "Lady, it would be a miracle to get off the roof of my car."

Eduardo leaned out of his window and called into the Mercury, "Are you here for a miracle, mi hijo?"

Pete started. "I'm here about a truck."

"He's here about a truck," Eduardo told his wife.

"Papa should shoot these dogs," Judith replied.

"Bullets are too afraid to hit them," Eduardo observed.

He took his time lighting another cigarette and smoking it as they all watched him. Then he kissed his wife, stroked his mustache, opened the door of the truck, and jumped lightly out, his sharp cowboy boots raising dust as he landed. Antonia's dogs turned to him. An owl hooted. A creature howled from inside one of the distant cabins. The moon smiled cunningly. Then Eduardo hurled down his cigarette butt and began to run. Man and dogs flew across the yard into the dark.

The Costas are known for their bravery, and for their smoking.

In the quiet left behind, Judith climbed from the truck. She was very nervous, but she did not show it as she walked over to the Mercury with a sway that matched her beauty. "Let's get you men a place to sleep and we can see about— Beatriz! What are you doing lurking over there?"

Beatriz was not lurking. She was standing motionless and observant in the deepest of the shadows beside her mother's house, so silent that even Antonia's dogs had not known she was there. She had been waiting for her opportunity to climb back into her bedroom, but Judith, with the uncanny intuition that sisters sometimes have, had seen her there.

"There are no beds," Beatriz told Judith. "None of the pilgrims have left since you did."

"No beds! Impossible!" Judith had not been back to Bicho Raro in months.

"It's true," said a voice from within the long stucco building. This was one of the pilgrims. They were always eavesdropping, as the forbidden lives of the Sorias were very interesting to them. They had been listening to the exchange outside just as much as the other Sorias had been, and now this voice floated out of the building in a way that seemed ghostly to Pete and Tony. It added, "The floor is available, though."

"Don't talk to me!" Judith snapped to the unseen pilgrim. Although this statement seemed unfriendly to Pete and Tony, her exhortation was actually colored by fear. All of the Sorias treated the pilgrims with caution, but Judith was more than cautious—she was frightened of them. This was one of the reasons Judith had moved away as soon as she'd gotten married and had not returned before now. She could not take the tension of living alongside them all day and all night long.

Beatriz said, "Michael's building a lodge, but it's not done."

"*A lodge?*" Judith was nearly overcome imagining an entire lodge full of pilgrims. "We are not a hotel. Fine, fine! These men can have the miracle and go on their way or sleep on the floor! Which of you wants to be first? The father or son?"

"Lady, just how old do I look?" Tony asked. "I only met this kid today."

"I'm just here about work, ma'am," Pete said quickly. He had been listening to this conversation with growing certainty that Tony had come here for a very different reason than him. He felt he needed to distance himself from it in case it was illegal.

"Work?" echoed Judith, with considerable confusion. "No miracle?"

"Not for me, ma'am."

This captured Beatriz's notice. People who came to Bicho Raro in the dark of night were always either a member of the Soria family or in search of a miracle. Here was this stranger, however, and he was neither. She interjected, "You aren't a pilgrim?"

"No more than any of us are, I suppose."

This exchange was when Pete and Beatriz first truly noticed each other. They used this moment of observation in two different but related ways.

Beatriz observed Pete with his arm crooked on the edge of the Mercury's open window and wondered what it would be like to press her thumb gently into the skin at the inside of his elbow. She could see this crook of his arm from where she stood, and it seemed as if it would be a soft and pleasant thing to do. Beatriz had never had this impulse before and was somewhat surprised by it. She was equally surprised by how the feeling, once noticed, did not go away, but instead extended to the other elbow as well.

Because she was Beatriz, she made a note to consider this impulse more acutely later, to determine where it might have come from. She did not consider this sensation to be a suggestion for future action, however.

Pete, for his part, observed Beatriz in the half shadow with her still, unblinking, eerie manner, her expression looking no warmer than those of the dark-eyed barn owls sitting on the roof above her. Although they had exchanged only a handful of words, Pete felt the most dangerous jolt to his heart so far, surpassing even what he had felt when he had fallen in love with the desert only hours before. He did not know the reason for this surge of intense curiosity, only that the scale of it felt deadly. It seemed that he should not repeat it if at all possible. He pressed his hand to his chest and vowed to keep his distance from Beatriz while he worked here.

"I'll wait in the car," he said hastily, and rolled the window back up.

"In *my* car?" Tony demanded.

There was no time for further discussion, as the sound of Antonia's dogs echoed back through Bicho Raro. Eduardo Costa had done a fine job leading them away, but he had run out of breath at a collapsed cattle barn near the highway and had climbed it to preserve his life. The dogs had left him marooned on the ruined spine of the building and were now returning to make a meal of Tony's other shoe.

"We should go before the dogs get to us," Judith said. She looked to Beatriz, but Beatriz had already vanished—she could not be persuaded to talk to strangers if there was anyone else who would do it instead, and she most certainly did not like to be volunteered to perform the miracle. (Also, unknown to Judith, she wanted to study the feeling she had had about Pete more closely and worried that another feeling might come along and make it more complicated to analyze.)

"*Beatriz*," Judith hissed. Then, to Tony, "Hurry up, follow me."

The sound of the dogs lent Tony speed. He limped after her on his one shod foot, one sock foot. "Where are we going?"

"Where do you think?" Judith replied angrily. "To get you your miracle!"

4

The Saint of Bicho Raro sat in the Shrine and listened to Tony DiRisio approach.

The Shrine was the oldest building in Bicho Raro. It had been designed and built by Felipe Soria, a member of the family now spoken of only in hushed tones. He had arrived in Bicho Raro on a large honey-colored horse and in a large honey-colored hat and promptly began work on a roadside altar after claiming that the Virgin had appeared to him with instructions to do so.

On the first day, he'd completed the stucco walls for a small structure the size of his stallion's box stall, and the other Sorias had been pleased. On the second day, he'd torn free a section of abandoned railroad and melted it into a beautifully intricate metal gate, and the other Sorias had been pleased. On the third day, he'd fired one thousand ceramic tiles with the heat of his own belief and installed a roof made of them, and the other Sorias had been pleased. On the fourth day, the Virgin had appeared again, this time surrounded by owls; he'd carved a statue of her in this state to place inside the Shrine, and the other Sorias had been pleased. On the fifth day, he'd made a rich pigment from some sky that had gotten too close to him and used it to paint the Shrine's exterior turquoise, and the other Sorias had been pleased. On the sixth day, he'd held up a passenger train, robbed the passengers, killed the sheriff on board, and used the sheriff's femurs to fashion a cross for the top of the shrine. The Sorias had not been pleased.

On the seventh day, Felipe Soria had gone missing forever, which was why the Sorias now spoke of him only in whispers.

When he was young, Joaquin had once told his mother, Rosa, that he'd seen Felipe Soria wandering the desert outside Bicho Raro, but Felipe would have been one hundred and thirty years old, so no one believed him. The Sorias were long-lived (except when they suddenly weren't), but such an age would have been exceptional even for a Soria.

As Judith Soria Costa escorted Tony to the Shrine, the current Saint of Bicho Raro kneeled inside its small interior. He had run all the way from the box truck in order to have time to prepare himself (spiritually) to perform the miracle and prepare himself (physically) to appear as the Saint. He did not have to do this, as even Sorias in poor standing with God remained miraculous, but he believed that the more spiritually prepared he was during the ritual, the more likely the pilgrim was to be completely healed. The miracles, he felt, were just as much about healing his own mortal spirit as theirs.

Daniel Lupe Soria had not always been on the path to holiness.

As a child, he'd been so terrible that Rosa Soria had sent him twice to be exorcised. He'd been so terrible that he'd chased a field of sheds out into the road one week and burned down a herd of cattle the next. He'd been so terrible that the cowboys at the neighboring ranch still used his name as a cuss word. In his teens, he and his school friends had decided to steal a painting of the Santo Niño de Atocha from a church outside Alamosa. As the disguised child Jesus gazed reproachfully from inside the frame, Daniel had carried the icon outside to where his friends waited in their truck. As he descended the few stairs, however, the painting grew heavier and heavier until he was compelled to put it down. His friends jeered, but they could not move it either. As Daniel had tried to decide if they should just leave the painting where it sat on the sidewalk, he'd seen an inscription on the back: *Donated by an anonymous benefactor, for all the crooked saints.*

Feeling suddenly and surprisingly heavy with the weight of both religious paintings and remorse, Daniel could not bring himself to abandon the painting to the elements his crime had exposed it to. He decided to wait with it until the priest returned in the morning, even if it meant confessing his theft. His friends abandoned him, but still Daniel waited. The wind began to kick up dirt, and still Daniel waited. A storm blew in, and hail began to fall, and he covered the painting with his body to protect it, and still he waited. As the hailstones pounded him, the frivolous and selfish nature of his childhood exploits hit him with equal pain. With each blow of the hail, he repented of another misdeed. Then the sky cleared and Daniel found that he could easily lift the painting: a miracle.

He'd returned it to its place in the church and had been the Saint of Bicho Raro ever since. He still had a divot in his shoulder from the first hailstone that had hit him that night, a physical reminder that regret stings.

Now, as he waited for Tony to come to him, he fell once more into prayer. He had been praying all day, stopping only to go out with Beatriz and Joaquin. The day of prayer was not unusual, as Daniel began to pray when the sun rose and often continued praying after the sun had set, setting out words and lighting candles for his family and each of the pilgrims who had already come and each of the pilgrims who were still on their way to him.

It was unusual for the Saint to pray for himself.

Now Judith's voice came to him from outside the Shrine. She was asking the pilgrim, "Are you prepared to change your life?"

"Yeah, yeah," the pilgrim replied.

The Saint turned back to his prayers. Some saints had a profound relationship with God or the Holy Child or a particular saint, but Daniel preferred to direct his prayers toward *Mother*. This figure in his mind was both the Virgin Mary and his own mother, the one he had never known, having been delivered from her dead body as a newborn. So now he prayed, *Mother, help me to help this man.* And he also prayed, *Mother, help me.*

The miracles at Bicho Raro always came in twos.

The first miracle was this: making the darkness visible.

Sadness is a little like darkness. They both begin the same way. A tiny, thin pool of uneasiness settles in the bottom of the gut. Sadness simmers fast and boils hard and then billows up and out, filling first the stomach, then heart, then lungs, then legs, then arms, then up into the throat, then pressing against eardrums, then swelling against skull and eventually spilling out of eyes in a hissing release. Darkness, though, grows like a cave formation. Slow drips from the uneasiness harden over the surface of a slick knob of pain. Over time, the darkness crusts in unpredictable layers, growing at such a pace that one doesn't notice it has filled every cavern under the skin until movement becomes difficult or even impossible.

Darkness never boils over. Darkness remains inside.

But a Soria could draw it out and give it form. They would feel a stirring of the pilgrim's darkness as it drew near, like the owls, and the promise of their gift inside their mouths, like a song they knew the words to. There was barely a pause between when they chose to draw the darkness out and when the darkness began to emerge.

Daniel's head was still bowed and his eyes closed when Tony entered the Shrine. Because of this, and the dim light afforded by one hundred tiny candles, Tony did not see young Daniel Lupe Soria when his eyes grew accustomed. He saw only the Saint.

The Saint had long black hair, parted evenly to his shoulders. His face was a ragged chalk white, his brown skin painted with a pale paste made from the dust of the surrounding area. His eye sockets were smeared black like a skull. His knuckles bore a spider's eight wide-open eyes. In this light he looked less like a human you would meet and more like a thing that you would discover. Tony noticed the Catholic artifacts in the Shrine, the rosary beads around the Saint's neck, but they seemed to belong to a different Catholicism than the perfunctory, godless form he had practiced back in Philadelphia.

Tony suddenly realized how cold it was here in the high desert night. The owls carved beside Mary seemed to be looking at him.

"Do you have darkness in you?" the Saint asked, his eyes still closed.

Tony's heart quailed inside him. He felt he had heard this story before, and it had ended badly for the radio DJ who'd driven his Mercury into the desert.

He thought he might just go. Leave that kid here pining after a truck and keep on driving west toward California, right into the sea.

The Saint of Bicho Raro opened his eyes.

Tony looked into them.

There were many reasons why Daniel Lupe Soria was the best saint that Bicho Raro had experienced for generations, but his eyes were on the top of the list. Eyes like his had not been seen for one hundred years. It might have been possible for someone else to look as gentle and holy as Daniel Lupe Soria did, but only if one had the right eyebrows. Eyebrows are extraordinarily important to expression. They say that if you shave off your eyebrows, babies cannot recognize you. Daniel, however, did not require his eyebrows to accomplish his mystical expression. Just his eyes alone would do the trick. They were wide-set, dark brown, and full of an otherworldly kindness that meant that not only did he love you, but any other possible otherworldly entity you believed in was looking through them and also loved you. If the Catholic Church had looked into Daniel Lupe Soria's eyes in the nineteenth century, they would have offered to do battle with the Mexican government on the Soria family's behalf. If the Mexican government had looked into Daniel Lupe Soria's eyes in the nineteenth century, they would have at once become better Catholics.

"Oh," said Tony.

He kneeled.

Daniel reached out and brushed Tony's eyes closed with his palm. Then he closed his own again.

They both sat this way in the complicated blackness that exists behind closed eyelids. Tony imagined static playing on his radio station. Daniel imagined the rain pouring on Marisita Lopez and the trapped butterflies on her dress.

The second miracle was this: getting rid of the darkness for good.

No one wanted to see their darkness made manifest, but the reality was that it could not be fought until you saw its shape. Unfortunately, the pilgrims had to do the fighting on their own, and only then, once they had seen their darkness and learned how to banish it, could they leave Bicho Raro healed and bright. There was a law laid down among the Sorias to not interfere. If a Soria lifted a hand or breathed a word in aid, a darkness would fall on the Soria as well, and a Saint's darkness was an even more terrible and powerful thing.

"Answer me now," Daniel said. "Do you have darkness inside you?"

"Yes," Tony said.

"And do you want to be rid of it?"

This is a harder question to answer than one might think at first blush. Almost no one would think it's correct to answer this question with a *no*, but the truth is that we men and women often hate to be rid of the familiar, and sometimes our darkness is the thing we know the best.

"Yes."

Outside, owls began to flap and call out. Horned owls hooted. Screech owls trilled. The barn owls gave their metallic hiss. Barred owls meowed. Spectacled owls barked hollowly. Pygmy owls peeped. The elf owls laughed nervously. The noise escalated to cacophony as the air turned ever more miraculous.

Daniel opened his eyes again.

The darkness began to appear.

5

The owls ordinarily roosted once the miracle took place. That night, they did not leave until the Saint told them to go.

6

The morning after a miracle is always bright.

This is because nearly every morning in Bicho Raro is bright. Colorado has long boasted that it enjoys three hundred days of sunshine a year, which is not actually true, but it is close enough to the truth to feel like it. The morning following Tony DiRisio's miracle did nothing to disprove the claim. The sun had been climbing hand over foot through the dry Colorado blue for several hours, and Bicho Raro was beginning to warm.

Beatriz Soria had woken up before everyone else, despite the lateness of the previous night. Her mind was very active while she was awake and didn't stop when she slept, so she usually did not spend much time doing the latter. That day, before dawn, she had used her retractable secret bridge to climb from her window without waking her mother in the room beside her. From there, she drifted across the silent compound to the telescope.

The telescope was a parabolic radio telescope, sixty feet wide and about eighty feet tall, a scooped dish of metal rods pointed hopefully at the sky. Its skeletal shadow moved around its base like a giant sundial. With the cooperation of some of the more tax-savvy Sorias, the telescope had been constructed during the fifties—ostensibly to monitor the weather but practically to spy on the Russians—and had been decommissioned after only one use. The head engineer on the project would not report on what his team had picked up with the tracker, only that everyone else would sleep better at night having not seen it. Later, everyone on the team quietly moved to colder climates in distant countries.

Beatriz now used it as a place to think. Sometimes she climbed the ladder forty feet into the air and observed Bicho Raro from the metal mesh platform. And sometimes she removed her shoes and climbed past even that, feet pressed into metal bars and legs hooked over supports on the back side of the dish, sometimes dangling, sometimes clinging, until she managed to heave herself over the rim of the dish and into it. Then she would lie inside the metallic nest of the dish and stare up at the sky, imagining herself—her mind, that is, the important part of herself—being projected as far up into the sky as she could see. She would hold her thoughts up there for hours at a time, breathing them back into the altitude if they started to drift down, and then, finally, she would turn those distant thoughts back down to Bicho Raro and consider her home from that great height instead. Things came into better perspective, she felt, when viewed from one thousand feet.

Sometimes, Daniel would join her, the only other person Beatriz had found so far who she could share her sanctuary with. Although they were very different, they shared one important trait: They did not try to change other people and rarely judged them unless the other person's values directly influenced their lives. For Daniel, this meant that he had, before his incident with the painting, hung out with young men whom others found to be of dubious character. For Beatriz, this meant that she had often frustrated Judith by refusing to take sides in moral discussions or disagreements.

This trait also made Daniel and Beatriz good conversation partners. A debate without a goal of philosophical interference can continue endlessly without drama. One of their earliest radio dish discussions had centered around who could receive a miracle. A pilgrim had just abandoned a fractious stallion at Bicho Raro, and the horse's famously ill temperament was the topic of every Soria conversation. Beatriz and Daniel, then ten and twelve, had looked down into the pasture from that great height and speculated upon whether they, as Sorias, could visit their miracle upon an animal.

Daniel argued that a horse's lack of humanity presented an insurmountable problem for the second miracle. Even if the Saint could manifest its darkness, surely the horse lacked the moral certainty to come to an understanding of how to banish it. The second miracle would never occur, and the horse would therefore live out its days plagued by the same darkness that had previously lived inside it, now made worse by being given concrete form.

Beatriz agreed that the horse's lack of humanity was indeed the obstacle, but she believed that the Saint wouldn't be able to perform even the first miracle. Humanity, she maintained, was necessary for darkness to exist. Without an understanding of the concept of darkness, morality, or other existential subjects, the unpleasantness inside the individual could not be darkness but rather simply nature, and thus could not be cured with a miracle, or perhaps at all.

"So that horse will be terrible forever?" Daniel had asked.

"I do not think the darkness is about being 'terrible.'" It had taken slightly longer for ten-year-old Beatriz to find the words that she needed. She had still been learning how to live with the hard truth that the most interesting parts of her thoughts usually got left behind when she tried to put them into words. There were often very long pauses as she strove for a perfect translation. "I think the darkness is about shame."

Daniel had contemplated the pilgrims he had already seen in his twelve years. "I think you're right."

"We were nearly in agreement in the beginning," Beatriz had added, in order to be a gracious winner.

Daniel had grinned. "Nearly."

On the day after Tony's miracle, Beatriz was alone as she climbed to the platform above the layer of dark dust. Then, as the sun slowly began to warm her cold blood into movement, she watched her home come to life. She could see most of it from her perch, as Bicho Raro occupied a fairly small footprint. There was a dusty, bare parking area at its heart. Buildings gathered around this like hands around a fire. Only a dozen or so were still standing: three houses, three barns, her father Francisco's greenhouse, her aunt Rosa's camper, three sheds, the Shrine. The dirt drive led through these, past a cistern, and then out to Highway 160, the only paved road for miles. Both the drive and the highway were barely better than the surrounding scrub, which one could drive through, too, if your vehicle was eager. One might even end up doing it even with an uneager vehicle if the night was thick enough, because there was not a lot of difference between the cracked asphalt and the dusty expanse it cut through. It was easy to lose your way without headlights (which is true of a lot of life).

Surrounding all of this was the high desert that Pete had fallen in love with, and that had fallen in love with him. It was broken only by scurfy tamarisk and sage and near-invisible twists of barbed wire until it got to the mountains.

Beatriz observed it all from her perch, paying less attention to the nature and more attention to the small humans moving below her. She did not particularly enjoy physical labor, but she found it satisfying to watch other people engaged in it. She liked to watch the things they did that were unnecessary. It is, after all, not the tasks people do but the things they do around the edges of them that reveal who they are.

For instance, from the dish's platform, she could see her second cousin Luis repairing some barbed wire that the cows had run through during the last big thunderstorm. He was cutting out some sections and restretching others. Every so often, however, he would move his fingers in the air and she would know that he was practicing his guitar in his mind. She could also see Nana working in the tomatoes behind her house. She was on her ancient hands and knees, weeding, but twice Beatriz saw her sit back on her rump and place a raw, fresh tomato in her mouth to savor. Beatriz also saw her aunt Rosa (Joaquin's mother) carrying peppers and the baby Lidia back to her home for cooking— the peppers, not the baby. Rosa's steps were slowed by pausing to sing and plant kisses into the top of Lidia's head; Beatriz knew from experience that this ratio increased throughout the course of the day until no work got done and only kisses were given.

A tremolo cry pulled Beatriz's attention from the ground to the sky just above her. Squinting against the brightness, she discovered that several owls had gathered on the rim above her head, their talons making familiar scratching sounds against the metal. The group was made up of multiple species: two barn owls, a barred owl, and a small owl of a kind Beatriz had not seen before. Most people, in fact, had not seen this kind of owl before, as it was the rare buff-fronted owl, a native of distant Peru. Because of how surely the miracles appealed to owls, Beatriz, like all the Sorias, was used to their presence, although, unlike most of the other Sorias, she had spent many long hours wondering if the owls' attraction to miracles was beneficial or harmful. There was, after all, a large difference between the way flowers drew hummingbirds and the way artificial light compelled moths.

A banded feather drifted down. Beatriz snatched for it, but the action of snatching displaced both air and feather, and it continued its slow descent to the ground below.

"Why are you still here?" she whistled in her invented language.

The owls didn't startle at her voice. Instead, they continued to stare at her in their wide-open way. The buff-fronted owl that had come so far turned its head on one side to better study her. She was not sure that they were the same owls from the night before after all, though if that was true, she wasn't sure what they were being attracted to.

"No darkness here," she whistled. "No miracles, anyway."

Their gazes continued to be so purposeful that she looked back to the ground to see if another pilgrim had arrived without her knowing. But the only person she saw was Michael, Rosa's husband, thrusting a shovel into a patch of dirt. For as long as Beatriz had known him, he had done nothing but work or sleep. To understand Michael, you only had to understand the project at hand, which in this case was the log lodge Beatriz had mentioned the night before. Currently, the lodge was only four pieces of wood sunk into the ground. It was merely the promise of a building, and had grown no further not because of Michael's unwillingness to do the work but rather because it was a point of contention, questioned at every stage. Judith was not the only one who argued that it didn't need to be built.

The building was not really the problem. The pilgrims were the problem.

There is a plant that still grows in Colorado today called the tamarisk. It is also called the salt cedar. It is not a native plant. In the 1930s, a dust storm had arrived in the middle of the United States and raged for years. To keep all the states between Colorado and Tennessee from blowing away, farmers had planted millions of tamarisk shrubs to hold the ground down. Once its job was done there, the enterprising tamarisk had packed its bags and moved to the southwestern corner of the United States to stay. In bloom, it is very lovely, with tiny pink flowers made beautiful by their unusual combination of tender color and physical durability. When it is not in bloom, it is an enormous plant of extreme hardiness, so suited to growing in Colorado that when it is present, no other plant can compete with it. Massive, unwieldy roots dig deep into the soil, drinking all the water and using all of the salt, eventually making the only suitable neighbor for tamarisk yet more tamarisk.

This is what the pilgrims had become at Bicho Raro.

They had been arriving at the same pace but leaving at a far slower one. For some reason, they could not seem to perform the second miracle on themselves with the same efficiency as past generations. So they loitered in their partially changed states, benevolently draining Bicho Raro's resources. The Sorias did not dare help. They had all been told the danger of interfering with miracles, and no one wanted to be the one to risk bringing darkness on themselves and the rest of their family.

The simplest solution would have been to throw these overflowing pilgrims into the desert to fend for themselves. But even if Daniel had not been around to protest the ethics of this, the memory of Elizabeth Pantazopoulus stopped the rest of the Sorias. Elizabeth Pantazopoulus had rolled into Bicho Raro at some point in the 1920s, wearing a man's striped prison uniform and bearing a bullet wound in her left arm. In the crook of her good arm, she had been carrying a long-haired cat that also had a bullet wound in one limb. She had not volunteered the circumstances that had brought her to this point; she'd merely received the first miracle and remained at Bicho Raro until her gunshot wound had healed and the cat no longer flinched at knocking sounds. Then she had managed to perform the second miracle on herself, and was gone the next morning. The Sorias had heard nothing more from her until four years later, when a packet had arrived from New York City with three things in it: (I) a piece of paper saying simply, *Thank you.—Yours, Elizabeth Pantazopoulus*; (2) a bullet, presumably from either her arm or the cat's; and (3) a pile of cash large enough to see Bicho Raro through the more difficult years of the Depression.

You just can't guess who will strike it big. So the pilgrims stayed, and the Sorias resentfully built a lodge.

Beatriz moved her attention beyond Michael and the lodge to the very large, wood-paneled Mercury station wagon still parked in the dust beyond it. Making binoculars of her hands to shield her eyes from the sun, she focused on the interior. She could see Pete Wyatt's boots through the back window; he was either sleeping or dead. To her continued surprise, the urge to place her thumb on his skin had not diminished, even though she could not even see his elbows from where she sat. In an effort to study this feeling objectively, Beatriz imagined it rising out of her mind and up into the air above the telescope, hoping to disentangle the emotion from her untrustworthy body. To her annoyance, however, it refused to float above her. Some feelings are rooted too strongly in the body to exist without it, and this one, desire, is one of them. Beatriz was aware of this form of attraction from observation but not from personal experience. She contemplated the absence of logic in the sensation and then considered the more emotional members of her family, wondering if this was what they felt like all the time.

Beatriz watched Pete's boots and pondered her puzzling feeling for such a duration and with such an intensity that she noticed neither the departure of the owls above her nor the arrival of Marisita Lopez below her.

Marisita stood at the telescope's base, one hand lifted to protect her eyes against the rain that always fell on her. The dust around her puffed and splattered under the assault of the precipitation. The butterflies on her dress moved their sluggish wings but did not fly.

She gazed uncertainly up at Beatriz. Her errand was urgent enough to encourage her to break the rule against speaking with Sorias, but still she hesitated. This was because Beatriz could be quite frightening from the outside. Right now, la chica sin sentimientos cut a stark and haunting image up on the telescope platform. Motionless, speechless, unblinking. She was, in many ways, like the owls that had just been perched above her, particularly the ghost-faced barn owls with their inscrutable expressions.

Marisita had come from Texas to Bicho Raro, and on the border where she lived, owls were considered with distrust. The problem lay not with the owls themselves but rather with the lechuzas, witches who could transform themselves into owls with human faces. Even though Marisita trusted the intentions of the Sorias, there was no pretending that they didn't have other-worldly abilities. And although she did not believe the Church had been correct to drive them from Abejones, it was not difficult for her to see how she, as one of the Sorias' troubled pilgrims, also did not belong in a church.

It was just that Marisita was not sure that saints and witches were very different in the end.

And Beatriz was the most saintly of the Sorias, apart from Daniel.

Which meant that Marisita did not feel bold enough to shout up to her that Daniel Soria had given her a letter meant for Beatriz. She merely trapped the paper between the metal rung of the ladder and the metal riser and made sure that it would not fall out on its own, moving quickly so that her rain-damp hands did not spoil it.

She didn't know what the letter said. She had been told not to read the letter, so she had not read it. She could not know how its contents would impact them all.

"Beatriz! Beatriz Soria! I have something for you!" she shouted, but only in her mind. Marisita often said things only in her mind. This is not generally an efficient way of speaking, as very few people are mind readers, apart from Delecta Marsh, who had received mind reading as a result of the first miracle back in 1899. But Delecta was long dead, shot by an immediately excommunicated and now-also-dead abbot, and so in reality,

Marisita merely twisted her hands together and hoped that Beatriz might notice her and come for the letter.

She did not, and Marisita grew no braver.

Marisita began to cry, just a little. Her tears were not only from anxiety. They were the kind of tears that come easily because earlier tears have already smoothed the path for them. The night before, when Tony and Pete had arrived, she had been considering a terrible decision. The decision was this: whether or not she should walk out into the desert without any food and proceed until she could no longer remember who she was. If you think this sounds like a painful way to die, know that Marisita had also considered this and decided upon it for that very reason; it was, she thought, what she deserved. But now Daniel had given her this mysterious letter to deliver, and he had told her it was important. She could not go into the desert until she knew what it meant.

She felt trapped in between. She had not truly wanted to go the night before, but she hadn't wanted to stay, either. It was this, in addition to her fear of Beatriz, that squeezed yet more tears from her.

The tears didn't make her any braver, however, so she left the letter clinging to the ladder, waiting to be discovered.

Beatriz, it began, *I am in love with Marisita Lopez.*

7

Pete Wyatt woke as a stranger in the world of miracles.

He was neither a saint nor a pilgrim. He was just a kid waking too late in the morning in the back of a stranger's egg-yellow Mercury.

Wiping the sweat from his forehead, he slithered into the boastful sunshine outside. The settlement's appearance surprised him. It was not at all what he'd imagined in the darkness the evening before. Bicho Raro by night was a god; Bicho Raro by day was a man. In the raw daylight, it was a place people lived—a place where a young man could work for a box truck.

One would think this unveiled truth would be encouraging, but it had the opposite effect on Pete. His journey before now had felt like a dream, and a dream can always be changed into something else. But when you are awake, the truth is bright and stark, not as willing to bend to the mind's will. So now Pete truly faced the reality of the plan he had made. He pressed a hand to his heart again and wondered if he had made a mistake. Perhaps, he thought, he had overestimated himself. Perhaps a place this vast and an adventure this curious were only for those without holes in their hearts.

Closing his eyes, he thought of his father.

George Wyatt was a man of action. George Wyatt had been supposed to die in the womb, as his umbilical cord had been wrapped around his neck, but he'd decided that death was not for him and had chewed himself free. He'd been born two weeks early, his baby hands still clutching the ragged stump of his umbilical cord, his baby mouth already full of teeth. He'd been the weakest of his eight siblings, but he'd begun lifting weights as a toddler and by the time he was fifteen, he could lift all of his siblings at once. His family had been dust-poor and he was meant to be, too, but he'd signed himself up for the army and worked hard. He saved a full colonel from choking on his rations in the field by punching him in the face and telling him to snap out of it and was made an officer.

George Wyatt would not have allowed himself to be disheartened at this early stage.

Pete opened his eyes. Resolve straightened his spine. He would search for someone who knew about his deal to work for the box truck.

Back in Oklahoma a few years before, he had enjoyed a brief stint as a firehouse fund-raiser. After a particularly difficult winter, the town's only fire truck had gone out of commission; an excess of chimney fires and poverty had clogged the fire truck's hose with prayers and despair and it had split from end to end. Pete had taken up a successful collection to replace it, going from door to door with a smile and a pledge sheet.

He knocked on doors now with the same vigor but got a very

different response. Although he was certain there must be people inside the buildings, every door remained closed to him. He got the sense that he was being watched, too, that eyes were on him through the windows, eyes that disappeared as soon as he squinted in their direction. At one point he even heard a baby cry out, hurriedly shushed as he knocked on Rosa Soria's camper door.

The problem was that he looked like a pilgrim. All of the Sorias knew that pilgrims had arrived the night before, and all of the Sorias knew that a miracle had taken place. They assumed that Pete had received the miracle alongside Tony, and therefore they would not risk speaking to him. Ordinarily, Daniel might have risked it, but today he was as absent as the others.

Pete did not know why he was being avoided, only that he was. He did the only thing he could think to do: He began to work.

He chose the log lodge site for his attention. Michael had made himself scarce as soon as Pete began to move about Bicho Raro, and it is difficult to jump usefully into the middle of someone else's tasks without instruction, but Pete had a lot of practice helping. Good helping is generally about taking quick and accurate stock of another's needs, and that was what he did now. He saw that dimensions for the lodge had been marked out, and he also saw that some holes had been started, and that it was slow going because of the rocky soil. He thought about what the unseen architect of this project might need, and then he began to move all the rocks from inside the dimensions of the lodge to the outside.

The occupants of Bicho Raro watched him work. They

watched him remove enough rocks to fill the wheelbarrow parked by the lodge site. They watched him remove enough rocks to pile one cairn, then two cairns, then three. They watched him remove enough rocks to begin to build a small structure beside it. He did not have the material to build a roof or put in glass windows or hang a wooden door, but he built four walls and a fireplace in the corner and had just begun on decorative windowsills when he ran out of rocks.

That was when Antonia Soria realized that she knew who he was.

Antonia was the one who had originally proposed the idea of labor-for-truck to Pete's aunt, sometime after Josefa had been cured with her second miracle, but sometime before she had left Bicho Raro. They were always short of hands, and it seemed to Antonia to be an ideal solution for disposing of the broken-down box truck.

Antonia put down her scissors.

Whenever she had a spare moment, she constructed elaborate paper flowers so realistic that sometimes even the flowers forgot they were not real and wilted for want of water. It was a painstaking process that required hours of concentration, and being made to stop in the middle put her in a terrible rage. Her desire to officially hire Pete warred with her hatred of interruption. The former won, but was a bitter victor.

Here was a thing Antonia wanted: to suck honey off a man's finger. Here was a thing she feared: that she would forget to shout at one of her family members and this family member's lack of care would lead to her house catching on fire.

With a furious exhalation, she rose from her paper roses. Securing her hair in a smooth bun, she pinched her cheeks a few times before marching out to Pete.

"Are you Josefa's boy?" she asked.

Pete had one remaining stone in his hand, which he put down in a hurry. He could see that she was angry and thought that he was the reason. "Her nephew, ma'am. Pete Wyatt."

"Watt?"

"Wyatt."

Antonia's annoyance at being interrupted faded as she looked at the structure he had started.

"Shake my hand," she told Pete, and he did. "Antonia Soria."

"Sora, ma'am?"

"Soria." Now she studied him closely. "Are you sure you don't have darkness in you?"

"No, ma'am, I've just got a hole in my heart."

"That hole in your heart going to kill you if you work too hard?"

The doctor who had diagnosed Pete, a man also named Pete, had explained that the hole in his heart was vulnerable to extremes of emotion—like shock, fear, and the complicated feelings one has when discovering other people want you dead, and generally all the things one might expect to encounter in the army. Pete the doctor told Pete the patient that as long as he lived in moderation and avoided situations where unexpected extremes of feeling might come at him, he would never notice the lack. As his parents and younger brother, Dexter, looked on, Pete the patient had asked if he could simply train his mind and join the army anyway. Pete the doctor had said he was afraid not; Pete the patient would always be the weakest link. Then he wrote, *Unfit for duty.*

Pete thought about this again, and he thought about Beatriz and the desert. Then he said, "No, I don't think so, ma'am. It's only shock that does it."

"Good. Very good," Antonia repeated. "Come on. I will show you where you'll put your boots at night."

As Pete fetched his bag from the car, Antonia spared a bitter glance at her husband Francisco's greenhouse. He was visible through the glass. While his wife spent her nights making paper flowers so beautiful they seemed real, Francisco spent his days growing real flowers so beautiful they seemed fake. Although the San Luis Valley was a good place to grow sturdy potatoes and hay and tomatoes, Francisco had instead turned his attention to raising roses. There were many impediments to growing show roses in Bicho Raro—hail to knock the petals off and elk to eat the leaves and searing sun to bleach the color from them all— but as a boy, he had been struck by the perfect beauty of a Fibonacci spiral in a rose's belly and had never lost the fire. Since then, he had been trying to breed the impossible: a black rose. He was in the greenhouse now, as he usually was, jotting notes in his tiny journal. They were numbers, although it was not arithmetic—it was a sentence written in the language he and Beatriz had invented. Translated, it meant, *I believe Antonia's dogs killed some men last night.*

Here was a thing Francisco wanted: to find a pitch-black bud on one of his roses. Here was a thing he feared: being asked to do anything else.

Antonia sneered again at her husband's figure, her temper warming again, and then she turned away. She pointed beyond the cistern. "That over there is the truck."

Pete felt a surge of gladness over the reality of the vehicle. If he tried hard enough, he could imagine his logo painted on its stained side. "Thank you, ma'am, for this opportunity."

"Don't thank me yet. I don't think it's running." She halted in front of a long and utilitarian adobe structure. "This is where you'll be staying. We're up to God's mustache in pilgrims, so you'll have a roommate."

"I don't mind, ma'am."

"You might," Antonia said.

The house Pete was to stay in had originally housed Daniel Lupe Soria's family, although it would have been difficult to identify it as a family home now, because it had since been divided into tiny apartments. Inside it was dark and cool, smelling of unfamiliar foods and years of woodsmoke.

"Kitchen," Antonia said, by way of tour. "Clean up after yourself."

"Yes, ma'am."

"Water closet," Antonia said, opening a door. "Clean up after yourself."

"Yes, ma'am."

"These rooms have pilgrims in them, so obviously don't enter without an invitation," Antonia said, gesturing to the four doors along the hall that stretched the length of the home.

"Yes, ma'am."

To prevent stuffiness in the house, all of these doors were open, and so in this way, Pete met the pilgrims who shared the house with him.

In the first room was Jennie Fitzgerald, a slight young brunette woman who waved at him as they passed.

"Hello," said Pete.

"Hello," said Jennie.

He didn't know it, but he'd just heard the result of her first miracle. It had left her with the inability to say anything but what other people had already said. She was the most obviously determined of the pilgrims to remove the darkness from herself. Since her first miracle, she had spent her days actively seeking conversation with others. Her conversation partner would speak first and then Jennie would try to reply in her own words, executing invisible techniques in an attempt to do more than simply echo. So far, the only success she'd had was in making the other pilgrims dread conversation with her, which was too bad, because she really was a nice young lady.

Pete nearly did not see the pilgrim in the second room they passed, as he blended in with the shadows of his room so well.

This was Theldon Bunch. The first miracle had left him with moss furring his entire body, and now he spent his days either in the rocker in the corner of his room or under the shaded patio beside the house, reading fat paperback novels that the postman brought from Alamosa. He had the same amount of moss covering his skin as he'd had the day the miracle had created it, and he did not appear to be doing anything to combat it.

"Hello," Pete said to him, but Theldon Bunch did not look up from his book until after Pete and Antonia had already passed.

The third room contained the glamorous California twins, Robbie and Betsy, who, after the miracle, were corded together by an enormous black snake with a head at both ends. It tangled their feet if they took too many steps away from each other, but it also snapped at them if they sat too close for too long. If one side of it was attacked, the other side came to the rescue. If it was fed constantly and kept at a continuously acceptable tension, they could carry on without noticing it. The twins had arrived at Bicho Raro alternately fighting and clinging, and remained thus. It had occurred to Beatriz, at the very least, that the solution was for a twin to hold one of the snake's heads while the other twin killed the second head, but of course she could not suggest such a thing. So they continued to complain that the snake was too strong for them to battle on their own, and lived with it wrapped around them both.

"Hello," Pete said to them.

He was turned slightly more toward Robbie, so the snake

71

head nearest Betsy jealously snapped at him. Pete's heart leaped first, and then his body leaped second. His back hit the hallway wall and his hand slapped his dangerously shocked heart. Betsy drew the snake up short.

"So sorry," she said, but she was looking at Robbie as if it were Robbie's fault.

"Sure, that's okay, miss," Pete said, although he wasn't sure if it really was. "I'm Pete."

"Pete," Betsy repeated, but she was looking at Robbie as if this, too, were Robbie's fault. Robbie refused to look at her; they were fighting.

"Wyatt," Antonia said, farther down the hall.

"So long," Pete told the twins, and caught up.

Antonia had not spoken to any of the pilgrims they had passed. Pete was remembering how the Sorias had ignored him as he'd knocked on their doors and he was thinking about how now she was ignoring these people, and he was thinking it was pretty rude. He was too polite to say anything about it, though; he just kept looking over his shoulder at the three rooms they'd passed.

Antonia was no fool, so she stopped before the final room and put a hand on Pete's shoulder.

"You are thinking I'm a pig."

"No, ma'am."

"You are. I can see it on your face."

"No, ma'am."

"Now you're being a liar and thinking I'm a pig, but that's all right. I understand. We have rules here, Pete, but they don't have to do with you. We Sorias must be careful with pilgrims; if we interfere with them after the first miracle, our own darkness will come down on us, and that is a terrible thing that no one would like to see, worse than any of their darkness. So that is the first rule: only room and board for the pilgrims, no other conversation, because you don't know what will help them. Rule two, if you want a wife or you want a husband, you go outside Bicho Raro. Love is a dangerous thing already, without a pilgrim in it. Rule three, only a saint performs the miracle, and no one else around, because you don't know when the darkness will bite like that snake you just saw. These are the rules."

"Yes, ma'am," Pete said. He wasn't sure what he was expected to say, as he was not a Soria and the rules didn't apply to him, but he also could see that it was a grave issue and wanted Antonia to see that he realized this.

"That's why I'm not talking to the pilgrims," Antonia said.

"Yes, ma'am."

"It's not because I'm a pig."

"No, ma'am."

"That's why no one came to talk to you, because we thought you were a pilgrim."

"Yes, ma'am."

"I'm telling you because all of the pilgrims know, and you should, too, so that you know what a Soria will or won't do, and you know we're not being rude."

"Yes, ma'am."

"Good. Here's your room," Antonia said, closing the distance to the final doorway. "Clean up after yourself."

"Yes, ma'am," Pete said.

Antonia leaned toward the room but did not look inside it. "Padre, this boy will be your roommate. He can have the floor." She was walking away before she even finished speaking. "Come find Michael or myself when you're ready to work, Wyatt."

The final room in the hall belonged to Padre Jiminez, a priest from northern Colorado. He was as benevolent and friendly and holy as you'd hope for a priest to be, so long as your skirt didn't blow up in the wind. The first miracle had left him with the head of a coyote but the hands of a man. He used the first to gobble up rabbits and the second to fasten on his white collar each morning. He did try to vanquish the darkness, but he could not stop his coyote's ears from pricking when a pretty girl came to Bicho Raro.

When Pete stepped into the doorway, Padre Jiminez was sitting at the end of a narrow mattress. The bed was made up as tidily as a business envelope, and there was nothing else in the room but a small table with a lamp on it and a cross hanging on the wall. At this sight—the spare decor, the coyote-headed man, the grimly made bed—Pete suddenly felt a second shock through him. This one was not surprise but homesickness, an understanding of how far he was from Oklahoma in every way, a fear that his plan was nothing but smoke tricks to fool himself into feeling better. The ferocity of this emotion sent an additional wave through his heart, and for the first time, Pete really believed that Pete the doctor may have been onto something, and that was a leash that felt shorter.

And so it was a somewhat more feeble version of Pete that Padre first saw—some might argue a truer version, if they are one of those who believes we are only as strong as our weakest moments. Luckily for Pete and for many people, Padre Jiminez was not one of them.

The priest leaped up and loped across the room to Pete. "Welcome, young man," he said. He had a very crisp enunciation, because he had to work hard to get the words out around his sharp canines and lolling tongue. "Welcome, welcome, welcome!"

Pete, like many a young rural Protestant, reeled back first from the priestly collar and second from the coyote head. "Oh—sir—thank you."

Padre Jiminez waited until the silence had become slightly uncomfortable, and then he gobbled it up with his flashing teeth. "Ah! So, have you had your miracle yet?"

"I'm just here about a truck," Pete said. "Just here to work."

"Is that so!"

"Just a truck."

"No secret darkness lurking inside you?"

Pete found himself once again telling the story of his aunt Josefa.

"Of course, of course, of course," Padre Jiminez said. "Josefa. Wonderful lady, though a little progressive. We court darkness when we swim nude."

"Do we?" Pete asked.

"Do you?"

Pete halted the conversation and restarted it. "Are you still—do you still—are you a priest here?"

"I am always a priest in my heart. Are you a Catholic?"

"I'm a Christian."

"Lucky," Padre Jiminez said. "So am I. Say, you came with the man last night, didn't you?"

Pete had not thought about Tony since waking up in his car. But the jolt of homesickness he'd just felt had the effect of softening the memory of his trip with Tony. His mind skipped over all the negative aspects and instead highlighted the camaraderie of the shared hours together.

Just a decade before, a scientist named Harry Harlow had studied the science of attachment by performing experiments on monkeys. The poor infant monkeys had been deprived of their real mothers but offered two substitutes: an artificial monkey covered with terry cloth and an artificial monkey made of wire. A terry-cloth mother is not much of a mother at all, but all of the infant monkeys agreed she was better than the wire mother. Harlow had not studied young men from Oklahoma in this experiment, but the results still held true for Pete. Padre and the other strange pilgrims felt like a wire mother to Pete, and the specter of Tony, though only a snarling terry-cloth mother, seemed to at least offer a semblance of comfort.

"Yes, I did come with him!" Pete said now. "Where is he? Is he still here?"

"Oh yes, yes." Padre Jiminez gestured out the tiny window.

Together, they peered out the window, but Pete did not see Tony. He saw the bright day, and a swath of shade across it. Pete's eyes followed that long, stretching shadow, deep blue in the late morning light. Shielding his eyes against the sun, he tipped his head back and then farther back, trying to clearly see what enormous structure cast it. He saw a smooth white surface stretching two stories up, with seams like enormous stitching. He did not understand the top of it, which was dark and so black as to be violet. It was not until he lowered his eyes to look at the base of the structure and saw a single, vast, bare foot that he realized what he was looking at, because he remembered clearly Antonia Soria's dogs eating the shoe that had been on it. Now he understood that the white surface was yards of white suit and that the black that topped it was a field of shiny hair, all of it the same as he had seen it the night before, except three times larger.

"Holy moly," Pete said. "Is that Tony?"

8

While Pete was eyeballing Tony's new stature, Beatriz was finally discovering Daniel's letter.

Daniel was not much of a letter writer. He was a slow reader and a slower writer, often reversing letters inside a word and sometimes transcribing numbers facing the wrong direction. His ears were more cunning than his hands, so he was easily distracted by any noises while he worked. He could not write while anyone was speaking to him, or else he would accidentally pen the words he heard spoken. In fact, before he was the Saint of Bicho Raro, he and his friends had driven into town after dark to paint the side of the local grocery. They were painting the grocery because the owner's son had spoken unfavorably of the Soria family during the school day, and they were arriving after dark because they presumed correctly that the grocer did not want his building painted. Daniel, the bravest, was given the role of painting, and so he began to slowly apply the words (in Spanish for his friends, who were not bilingual like the Soria children) as the others kept watch, being careful to not form the letter *e* backward. He had intended to paint the proverb ¡*Vivir con miedo, es cómo vivir a medias!*—*A life lived in fear is a life half-lived!*—but his fellows, too drunk and jolly to cleave close to that noble sentiment, began to softly chant as Daniel painted, knowing how his letters would obey them rather than him. He ended up decorating the building instead with *¡Vivir con mierda, es cómo vivir a medias!*, which has a different meaning, as the corruption of only two letters transforms *miedo* from *fear* to *shit*.

This difficulty in writing had followed Daniel into his young adulthood, so when Beatriz got a letter from him, she knew immediately that something was amiss. He would not have written if there had been any other way to convey his meaning.

She had stepped on the letter as she'd descended the ladder. The paper had provided less grip than the rung and so her foot had slipped and she'd nearly fallen. She jumped to the ground to avoid twisting her ankle—and there it had been before her eyes. She opened it, saw Daniel's handwriting, and closed it back up again, quick. The sight of so much of Daniel's handwriting was as troubling as the sound of his voice had been the night before.

Beatriz preferred to do her hard thinking in private whenever possible, so she moved quietly away from the radio telescope, behind the buildings of Bicho Raro and over to the box truck. There was not much room beneath the truck, but she nevertheless managed to slide herself beneath it with some wiggling of first her hips and then her shoulders. Then, in the safety of that dim, small space, she sighed and opened the letter back up again.

She read it. She read it again, because the letter asked her to. She read it a third time. The letter didn't ask for that, but twice had not been enough.

Beatriz,

I am in love with Marisita Lopez. It was an accident.

Last night after I was done with Tony, I helped her. That wasn't an accident. I couldn't be a coward and watch her suffer anymore.

The darkness has already started to come to me.

I am going away from Bicho Raro to the wilderness, where it can't hurt anyone but me. I am worried that if I stay, the family will be tempted to help me, and bring darkness on themselves, too. I cannot live with that.

I am telling her to give this letter to you and no one else because you are the only one I can trust to be reasonable instead of kind. I'm trusting you to make them understand they can't try to find me. You better wait several hours before telling anyone to give me a head start just in case. Please. It's what I want. Read this another time so you see how much I mean it. This is only my fault and no one else should get hurt. Maybe I will be able to beat it and you will all see me again.

I am sorry, but I am taking the kitchen radio. Maybe I'll be able to pick up Diablo Diablo in the evenings, and it will be like you two are there with me.

Please don't tell Marisita that I love her. I don't want to make her any more hurt than she already is.

Daniel

Several of the words were spelled incorrectly and he had left out a few of them and his emphatic but messy underline for emphasis had nearly crossed out a few syllables, but Beatriz figured it out.

For several long minutes she remained under the truck, gazing at the lacy rust next to the wheels. The truck would not have ordinarily rusted so soon, not here in the dry heat of Bicho Raro, but earlier in the year it had been parked too close to Marisita's lodgings and had been flooded with the salt water of her tears.

Beatriz always carried a pen and one or two pieces of notebook paper folded into fourths, and now she removed them from her pocket. Previously, she had kept a stub of a pencil instead of the pen, as she preferred the feeling of its scratching—it felt quivery and alive as it shuddered across the paper—but once she had been knocked over by the cows when they escaped their paddock and had impaled her arm. Now she carried a pen. It was more inanimate but also more easily hooded.

Rolling onto her stomach, she began to jot down thoughts in the numbers of her secret language. How long, she mused, had Daniel been in love with Marisita Lopez, and how had it even happened? They'd been told their entire lives to keep their distance from the pilgrims, and one couldn't fall in love without getting close. Perhaps, she wrote, he was wrong. Perhaps he only felt he was in love with Marisita.

But Beatriz immediately crossed this out. Daniel knew himself and his emotions in a way that no one else in Bicho Raro did. If he said he was in love, he was in love. More to the point, she wrote to herself, using increasingly small numbers to preserve her paper, love would not be what killed him. He would need water in the desert, and food. He would need shelter from the bitter night cold and the attentive afternoon sun. It did not seem to be possible to bring him food or water without violating the taboo. There was also the question of his darkness. Darkness came in all shapes and sizes, and it was difficult and unpleasant to imagine what might have been lurking inside Daniel. They had all been told that a Soria's darkness was more dangerous than an ordinary pilgrim's darkness, and Beatriz had seen some fairly ominous manifestations. There was, Beatriz wrote, the possibility that his darkness was fatal.

After she recorded this thought, she had to put the pen down in the dust.

With a cluck of her tongue, she picked it back up. What she worried was that if she, the girl without feelings, was tempted to ignore Daniel's warning and search for him in the high desert, with the risk of bringing darkness upon them all, then the more passionate of the Sorias would be even more tempted. A pragmatic worry also pressed on Beatriz: If Daniel did not return, it would fall to her to be the Saint. Like all of the Sorias, she could manage the miracle. But when a real saint performed it, it was important. Spiritual. To Beatriz, it was a thing she could do, like brushing her teeth or changing oil in the truck.

It did not feel like enough.

If only the process was easier on the pilgrims. Often they journeyed for hundreds of miles to Bicho Raro and were already wearing thin on optimism by the time they arrived. Then, when the Saint performed the first miracle, many pilgrims found their

newly visible darkness just as daunting as invisible darkness—
possibly more so. Despair, that opportunistic companion, slunk
in, preventing them from examining themselves to perform the
second miracle necessary for complete healing. And of course
the Saint could not interfere. It was important, then, that the
pilgrim's emotional healing be well set in motion before the first
miracle ever took place, with prayer and counseling and atmosphere. With holiness, Daniel would say. Legend had it that the
greatest Soria saint of all, Catalina de Luna Soria, was so holy
that the first and second miracles always happened right on top
of each other, the darkness appearing only to be almost immediately vanquished by the euphoric pilgrim. It was hard to imagine
that now, with Bicho Raro brimming with unhealed pilgrims.

It was beginning to be uncomfortable beneath the truck.
Beatriz's shoulder blades pressed up against the exhaust. Her hair
tangled in a drivetrain component. The world outside the truck
was growing louder as well. A shovel pinged against rock, and
Antonia's voice lifted. She had set Pete Wyatt to work, and the
sounds of their industry intruded into Beatriz's thoughts.

Beatriz tried to write down a scenario where she successfully
filled Daniel's shoes, but it was not a pleasant thought exercise
for either her or any future pilgrims. Beatriz had acted as the
Saint only once, during the brief time before Daniel had repented
of his sins, and after Michael had stepped down as Saint to lose
himself in mundane work. Although not eager to take on the
role, she had been universally suggested as Michael's replacement
because of her otherworldliness. Shortly after, a smart-looking

financier had arrived in a smart-looking car with New York plates. Everything about him was in order; he did not even appear to have darkness inside him. But he was there for the miracle, and so she performed the miracle. Because of Beatriz's pragmatism, there was no ceremony or mystery, but because of her Soria blood, it worked anyway. The hair on the financier's head swiftly grew and curled, cascading long and lank around his face, and at the same time, his beard swiftly grew and curled, cascading long and lank down his chest. His clothing melted away, leaving him naked as the day he was born.

"This is unacceptable," the financier said, reaching to cover himself with the rug he had sat upon. But it, too, melted away when it touched his skin, leaving him once more naked and unshaven before Beatriz. He grasped for a wall hanging of Mary, but when the Virgin also vanished in his hands (a pity, as it was an heirloom), the truth of his miracle dawned on him. The miracle had reduced him to a primitive man, bare-bodied and shaggy-headed.

With poisonous anger, the financier turned upon Beatriz. This was no miracle, he told her. This was merely witchcraft, and not very good witchcraft at that. In previous generations, he continued, she would have been burned, or stoned, or worse. He went on to say that he could not imagine what sadistic pleasure she took in ruining successful men but he certainly hoped she was not angling for money since his finances had been in his pockets, which her curse had melted away. Beatriz could only quietly listen as he coldly berated her. She could not even remind him of his own role in the second miracle, lest she bring the darkness upon herself.

Finally he stood, naked of his dignity, his still-growing beard covering his manhood. With a last snarl in her direction, he stormed out of the Shrine and into the night, leaving his fancy car behind. He never returned for it; eventually, Luis sold it to a man he knew across the border. Rumors of him wandering the desert had joined those of Felipe Soria. Together, they were the wild men of Colorado.

Beatriz had never performed a miracle again.

"Beatriz, Judith's looking for you," Joaquin said, on one knee beside the truck.

Most people pass by box trucks without checking underneath them for other people, so it may seem surprising that Joaquin found Beatriz there. But Joaquin had many years of practice looking for Beatriz, and he knew to search for her in all of the places you might hope to find a cat or a venomous lizard— on top of roofs, hooked on tree branches, stretched in the dust beneath trucks.

"Hey. I see you under there. I said, Judith is looking for you."

Beatriz had not reached a satisfactory conclusion on her scratch paper and so did not emerge.

Joaquin picked up a stick to poke at her and then poured a little of the water from the bottle in his hand so that a slow, dusty river started moving her way. "Your mother is yelling at your father, and Judith is yelling now, too."

She made no move to emerge and the water stopped before it

reached her, so Joaquin unbuttoned his Hawaiian shirt and hung it on the truck's mirror to spare it from the dust and grime. Then he, too, squeezed his way under the truck to lie beside his cousin. In the background was the sound of Pete's shovel dinging off hard soil, and chickens barking at one another. Joaquin had managed to convince Luis to acquire aftershave for him and had doused himself in it. This musk spoke more loudly than the cousins did for several minutes, and then Joaquin said, "What?"

Beatriz handed him her notes.

"I can't read your—your—math recipes."

Beatriz handed him Daniel's letter.

Joaquin read it, and then he read it a second time, as Daniel had advised, and then, like Beatriz, he read it a third time. He let it flutter onto his bare chest so that he could grip his hair in his palms. The theatricality of this gesture might have convinced an outsider that his feelings were spurious, but anyone who knew how Joaquin felt about his hairstyle would have realized the opposite was true.

"I hate them," he said, eventually.

Beatriz replied to this in the same even way that she replied to all of Joaquin's untruths. "No, you don't."

"Fine. It's not their fault, they are all children of God and Mary, el alma generosa será prosperada, y el que riega será también regado, I know, I know," Joaquin said in Nana's quavering voice. Then, in his own: "We have to find a way to bring him water."

"Did you even read what he wrote?"

"Yes, but it's stupid."

"Don't make me regret showing you."

"We could ask a pilgrim to bring him water," Joaquin said, but almost immediately understood the impossibility of his own suggestion. ". . . if we could only speak to the pilgrims."

Beatriz gazed at the rust holes until they became a ruddy bug-eaten leaf and then focused into a rust hole again. To her vexation, her mind drifted to Pete Wyatt and his elbows, but her irritation dissipated when this thought solidified into an idea. "What do you know about that man who came to work last night?"

"Man? What man? Oh," Joaquin said dismissively. "That boy, you mean."

Beatriz ignored the demotion. "He's not a pilgrim. He could bring Daniel food and water."

There was silence as both cousins examined this idea for fault. When neither found any, Joaquin handed Beatriz the letter and she folded it up again neatly. They both rolled out from underneath the truck. Joaquin collected his shirt but didn't put it on; his skin was too dusty for him to risk sullying the fabric.

Both cousins looked in the direction of Francisco Soria's greenhouse. Voices still battled from within.

Joaquin said, "We could wait until they're done."

But Beatriz set off without hesitation. If Daniel could face his darkness head-on, she could face one of her parents' arguments.

9

At one point, the tale of Francisco and Antonia Soria had been the greatest love story to ever grace Bicho Raro, which was saying a lot.

Love in the high desert is a strange thing. There is something about the climate—the remoteness, the severity of the seasons, the dryness of the air, the extreme beauty—that makes people feel more deeply. Perhaps without trees or cities to dampen the enormity of the feelings, they spread out hugely. Perhaps the hard-packed dust of the San Luis Valley amplifies them, like a shout into a canyon. Whatever it is, the people of Bicho Raro were no exception. Everything was bigger: anger, humor, terror, jubilance, love. Perhaps this was why the darkness of the Sorias was considered a more dangerous thing, too. It, like everything else, was deeper and more uncompromising.

Antonia and Francisco had been born on the same minute of the same day, one hundred miles apart. They might not have met if not for the weather. In the dirty 1930s, drought had struck Bicho Raro, and the air was orange and thick from dawn until dusk. There was rarely wind, and when there was, it was also orange and thick. Temperatures seared. Cattle turned to statues in the fields and birds fell out of the sky.

One day, however, a cool, clear breeze caught Francisco's hair as he was digging the family sheepdog out of a sand dune that had formed overnight. It was a strange breeze—from the north, unlike the usual southwestern weather—and when he lifted his head, he could see that the breeze was carrying blue sky with it: clear blue air that a man could breathe without choking. He put down his shovel, and he and the dog followed the breeze clear out of Bicho Raro, down through San Luis, over the border to New Mexico, past Costilla, past Questa, and clear into Taos, where they were having a fiesta.

Francisco, who had lived in the San Luis Valley his entire life and under the drought for half of that life, could barely fathom such festivities. Little girls in fiesta dresses rode painted carousel horses on a merry-go-round powered by men turning a massive wooden gear. Boys one-third his height wore crisp and dustless sombreros. The dancing was so vigorous that he felt his legs stepping out without his permission, his body an unwitting mirror. The music replaced Francisco's blood, and he felt he could do anything. That was when the blue sky stopped, right over Antonia Alamilla, who was dancing in a white dress. He saw now that it was not blue sky at all, but rather a blue balloon whose string was tied around her wrist. When she saw Francisco in his dust-covered overalls, she immediately stopped dancing and declared, in facile Spanish, "I love dogs."

The rest of the townspeople looked on in shock. No one had heard Antonia speak since she'd been born, and once she had met Francisco, she did not stop. He asked her to be his wife, and when they were married in Bicho Raro two months later, Antonia's tears of joy coaxed rain from the sky and ended the decade-long drought.

But that was *before*.

On the day Beatriz climbed beneath the box truck to think, it was precisely one week before Francisco and Antonia's fiftieth birthdays. In honor of such a distinguished occasion, Judith had proposed a massive celebration; this was the reason she and Eduardo had returned the night before, to help prepare for such a feast. But Francisco and Antonia's union was becoming ever more fretful; unbeknownst to Judith, they had stopped talking to each other almost entirely.

Or rather, Francisco had stopped talking to Antonia. Once Antonia had begun to speak to Francisco, she had not decided to stop simply because he was not listening.

The yelling Joaquin had heard was because Antonia and Judith were confronting Francisco in his greenhouse. The greenhouse was a laboratory for plants, as Francisco believed in being scientific about his quest for the art of the black rose. A system of narrow metal pipes delivered precious water precisely where he intended it to go, and reflectors were attached to shutters so that he could direct the sun similarly. There were not only roses but also delicate lettuces that grew in a vertical grid arranged above an old claw bathtub, and secretive mushrooms that flourished in an old set of printmaker's drawers. Francisco stood among them, his hands covered in soil, his clothing covered with soil, but his hair impeccably oiled back. He had only a very few things he required to be in their places, but those things were non-negotiable.

"People will not come all this way just for you to stay in here with your roses!" Antonia told him. "And do not say that there are plenty of other people here!"

"No one is even asking you to help with the preparations!" Judith added.

"Although she would be well within her rights," Antonia continued. "She and Eduardo came back entirely for this. We only ask for you to promise to appear for one day out of the year. That is not so much for a wife to ask!"

"And don't say that your roses won't bear it!" Judith said. "*We* are supposed to be your roses!"

Judith was near tears at this point. Terror had accompanied her dreams that night, even though she had slept tangled with Eduardo's warm body. She could not stop thinking of the pilgrims lurking so close to her mother's home. All her life, Antonia had warned her shrilly of the dangers of the unhealed pilgrim, and Judith had forgotten what it was like to spend every minute alongside them. She did not know how her sister, Beatriz, could bear it—but then again, her sister had no feelings, and fear was a feeling.

"We *were* your roses," Antonia countered hotly.

Beatriz and Joaquin arrived at this moment, and for the first time, Francisco made a sound. He said, "Close the door! The humidity!"

"What was that?" shrilled Antonia. "Do you believe this is a game?" Because, to her, it had not sounded like he had spoken. It had sounded as if he was making light of the situation by whistling. This was what Beatriz's invented language sounded like when it was articulated aloud. Since it was mathematical, it was far more usable in musical form than with words.

Beatriz closed the door.

"Beatriz!" Judith said gratefully. "*You* speak sense to him."

"How are your roses?" Beatriz whistled to Francisco. "Any luck?"

"Too soon to tell," Francisco replied to her. Father and daughter had an easy relationship that came from possessing complementary needs. Roses and tomatoes are not precisely the same, but they both flourish in the same soil. He caught the dissonant, sour note in her sentence and asked, "Is everything all right?"

"What was that?" Antonia stormed again. "I don't understand why I must be deliberately excluded!"

The appearance of Beatriz gave Judith more strength. She said, "What Father is doing is despicable. He is deliberately ignoring her. I arrive home last night and she tells me that Ed and I can stay in their bedroom as she has moved into mine! 'Mama,' I asked, 'how do you and Papa fit in that room?' And she tells me that Papa stays in the greenhouse all the time and never sleeps, so she is sleeping alone now! She stays in my room because the loneliness there is smaller! How do you think I felt coming home to that news, Beatriz?"

Beatriz didn't believe she needed to think about the answer, as it seemed clearly telegraphed in Judith's tone.

Judith went on. "I don't care what they are fighting about. Papa cannot extort her in this way! It is not fair and it is not how a husband of forty years behaves!"

"Gosh, forty years?" Joaquin said.

"I was estimating," Judith snapped.

"Is that how old you think we are?" Antonia demanded.

Judith told Francisco, "This mistreatment won't do. You must move back into the house. You cannot turn your back on her this way! If you don't like her moods, you have to know that withholding your presence will only make it worse!"

Some may have felt she was being unfair or frivolous. But for newly wed Judith, the party represented something else—a promise that a pure and passionate love was still a pure and passionate love years down the road, despite tragedy and differences in personality. It also represented security. She had remained safe at Bicho Raro all these years only because she had her mother and her father standing guard over her sister and her. But now, if they had separated, anything could happen. Darkness could swallow them all. If there was not going to be a party, she wanted to flee again immediately. She *would* have fled again immediately, if she did not love her family too much to leave them to their fates.

Francisco did not reply. When he did not like the sound of

something, he merely went away inside his head, where it was quieter.

Beatriz joined her father and inspected the plants before him. These were not roses nor mushrooms nor lettuces but instead tender garlic bulbs, broken open for investigation. He offered her two to smell and she did, experimentally, one then the other.

"Make him understand, Beatriz, that really all I want is to make certain that he will celebrate his birthday with the rest of us!" Antonia said. When Judith had lived at home, both she and Antonia had often exhorted either Beatriz or Francisco in this way, as if Beatriz and Francisco had feelings as a second language and that someone who spoke fluent logic was needed to accurately convey their meaning. In reality, father and daughter were capable of deep feelings, but both were victims of that old saying, "believing your own press." After years of being told they had no feelings, they began to give the opinion credence themselves, which was why Beatriz was having the crisis of decision over Daniel's letter in the first place. If she had recognized herself capable of such deep distress, she might have been able to better address it.

When Beatriz didn't answer, Antonia said, clearly hurt, "You always take his side."

Beatriz said, "That is *not* true." She did not take sides.

"It isn't," Joaquin agreed. "Beatriz is very fair."

This statement reminded Beatriz very acutely of a similar statement made by Daniel in his letter. Realizing that there would be no good time to address the task at hand, she produced the letter now without unfolding it.

"I need to tell you something. I have a letter from Daniel," she said.

"A letter?" Antonia asked, with confusion, unable to imagine what would drive Daniel to do such a thing.

Beatriz went on. "He helped one of the pilgrims."

This news traveled into the interior of the brains in the room at different speeds. Francisco put down the garlic bulb he had been holding. Judith blinked, and then her eyes widened.

Rage seized Antonia.

Here are things that happen when rage overtakes you: First, your blood pressure begins to tick upward, every escalating beat of your heart punching angrily against the walls that contain it. Your muscles tense, fisting in preparation for action. Adrenaline and testosterone leap from your glands, twin horses dragging a red-faced chariot through your thoughts. It is an interesting and peculiar twist of anger that it is jump-started in the part of our brains responsible for emotions, and it is only after the blood-boiling process has taken hold that our good old cortex, the part of the brain we rely on for thought and logic, has a chance to catch up. This is why we say stupid things when we are angry.

Antonia was nearly always angry.

Pacing, she ranted, "What an idiot! He knew better! We told you all!"

"Did he say what form his darkness took?" Francisco asked calmly. His tone further fanned Antonia's rage.

Beatriz shook her head.

"Soria darkness?" Judith whispered. Fear built in her just as rage had mounted in Antonia, only it was a lighter, more feathery structure, batting around in her rib cage.

Joaquin broke in. "But we have an idea. Even if we can't help him with his darkness, he doesn't have to be helpless."

Francisco, Antonia, and Judith stared at them both, as intent as the owls that had gazed at Beatriz earlier.

Beatriz added her thought. "That boy from last night could bring him food and water. Pete Wyatt. A Soria can't help, but there is no reason why he can't interfere."

Immediately, Antonia said, "Absolutely not!"

"No," Francisco agreed. Everyone stared at him, shocked by the agreement and by the firm denial of such a simple solution.

"But why not?" demanded Joaquin.

Antonia said, "We can't know if helping him in any way would count as interfering with his miracle, even if it is through Pete Wyatt. If it counted against us as interference . . . where would we be? In the same foolish place he is! And what good would that do any of us?" She opened the door—humidity escaped—and shouted, "Rosa! Rosa! Rosa! Come here! Oh, come here." She swooned against the door. Judith gasped as if she was sobbing, but she did not cry.

"Oh, Mama, Judith, you're being dramatic," Beatriz started.

"You're just like your father," snarled Antonia.

Neither Francisco nor Beatriz rose to this remark; they never did.

"I don't see why going through that guy is a risk," Joaquin insisted. "We don't avoid the pilgrims who live here any more than that."

"We can't do nothing," Beatriz said.

"Look, all of you. A Soria's darkness spreads like nothing you have seen before." Antonia's voice was ironclad. "I forbid all of you from going to find Daniel. Over my dead body!"

10

To understand Antonia's response to Beatriz's suggestion, you must know the story of the last time darkness came to Bicho Raro. None of the cousins except Judith had been born yet; it was only a few years after Antonia had come to live with Francisco. There were more Sorias and fewer pilgrims at Bicho Raro then; the pilgrims back then seemed to be swifter about vanquishing their darkness and heading back on their way. The Soria siblings at that time were as close as Daniel and Beatriz and Joaquin were.

It was 1944, and the world was at war. Even if you had not gone to enemy territory, the enemy could come to you. In Colorado Springs, twelve thousand interned German prisoners of war harvested sugar beets in work camps. Trinidad housed another two thousand Germans. Tiny Saguache kept two hundred prisoners of war within their high school. Even Bicho Raro was not exempt: A branch work camp operated in the sugar beet field ten miles away, and on a clear day, the sounds of Germans singing as they worked could be heard in the grazing pastures above the houses.

The prisoners, separated as they were from ordinary life, were the source of much curiosity and contention. The government promised these young German men were the answer to the labor shortage in Colorado, but the Germans did not look like they belonged, with their fair, easily burned skin and their pale hair, nor did they sound like they belonged, with their marching, deliberate syllables. They did not dress like they belonged: Prisoners of war were allowed to wear their uniforms if they wished, and most of them wished, although their khaki shorts grew increasingly improbable as the year marched toward winter.

And winter was dark that year.

Winter in this part of the country was a frozen place. Temperatures plummeted in the desert and snow heaped over the memory of the scrub. Nothing moved. Survival happened by having a warm hole to wait in; if you had not built or found one by the time the blizzards hit, folks relayed the ending of your story with tears and a beer.

Unlike much of the world, Bicho Raro was enjoying a time of prosperity due to the previously mentioned windfall from Elizabeth Pantazopoulus. So although it was bitter outside, and claustrophobic inside, there was plenty of food and comfort to be had.

It was a grim evening when a strange pilgrim came to Bicho Raro. It had been snowing for the entire week, and it was still snowing then, the bored snowfall of a sky that cannot think of anything better to do. It was neither light nor dark—just gray. Everyone was inside when the owls began to make a commotion. They lifted from roofs, sending snow coughing down to the ground, and launched themselves in the direction of the newcomer. He was still trudging a half a mile off, but the owls went straight to him and doubled back to Bicho Raro, and then back to him again, half-mad with the promise of the darkness and the miracle.

Antonia Soria was the first out to greet him when he stumbled into Bicho Raro. She had made it only a few yards into the knee-high snow when she stopped; it had become clear to her that he was one of the Germans. She didn't see much more than his uniform before she went back into the house for Francisco and a gun. She was joined by others: the oldest brother, José, and also Michael and Rosa Soria and their curious sister, Loyola, who was Daniel's mother, and gentle Benjamin, who was Daniel's father (and the current Saint). Loyola was very pregnant at this time with Daniel and should not have been out in the cold, but she did not take many steps without Antonia; the two had been the very best of friends since Antonia had come to live at Bicho Raro.

"Bitte," the German said. His knees were knocking together with the cold, and they were bright red. He was wearing his uniform shorts, and the snow had soaked right through his socks and pressed up against his bare knees for miles.

Antonia raised the shotgun warningly.

"Bitte," the German said again. This was because his arms had a child in them. The child's face was the same color as the German's knees, the ugly red of too much cold. Because he spoke very little English and no Spanish, there was no way for the

German to tell the Sorias how he came to be holding the child. He was barely a child himself.

"Where did you escape from?" asked Francisco, but of course the German didn't understand this, either. The owls were sweeping low and desperate around him as he staggered close, not looking at the shotgun, and offered the child to Michael.

Now, it must be said that it is a funny thing to be able to perform miracles. Having the ability to help someone does not automatically go hand in hand with the ability to know when it's the right time to help someone. One is left looking at strangers who are clearly in need of aid and wondering if the Saint can merely attend to their needs, or if the Saint is required to ask the would-be recipient first.

The German clearly needed a miracle.

It was not as if they could ask him, though. No one there spoke a lick of German.

Benjamin weighed his responsibility in the matter and the level of earnestness on the German's face, and made the decision that because the German had been kind to this child, Benjamin owed him kindness as well. He performed the miracle.

At once, the German let out a small cry of surprise, put down the child in his arms, and transformed into a large-eared kit fox. Benjamin had anticipated this, or something like it. What he hadn't anticipated was that the miracle would also operate on the child the German had brought—Benjamin had not considered it would be possible for such a small toddler to have darkness in him. But the child's hands began to turn into dragon scales, and as they did, the child roused from his stupor and, in fright, began to cry.

What does it mean to interfere with a miracle? It is not rightly known what counts as helping pilgrims to heal themselves. It is not the indirect care of providing a roof over their heads, as they did at Bicho Raro, or the direct care of providing food for their bowl. But it was sometimes the indirect kindness of allowing a pilgrim to play a card game with you, or the direct kindness of offering advice. Better to keep one's distance, the Sorias had decided, than to try to predict what might count as interference.

But Benjamin did not think about this as he offered comfort to the crying child. He was not thinking about the child's miracle at all, really, as he had only intended to help the German. And for him, like for most, there was not much that the head had to do with hearing a crying child and moving toward it; that was all in the heart.

It took no time for the Soria darkness to manifest in Benjamin. Soria darkness, as said before, is faster and more terrible than the usual pilgrim's darkness. Benjamin had barely spoken to the child when he let out a gasp. His legs had gone sprawled and odd, a foal's legs scrabbling for footing in the snow. He could not see it, but his legs were beginning to turn to wood. Loyola, unknowing, asked him what was wrong. She tugged up his snow-crusted pants leg to reveal gray, spindly wood, dry logs like you would find left in the sand.

"Oh, Benjamin, I will love you anyway!" she told him, and

even this phrase, this small comfort, counted against her, and now the darkness began to fall upon her, too. She became wood from the top down, the opposite from Benjamin, and as Benjamin's chest and arms became wood, her head and neck and shoulders became wood.

"¡El niño!" José cried. He did not mean the dragon-scaled child, but rather the infant that the now-wooden Loyola had been carrying. As Antonia began to scream Loyola's name, the sound swirling away in the powder, José seized a shovel and leaped forward to chop Daniel's small body out of the now-wooden Loyola before he was sealed in forever. Even as José hacked at Loyola's lifeless form, his own legs became wood from this interference. He shouted for his brothers to leave him.

Francisco and Michael and Rosa dragged Antonia into the house and slammed the door.

The fox ran away, and so did the dragon-scaled boy.

It was only after the sounds of destruction had died away that Antonia, Francisco, Michael, and Rosa reemerged. José's sacrifice had worked: The baby Daniel had been hewn from his wooden mother and now sobbed in the dust beside his wooden father and wooden uncle. He was fully flesh and blood, and untouched by the darkness. As a helpless newborn, he had no way to accidentally interfere with his parents' or uncle's miracle, and moreover, as an innocent infant, he had no darkness inside him yet to be provoked by such a disaster.

Rosa lifted Daniel from the wooden remains of his family. Antonia touched the place where Loyola's wooden frame had been cleaved to remove him. Francisco took the shovel from where it had fallen beside José and leaned it back up against the house. He did not say anything.

This was when Antonia became angry, and she had never become unangry since. This was also when Francisco began to use fewer and fewer words each year. Michael stopped cutting his hair. Rosa remained Rosa.

Antonia finished telling this story as she led the cousins toward a small shed by the chickens. The door was barred and never opened, but she opened it now. The light sprawled over the dust inside.

She threw her hand outward to demonstrate the contents of the shed. She said, "And there they still are today!"

"That just looks like wood," Joaquin said.

"Exactly," replied Antonia.

"But Loyola was not a Soria," Beatriz pointed out. "Why wasn't she allowed to help Benjamin?"

"If you love a Soria, their darkness is yours, too," Antonia said.

"Hm," said Beatriz.

They all peered at the pile of gray wood inside the shed for several long minutes. Beatriz was thinking it was fortunate that she had never opened the door before, as she would have thoughtlessly burned her relatives as firewood. Antonia was thinking that she was even angrier now than she was the day she lost her best friend. Joaquin was thinking that Daniel was only alive because of José's quick and selfless bravery ... and now Daniel had been felled by the precise same thing that had claimed his parents. Judith was thinking about how she had never even con-sidered that Eduardo was just as endangered now by the Soria taboo, by virtue of his love for her. Francisco was thinking about how long it had taken them to decide on a name for his dead sister's baby once they had removed him from the scene of the tale.

They were all thinking about what Daniel's darkness might look like.

"If only we could train your dogs to take food to him," Beatriz said.

"Without killing him directly afterward," Joaquin murmured.

Antonia snarled.

"In any case, that settles the issue of the birthday party for now," Francisco said finally. "I won't celebrate until Daniel returns to us."

11

Pete worked.

He began to work as soon as he tossed his bags into the room he was to share with Padre Jiminez, and he worked without pause all day long. He worked for six hours straight, pausing only to suddenly divert his path when he caught sight of Beatriz Soria, waiting until the coast was clear and his heart was safe before he began work again.

"New boy!" called Robbie, one of the twins, who could not remember his name. "Come talk to us."

Pete said, "I can't. I'm working."

"Pete?" Marisita called as he walked through Bicho Raro, his arms full of boxes. "Will you be stopping for almuerzo?"

Pete said, "I can't. I'm working."

"You're making me tired to look at you," said mossy Theldon from his seat on the porch. "Take a load off."

Pete said, "I can't. I'm working."

Antonia had set Pete on tasks that required little skill but much sweat. Pete found himself digging out collapsed irrigation ditches and picking individual nails out of the driveway, sweeping unoccupied (and sometimes occupied) wasp nests out of

eaves, and plucking malevolently red Colorado potato beetle larvae off the tomato and potato crops.

The last of these tasks nearly broke him. As relentless as Pete
was, the Colorado potato beetle was more so. As fast as he could
destroy them, they made more of themselves. He did not know
that the Colorado potato beetle, also known as the ten-lined potato
beetle, was also currently persecuting the East Germans. Plagues
of potato beetles were blamed upon American planes. Communist
propaganda shouted that the Sechsbeiniger Botschafter del Wall
Street (six-legged ambassadors of Wall Street) would eat them out
of house and home and right into capitalism. East German school-
children were sent into the fields to pluck larvae, just as Pete was
doing, and they, too, learned to hate the small, fleshy, scarlet
creatures.

It was possible that this particularly unwinnable game might
have broken Pete's will to work, but luckily for him, a thunderstorm came in, fast and roaring. The desert caught his attention
with a puff of dust and weeds, so he just had time to take cover
in the six-stall barn before the rain really began to come down.
Inside the barn, Pete began to shovel manure and sweep the aisle.
It was hard work, but it was better than the never-ending drudg-
ery of beetle picking.

Inside, it was dim and comforting, either because of or
despite Pete not being raised around horses. There were only two
horses in the stable at the moment—three if you counted the one
the mare was carrying inside her—but they were all terrible
horses. The mare was a savage creature kept mostly because she

was the fastest barrel racer to come out of Colorado in a generation. She was so mean that she even killed her own name, and
now people just pointed to her. They kept breeding her, hoping
that she'd throw a foal with all the speed and none of the malice,
but so far, no dice. They had great hopes for the foal she was
carrying now, but the truth was that the tiny filly inside her
would, in six years, bear the state's current barrel-racing champion out of a competition and through the display window of a
local furniture store.

The other horse in the barn was Salto, a saddlebred stallion
that one of the pilgrims had come riding in on five years before.
He was a very fancy horse, it turned out, one of the last of a very
rare bloodline, and so although the Sorias were not particularly
interested in saddlebreds, he was nonetheless valuable for his
progeny. Every so often, people would come from very far away
to breed their mares to him and would pay an enormous sum for
this privilege. And so he remained. The only problem with Salto
was that he was extremely high-strung and would not respect a
fence. He had to remain in his box stall day in and day out, and
as he was so anxious and excitable, he had to wear a small bit of
padding strapped between his ears to prevent him from rearing
up and murdering himself on the ceiling of his own stall. Michael
had put a radio in the stable to soothe Salto and prevent him
from attempting escape.

Pete was looking at Salto when he realized that he was not
the only human in the barn. There was another man scrubbing

buckets in one of the empty stalls. To break the silence and to be friendly, Pete said, "Crazy weather, right?"

Pete did not know it, but he was talking to Luis the one-handed, who was not actually one-handed but was called that because his left hand was a full one-inch wider than his right. Luis used the spread of those left fingers to great advantage: He was the finest guitar player in a fifty-mile radius and no one could catch a baseball like he could. There were two things that people did not know about Luis: First, that he was a collector of gloves. He bought two pairs of gloves each time, as he needed two different sizes, and he kept the too-small left gloves in a box that he stored between his mattress and the wall. Second, Luis the one-handed was a great romantic, and he daydreamed that there existed a love of his life who also had mismatched hands, and that his useless left-hand gloves would one day fit her. So he kept those gloves in a box like a stack of prewritten love letters, waiting for the heart that was longing to read them.

"It's a big change from Oklahoma," Pete tried.

"Llueve a cántaros," said Luis.

This exchange was unproductive as Luis the one-handed did not speak very good English and Pete was from Oklahoma and had only loneliness as his second language.

They both shrugged, and, his bucket scrubbing done, Luis went into the hayloft to nap until the rain was over.

So Pete worked with only the galloping rain on the roof for company. He was happier than he'd been in a while. Although homesickness still plucked at him, his overall mood had been so poor in the days leading up to his exodus from Oklahoma that everything else seemed brighter in comparison.

It would be easy to think that the reason Pete's failure to serve hit him so hard was because his family wasn't understanding. But the truth was the opposite. If one lives with a brood of ogres, it is not a hard thing at all to let them down. One can even feel, perhaps, that the ogres had it coming—they were ogres, after all. But the Wyatts were not ogres. George Wyatt was a brusque and realistic man, but he was not cruel. He eyed the situation at hand and took the steps needed to correct for it. When Pete the doctor handed Pete the son back to him with the verdict of *unfit for service*, he surveyed the situation and told Pete, factually, that Pete would find something else to do and, in any case, he was sure that Dexter would continue the family's military legacy, so Pete didn't have to feel he was letting down the home front. Flor Wyatt, Pete's mother, was married to a military man, and her mother had been married to a military man, and her mother's mother had been married to a military man, and even back in Spain her mother's mother's mother had been married to a military man, and so on and so forth until the beginning of both women and the military, but she did not shame Pete's inability to enlist. Instead, she said, "I'm sure you'll find another way to serve your country." And Dexter Wyatt, Pete's slightly younger brother, who was the closest to an ogre the Wyatt family had, said, "I'll shoot 'em for you, Pete."

This kindness, however, only made the situation worse for Pete. It emphasized that the person who was being cruelest to Pete was actually Pete.

He knew that leaving wouldn't change the way he felt. He didn't pretend that he would outrun himself. But he did think he might find something to feed that voracious sense of duty inside him, unless that hungry feeling was just the gaping hole in his heart.

The box truck, he thought, had to be the answer.

Pete peered at the vehicle as he worked in the barn, looking out the windows to where it was parked at every opportunity. It was a touchstone, reminding him of what all of his new blisters would eventually be traded for. He thought he saw the back of the truck open at one point, but when he looked back out the window, it was closed again.

After a few hours of work, Pete realized that there were sounds coming from within the barn that could not be accounted for by the storm, the horses, or Luis's snores. Following the sounds to their source, he discovered a low crawl space with a door in it. On the other side of the door, standing in the rain, was Michael Soria, Joaquin's father.

Michael was working. He had not yet been told about Daniel, but even if he had been, he would have still been working. Ever since he had lost so much of his family to the incident with the German and the child, all he did was work from the moment he opened his eyes until the moment he closed them, taking his meals standing up and saving all of his non-negotiable body functions for the two minutes before he retired to bed. He was a very old-fashioned kind of person. Many people mistook Michael for Joaquin's grandfather. He had already been quite old when he'd had children, and he appeared even older than he was because of his beard. Ever since the incident with the German and the child, he had stopped cutting both his hair and his beard and instead allowed them to grow as long as they wanted. Now both were so long that he had to wrap each up into a knot he secured with bands, one at the nape of his neck and one at his chin. Because his bones troubled him so much from all of his age and all of his work, he would unknot his beard and hair when he climbed into bed and, spreading it out, he would lie on top of it and find that it was the only thing that eased his aches and pains.

Here was a thing he wanted: to work. Here was a thing he feared: that he would become too feeble to work.

When Pete heard Michael, he was repairing the barn foundation in the rain. A scourge of pocket gophers had arrived at the beginning of the year with only two purposes: to make more pocket gophers and to dig their home directly beneath the barn. They had been so successful in the first pursuit that Antonia's dogs could now subsist entirely on a diet of slow pocket gophers, and they had been so successful with the second pursuit that the barn foundation now tipped precariously, weakened by a network of gopher sitting rooms. Michael had previously performed a temporary repair by filling the holes with Rosa's failed, rock-hard milk cakes, but the holes had outgrown Rosa's baking habit and now he had no choice but to rebuild it properly.

Pete surveyed the situation and formed an opinion. "Need a hand?"

Michael surveyed Pete and formed an opinion. "It's raining."

"Yes, sir," Pete agreed. He joined Michael in the rain, and together they worked side by side until their clothing was as soaked through as Marisita's. They reached the end of the section Michael had hoped to finish that day, and wordlessly they began the next. They finished the next day's section and began on the next. And so on and so forth until they had repaired the entirety of the barn's foundation and it had stopped raining and the sun had come back out again and they both stopped to rest their hands on their knees and look at what they had done.

"You're Josefa's boy," Michael said finally.

"Nephew, sir."

"You're here about the truck."

"Yes, sir."

"Good," said Michael, which might not seem like much of a reply, but put together, was more than he'd said to most anyone for years.

"Sir, do you mind me asking—" Pete began. "Do folks mostly come here for miracles?"

"Why else would they come out here?" This statement was not as dour as it sounded; Beatriz was not the only one in Bicho Raro who could be strictly pragmatic.

Pete gestured to the land around them. "Because it's pretty."

The desert preened and Michael regarded Pete anew. One compliments a man when one compliments his chosen home, and Michael felt nearly as good as the desert about Pete's words. Kindly, he said, "You better get into some dry clothes now."

Straightening up, Pete finger-combed his rain-flat hair into its usual style. "Soon. Got to pick some beetles first. See you later, sir!"

He left Michael standing there by the side of the barn, sheering off hard left to avoid a shadow he thought might be Beatriz, and then threw himself back into beetle picking. Ordinarily, Michael would have also thrown himself directly back into work, but for the first time in a very long time, Michael stood there for a full five minutes before beginning his next job, just watching Pete start on his next project. Humans have always been fascinated by mirrors, after all. Michael had never seen from the outside how it looked to work constantly to avoid feeling, and he could not look away.

12

That night, Beatriz and Joaquin went out in the box truck with a renewed purpose. Before, the identity of their desired audience had been nebulous, distant. Now, in light of the day's events, all of their audience was wrapped up in a single person. Daniel Lupe Soria, their beloved cousin. Daniel Lupe Soria, their cherished Saint. Daniel Lupe Soria, lost in darkness.

"This one goes out to Daniel, if he's listening," said Diablo Diablo. "Some light for your darkness: This is 'There's a Moon Out Tonight' by the Capris."

"There's a Moon Out Tonight" began to croon, although there was no moon out that night. Diablo Diablo's pretaped voice remained inside the back of the box truck as Joaquin, the body of Diablo Diablo, sat in the cab of the truck with Beatriz, listening.

Joaquin was torn every which way inside. He was a passionate person, but not good at being passionate at more than one thing at a time. On the one hand, he was thinking about Daniel's plight. Joaquin had always admired Daniel. He did not want to *be* him, as all of the praying and holiness seemed as if it would conflict with Joaquin's sense of panache, but he deeply appreciated everything his cousin stood for and all of the kindnesses Daniel had ever shown him. It seemed to Joaquin now, in misty and faulty retrospect, that Daniel was soft and vulnerable, too kindly to protect himself, a saint made for martyring. He could not imagine how the older Sorias could live with themselves, knowing that Daniel was out in the desert alone. Where was their courage?

But this was not all that Joaquin was thinking about. It felt unfair to his cousin to be anything but consumed by thoughts of him, and yet Joaquin was also guiltily thinking about the radio. Joaquin had long been obsessed with radio personalities and modern music. He listened to Denver's KLZ-FM with both resentment and hope, comparing himself to the local personalities and measuring if he could do better. He listened to the wild howl of the border blasters' DJs—those cowboys of the high-powered stations that screamed out from just across the Mexican border, skirting American regulations through sheer force of power. And, signal permitting, he listened to the sweet fast patter of the more famous personalities of the time, like Jocko Henderson and Hy Lit. He was an ardent follower of *American Bandstand*, that daytime Philadelphia-based television show featuring teens dancing to the latest hits. The Sorias did not have a television, so twice a week, Joaquin rode into town with Luis and watched it on Elmer Farkas's television before hitching a ride back home, an arrangement that had been established during the school year and had not yet expired. This program formed the basis for most of Joaquin's hair and clothing decisions. He studied the screen diligently for evidence of fashions that had yet to reach southern Colorado (most never would) and did his credible best to duplicate them. For this progressive attitude, he received considerable ridicule from his family, which he never appeared to notice (although he did). He dreamed of a day when he would be infamous behind the microphone, Diablo Diablo, devil of the airwaves, and teens would be looking to *him* to set trends.

Joaquin tried to make himself think only about Daniel, but here in the box truck, the radio could not help but intrude.

Beatriz, however, had only one thought in her head. This was unusual because she was ordinarily likely to hold many thoughts in her head and, unlike Joaquin, was good at it.

The one thought was Pete Wyatt.

Over the course of the day, Beatriz had learned that Pete— he of the potentially soft elbow skin—was in Bicho Raro to work for the very same truck they were sitting in now. Her first impression had been that this deal wasn't fair, which she almost immediately rejected as her personal bias, and then revisited when she considered that actually, after a consultation with the facts, it really *wasn't* fair. The truck, after all, had been a wreck before this summer, overgrown and inoperable, and Beatriz had spent many long hours restoring it to life. Surely that gave her some claim to it. She didn't blame Pete for this conundrum; he could not have known before making the work arrangement that Beatriz was going to restore the truck. But it didn't erase the conflict.

It would not have mattered if the truck hadn't been their only way to communicate with Daniel.

Annoyed at the impasse, she opened the passenger door.

"Where are you going?" Joaquin asked.

"I'm checking the range." During the course of the afternoon, Beatriz had double-checked her soldering job on each connection—this was when Pete had glimpsed her earlier. Although there was no way to find out if Daniel and the kitchen radio were anywhere within the listening radius, she could at least do her best to cast the signal as far as possible. Both cousins were desperate to communicate with him safely.

They had their ideas of what he might be doing at that moment. Although it defied his sense of nobility, Joaquin imagined Daniel huddled in a grotto like a caveman, gnawing on the desiccated leg of a kangaroo rat, his clothing already tattered rags. Although it defied Beatriz's sense of probability, she imagined Daniel padding silently across the dusty desert, his form the opposite of Padre Jiminez's: the body of a coyote, the head of a man.

With a shiver, Joaquin removed the keys from the ignition. He didn't want to stay in the truck by himself; there was something more ominous about being in a dark vehicle alone than being in the dark night with Beatriz. He made sure to snatch a bottle of water, lest he dry out in the desert (he put it inside his shirt), and also the flashlight (he did not put it inside his shirt).

Beatriz had already climbed from the truck with a radio in hand. Because Daniel had taken the kitchen Motorola, they had taken the only other radio that was in Bicho Raro. This was the one Pete had heard playing in the barn earlier. Joaquin had been anxious that the horses would somehow stampede without the benefit of the radio's static, but Beatriz had considered the likelihood of that and found the odds acceptable. Statistically, the horses had never stampeded in her lifetime; factually, it was impossible for the radio to have been playing programming for all of those hours; statistically, the horses would not stampede in her lifetime; factually, the cousins would be fine to take it for a few hours.

Beatriz also carried a shotgun. She did not think she would have to use it, but the world seemed like a more dangerous place than it had only a few days before.

"Joaquin," she ordered, "please point that flashlight where we're going."

Joaquin was caught equally between a fear of invisible wild animals and detection by the FCC, and so he alternately pointed the light where they were walking and into his palm when he felt they were too obvious to prying distant eyes. "I heard that sometimes Soria darkness will attack other Sorias, even without interference."

"All the more reason to see it coming. Who told you that?"

"Nana."

"I don't believe you."

"Okay," Joaquin admitted. "It's just this: I saw Mama tell her about Daniel, and Nana immediately got up and locked her back door. What do you think about that?"

Grudgingly, Beatriz had to admit that Joaquin's thesis was

not a bad one. Joaquin made a triumphant noise not in keeping with secrecy.

"If you're going to shout, you might as well point the flashlight so we can see!" Beatriz ordered.

Distant thunder made them pause.

Joaquin ran an anxious hand over his hair and cast an anxious glance at the sky. "Are we going to be killed?"

"Unlikely," Beatriz replied.

Although the sky above them was clear, lightning was visible on the horizon: a storm, many dozens of miles away—in a place as flat as this high desert, weather was often something that happened to other people. Beatriz was not particularly worried about being struck by that storm's lightning, although she did devote a passing thought to the antenna connected to the box truck; they would turn back to take it down if the storm got too close. A lightning strike would be potentially deadly to the station.

"Can we make the signal stop crackling like that?" Joaquin asked.

"Not tonight," Beatriz replied. "It needs more work." This reminded her of Pete Wyatt and how she was not at all sure how much more time she had with the truck. She felt obliged to tell Joaquin all of this, and did, in a low voice, so that she could still have one ear on the signal strength.

After she was through, Joaquin kicked the dirt, but not hard, because he didn't want to dirty his paisley pants, and he also cursed a little. "Pete Wyatt!"

Joaquin didn't know much about Pete Wyatt, but he was not

a fan. This had nothing to do with Pete Wyatt and everything to do with Michael, who had actually stopped working in order to sing the praises of Pete's work ethic to Rosa and Joaquin. He began with small gestures, complimenting Pete's quick ability to grasp the meat of any new job, and then moved out from there to admiring how hard Pete worked even under the harsh rain, expanded further to how satisfying it was to see a young person who actually appreciated the land, and then ultimately ending up with a somewhat tone-deaf statement that Pete was the son every man deserved but never had.

Joaquin, as the son that Michael may not have deserved but definitely actually had, was less than thrilled by the statements. His mother, Rosa, defended Joaquin, but not in a way that brought Joaquin any satisfaction.

"If only Joaquin could bring himself to work at anything like Wyatt does," Michael said.

"Oh, you know Quino," Rosa replied, "he is a gentle boy and he will come into his own one day!"

"When I was Joaquin's age, I knew what I wanted to do with myself, and that was leave a print on the world with the dint of my labor," Michael said.

"We need soft men, too. Sweet gentle boys whose mothers love them just the way they are!"

"I never see Joaquin doing anything but oiling his hair. A man is more than his hair."

"He is also his mustache," Rosa agreed. "But Quino is still just a boy and soon enough he will have a mustache. Not like yours, of course. You cannot expect that of anyone, even your own son. But he will have his own sort."

This infuriated Joaquin. He did not want to be a soft, gentle man who had accomplished nothing. He was *not* a soft, gentle man who had accomplished nothing. He longed to tell them that he already had plans, and that he was going to be a radio DJ, Diablo Diablo, and that one day they would compare Pete Wyatt to *him* and find Pete wanting.

"I'll talk to him," Beatriz said. "Pete, I mean."

"What are you going to say?"

"I think that will depend on him. I—"

Quick as death, Joaquin halted and held a hand out to Beatriz, snatching her to a standstill. Everyone has two faces: the one they wear, and the one that is beneath it. Joaquin quite suddenly wore the latter.

Beatriz stopped. She gently lifted the shotgun.

A desert is a lot like an ocean, if you replace all of the water with air. It stretches out and out and out in unfathomable distance and, in the absence of sunlight, turns to pure black. Sounds become secrets, impossible to verify as true until the light returns. It is not empty merely because you cannot see all of it. And you know in your heart that it isn't—that it is the opposite of empty once it is dark, because things that do not like to be watched emerge when all of the light is gone. There is no way to know the shape of them, though, until your hand is on them.

Something was there in the desert.

The creature was moving slowly among the distant brush,

dark against the night-purple horizon, nearly human-shaped. There was a rattling or hissing as it moved, like dry beans shaken gently in a pan.

Joaquin was suddenly reminded of Nana locking her back door. Beatriz was suddenly reminded of long-lived Felipe Soria, wandering forever, looking for that femur-made cross, and of the furious businessman she had failed to help, tangled in his beard.

Diablo Diablo said, "If there wasn't a moon out there before, there is one now. Coming up next we've got something to put a smile on that moon's face."

At the sound of his voice, the figure stopped.

Every head turned toward the radio. It continued to prattle on in a way that we do not notice when we are not trying to be silent in the desert night. Diablo Diablo said, "The moon loves company, so get your teeth ready."

The creature stepped toward them.

It was difficult to terrify Beatriz Soria, for the same reason that it was difficult to get her angry. Fear and rage are not very different when you think about it, two hungry animals that often hunt the same prey—emotion—and hide from the same predator—logic. So Beatriz's surfeit of logic usually protected her from terror. (Although it easily delivered her to anxiety. Anxiety was merely another brand of her usual considered thought, after all, just one that refused to go away when she asked it nicely or was trying to sleep.) Beatriz's fear, though, required enough information to conclude that almost certainly something bad was going to happen, and also that the something bad was awful enough that it could not be easily remedied, and that rarely happened.

So Beatriz was not afraid in this moment, but only because she didn't have enough information to be afraid.

"The flashlight," she said, without taking her eyes from the figure.

Joaquin did not require information to be afraid and was accordingly out of his mind with fear. He managed to collect himself just enough to point the light directly at the intruder.

Butterflies moved their wings slowly in the flashlight's beam.

It was not Felipe Soria, nor Daniel's darkness.

It was Marisita Lopez.

Marisita's ever-present wedding dress and the weighty bag upon her back had created the strange silhouette the cousins had spotted. The hissing sound was nothing but the sound of the raindrops dashing against the tumbleweed and brush around her.

Joaquin recoiled. She was not a monster, but she was a pilgrim, and that was just as dangerous.

Beatriz, however, scrutinized Marisita. This was the first time she had seen the young woman since reading Daniel's letter, and she was now trying to see Marisita through Daniel's eyes. As anything but a pilgrim, because Daniel must have seen past that to fall in love with her.

Joaquin twisted his fingers in Beatriz's sleeve and tugged.

But Beatriz lingered. "Were you running away into the desert?"

"*Beatriz,*" Joaquin hissed.

"I—I am looking for Daniel. The Saint," Marisita said. "I couldn't—I couldn't imagine him out there without supplies."

This was what filled the overfilled bag she carried. Marisita had thought very hard about what Daniel might need, and had taken quite a long time to assemble it into the pack. Here was what she had brought: ten cured sausages, a pot of cheese, twelve avocados, three oranges, two cups of lard, a small pile of tortillas, four tins of beans, cornmeal, a skillet, one hundred matches, three pairs of dry socks, four clean shirts, a harmonica, a small blanket, a pocketknife, a paring knife, a votive candle, a hairbrush, a bar of soap, a notebook that was only halfway used up, a pen, three ciga-rettes, a sheep-collared coat, a cup for water, a pellet gun, a flashlight, and a small satchel of Francisco's rose petals in case Daniel needed to smell it in order to cure homesickness.

The tenderness of this gesture finally provided Beatriz a window into Marisita's heart. For the first time, she began to see Marisita as not merely a pilgrim but rather a person, and not just a person, but someone who showed her care for someone else in intensely practical ways.

Joaquin, on the other hand, had reached the end of his stam-ina for uncertainty. "Beatriz! Let's go! We can't be talking to her! This is madness! She could kill us both!"

Marisita knew the taboo as well as a Soria, perhaps better, after the events of the night before. She was already ducking away as she said, "You should! I don't want something else ter-rible to happen. I'm so sorry! I didn't mean to meet anyone tonight."

"Wait," Beatriz said, although she did not yet know the words that were going to follow. The problem with ideas is that they never come all at once. They emerge like prairie dogs. An edge of ear, or the tip of a nose, and sometimes even the whole head. But if you look straight at an idea too fast, it can vanish back into the ground before you're even sure of what you've seen. Instead, you have to sneak up on it slowly, looking out of the corner of your eye, and then and only then you might glance up to get a clear look.

Beatriz was having an idea now, but she'd only seen an ear or a whisker.

"Wait?" echoed Joaquin.

"I just—I have questions," Beatriz confessed.

"*Beatriz*," Joaquin exhorted.

"She's the pilgrim Daniel helped," Beatriz told him. "She's the last one to see him. This is Marisita."

"Oh," said Joaquin.

There was a pregnant pause. An unusual and elegant intersection of needs and wants had formed in that moment, and they could all sense it. They all longed to talk to one another about their common interest: Daniel. As pressing as this urge was, if it had only been a desire for information, it might have died there. But there was something else. When Daniel had asked Beatriz if she ever thought they were doing it wrong, he had merely voiced an unspoken question both of them had been carrying for a while. For Daniel, it was because ethics pressed badly at him, with all of the pilgrims falling between the cracks. For Beatriz, it was the sense that the facts were being made to add up to something that was not quite true. All of these truths were being bundled together and sealed with superstition and fear instead of science and reason.

Marisita lingered, but didn't speak. Beatriz's mind worked busily. Joaquin's mouth still held the shape of his last word. None of them knew precisely how far they could press this meeting.

Before he'd moved into the greenhouse, Francisco would sometimes tell Beatriz stories of scientists, like Guillermo González Camarena, the teenage inventor of the color TV, or Helia Bravo Hollis, the botanist who'd catalogued hundreds of succulent plants and founded the Sociedad Mexicana de Cactología. These great minds organized facts in new ways and performed experiments on the accepted truth, changing one variable here or there to test just how factual their facts really were. Beatriz and Daniel had been eyeing the facts they'd been given for quite a while, though they'd had no way to test them. But now—

Beatriz's thoughts moved to the radio, which was still noisy with Diablo Diablo's banter. It sounded as if they were still hearing Joaquin's voice, but really, it was not Joaquin at all. It was the sound of his voice encoded onto a signal, which the transmitter then modified so that the stable-stolen radio could pick it up and play it from the speaker. It was no more Joaquin than a drawing of him would be him.

"What do you think about . . ." Beatriz began. The prairie dog of an idea had lifted its head from the hole. "Doing a radio interview?"

13

We don't quite understand miracles. This is the way of most divine things; saints and miracles belong to a different world and use a different set of rules. It is hard to tell the human purpose of St. Joseph of Cupertino's miraculous levitation, for instance. Whenever he was transported by faith, he was also transported by physics, often several feet into the air, sometimes in the middle of a homily. He would at times remain up there for hours, paused in mid-speech, while his fellow brothers waited for him to descend and finish his thought. It is also difficult to tell the usefulness of the miracles of St. Christina the Astonishing—after rising from the dead in her twenties, she would upon occasion hurl herself into a river and allow herself to be carried downstream into the path of a churning mill wheel. There she would be thrown in violent circles before emerging unscathed: a miracle. And then there was St. Anthony of Padua. His miracles were varied, all beyond understanding, but perhaps the most inscrutable was the miracle at the water's edge. Finding no human company to address, he preached at the water's edge so piously that a school of fish broke the surface to listen—a miracle difficult to understand, as fish have no souls to save and no voices to convert unbelievers.

Compared to these, the Soria miracles were quite palatable. Yes, sometimes the pilgrims to Bicho Raro became impossibly ugly or fearfully radiant, intensely practical or clumsily fanciful. Some grew feathers. Some shrank to the size of a mouse. Sometimes shadows came to life and scampered around the pilgrim. Sometimes wounds formed that refused to heal. But these oddities were no random punishments but rather messages specific to each pilgrim. The darkness made flesh was a concrete puzzle that, if solved, provided the mental tools the pilgrim needed to move on.

The intention of every Soria miracle was the same: to heal the mind.

Daniel Soria had been telling himself this over and over since the night before. This trial was not a punishment, he reminded himself. This trial was a miracle.

But it did not feel like a miracle.

He was out in the high desert night, sitting cross-legged by a smoldering fire. Although it was very cold, it was a very small fire, because Daniel could not shake the image of Joaquin coming after him despite all warnings and finding him by the light of the blaze. So he kept it near-suffocated, and sat with his palms pressed against the still-warm ground.

It was so dark. Although he was curved into the small orange circle of light provided by a smoldering fire, everything he looked at appeared dull. He seemed to be having difficulty seeing light the same way he had this time yesterday. It was as if there was a gauzy curtain hung between his eyes and the fire, and two heavier curtains on either side of his vision, threatening to close. It was possible, he thought, that they had already closed a little more since he had left Bicho Raro. He did not know what he would do if he went blind out here in the wild scrub.

He knew the miracles were meant to teach the pilgrims something about themselves. Take Tony, for instance, and his newfound gigantism. Daniel figured Tony was someone famous. He didn't recognize him personally, but he'd seen many celebrities come through Bicho Raro, and he'd gotten pretty good at noting the posturing and style that marked public figures. So Tony, suffering under the public eye as most celebrities do, had received a miracle that ensured he was under even more constant scrutiny. The miracle's purpose was then clear: If Tony could learn to live as a giant, he would once again be able to live as a man.

This meant that Daniel's narrowing vision was supposed to teach him something, but he didn't know what it might be. He had thought that he knew himself pretty well, and yet meaning eluded him. Perhaps this darkness was meant to teach him trust, or humility, or despair. Nothing seemed obvious. Possibly an outsider might have been able to immediately identify the truth of it, just as the meaning of Tony's darkness was obvious to Daniel. But there was no one else to observe Daniel, and he meant to keep it that way.

Daniel tried not to devote too much time to the most hopeless outcome, which was that Daniel might discover what the darkness truly meant, and still be unable to overcome it. He recalled a pilgrim from Utah whose miracle had left him with a bulbous red face and a helpless desire to gag whenever he tried to put food in his mouth. The man seemed to understand at once what this darkness stood for, because he became overwhelmed with grief and guilt. Daniel, of course, had been unable to speak to him because of the taboo, and the pilgrim had disappeared into the desert overnight. Later he was found dead, his face no longer red; the miracle had died with the pilgrim. The knowing had not helped him.

Perhaps Daniel was meant to learn how difficult miracles were.

No. He thought he knew that already.

"If there wasn't a moon out tonight, there is one now," Diablo Diablo said. "Coming up next we've got something to put a smile on that moon's face."

The radio had managed to snatch the signal of his cousins' station, and though Daniel knew it would be as easy to die with the sound of Diablo Diablo playing as not, he preferred the company. It distracted him from the black at the corners of his vision, from the cold, and from the distinct feeling that he wasn't alone. There was *something* out there in the night, something that had drawn near as soon as he'd broken the taboo. Although he knew that it must be a concrete form of his own darkness, it didn't feel like an extension of himself. It felt like the concrete manifestation of the strangeness of this valley instead. Perhaps this was what was meant when they said that a Saint's darkness was worse than an ordinary pilgrim's. Perhaps that was the reason why he couldn't find meaning in his miracle. Perhaps this was not healing darkness at all but rather the opposite: a hellish entity sent to caper around and gobble up a fallen saint.

He did not know if it was better or worse that the thing remained out of sight.

Daniel mouthed a prayer. *"Mother—"*

"Ladies and gentlemen of the San Luis Valley," said Diablo Diablo, "we interrupt our normal broadcast for a live interview."

Daniel's prayer silenced in his mouth. His hand with its spider eyes walked to the knob and turned up the volume. Static hissed in the background.

Diablo Diablo continued, "This is our first interview, so excuse us, excuse us mightily, if we experience any technical difficulties. The first man to walk a road always has to clear a few rocks. Señorita, would you tell all our listeners at home your name? For your privacy, just your first name. We don't want anyone to stop you on the street and tell you your face is as pretty as your voice."

Marisita said, "Marisita."

It was obvious now that the hissing in the background was not static after all; it was the patter of rain falling around Marisita. "Welcome to our show, Marisita."

"Marisita," Daniel said out loud, with wonder. Then, understanding what this meant, with worry—*"Joaquin."*

Diablo Diablo continued, "Let me catch our listeners up on

the situation, because you will not be able to understand Marisita's story unless you know about the Saint of Bicho Raro."

Joaquin was not being entirely aspirational by suggesting they had an audience. Apart from Daniel, the station did actually have a few other listeners that night, including two long-distance truckers, a man in a farm truck two ranches over, an old woman with insomnia who was passing the time jarring cactus jelly while her four dogs watched her, and, by a twist of AM radio wave magic, a group of Swedish fishermen who had turned on the radio to listen to as they woke themselves up for their work of catching halibut.

"Imagine . . . you have a tormented mind," Diablo Diablo said, his voice dramatic. "You barter with sadness or you fight with grief or you eat arrogance every morning with your coffee. There are saints in this valley who can heal you. You and every other pilgrim can canter to Bicho Raro to receive a miracle. A miracle, you say? A miracle. This miracle makes the darkness inside you visible in amazing and peculiar ways. Now that you see what has been haunting you, you overthrow it, and then you leave this place free and easy. Don't believe me? Hey, hey, I don't make the news, I just report it. There's only one catch: The saints cannot help you tackle your darkness after you receive the miracle, or they will, ah, they will bring darkness on themselves, a worse darkness than any ordinary man's. Or woman's, golly."

And now Daniel laughed out loud, helplessly, because he could hear the crack in Joaquin's voice that meant Beatriz must have shot him a look. The familiarity of it both comforted and tormented him.

"Now, Marisita, who we have on the show tonight, was recently in the presence of a saint when darkness overtook him. That's right, isn't it, Marisita?"

"Yes," Marisita said.

"And did you see what form his darkness took?"

Marisita said, "I'm sorry, I'm crying. May I have a minute?"

"Oh," said Diablo Diablo, sounding a little cross and a lot like Joaquin. He pulled it back together. "While you have a cry, the rest of us can join you, including Elvis. Let's have a listen to 'Are You Lonesome Tonight?'"

You can imagine the effect that this exchange had on Daniel, who was in love with Marisita. He had heard the tears in her voice and it made tears rise up in his throat as well. It was only because he knew that he had brought only so much water with him and could not spare it that he did not allow himself to weep with her.

The song drew to a baleful close, and Diablo Diablo's voice cut in. "And we're back. Wipe your eyes, everyone, it'll be all right, and if it won't, it'll be a good story for someone else. Marisita, are you still there?"

"I am."

"Let's try this again. Did you see Daniel's darkness?"

Daniel was as interested in this answer as his cousins were, as he had not yet seen whatever it was that he felt shadowing him. He was certain that Marisita had looked out the window after him as he left—he had been able to feel the familiar weight of her gaze wrapped around him. So it was possible she had seen whatever it was that watched him now.

"No, I did not," Marisita said in her sweet, sad voice. "Nothing except for the owls. I'm sorry. I want to be able to help. But I didn't see any change at all. It's hard for me to imagine that he even had any darkness inside him, because he is—he was—you know how he is."

Yes, they all knew how he was. But we all have darkness inside us. It is just a question of how much of us is light as well.

"Yes," Diablo Diablo said bleakly. "He was a Saint."

"I didn't see him up close, though. He passed me a note through my door and told me not to come out," Marisita continued. "It said he was dangerous and that I shouldn't follow him."

"*Dangerous*," Diablo Diablo repeated, and the word thrilled over teeth. "Did you happen to see which way Daniel went when he left?"

"I looked out the window after him. I saw him going into the night. He stopped near the edge of Bicho Raro, but I don't know why."

This had been because Daniel had encountered Antonia Soria's dogs. They had not yet become aware of his presence. Some were sleeping, some were dozing warily, and yet another was worrying at what was left of Tony's white jacket. Some men might have tried to sneak past the dogs, or to trick or intimidate them. Daniel did none of these things. Instead, he prayed. He prayed to his mother that the dogs might know how he was feeling. The dogs at once began to weep. They tipped their heads back and instead of howling, they let big tears roll out of their eyes and into their fur. They wept as they understood that Daniel was afraid that he might be going into the desert to die alone. They wept as they understood that Daniel could not bear the thought that he might not see Bicho Raro or his family again. They wept as they understood that he was in love with Marisita Lopez and still, even after all of this, longed for there to be a way to spend his life with her.

As the dogs cried and whimpered, Daniel walked past them. He did not try to comfort them, because he knew there was no comfort. He could hear the strange sound of his darkness moving in the shadows on the other side of the house, but he did not flinch. He was the Saint of Bicho Raro, and he was determined to walk out of Bicho Raro without harming his home.

Diablo Diablo persisted. "You didn't see where he went after that?"

"No."

"Just now, you were wandering in the desert after him with no idea of where he went?"

"I had to start somewhere. I can't imagine him out here alone. And his family can't help him. I can do something, and so I will."

"How long are you intending to wander?"

"As long as I need to," Marisita said.

Daniel was overcome then, and allowed one tear to fall. He would spare one drop of his precious water for this feeling to escape him.

"As long as you need to? And what if you haven't found him by tomorrow?"

"I will eat some of the food I packed for him and keep looking."

"And the next day?"

"The same."

"And the next? And the next?"

"I'm going to look for him until I find him," Marisita insisted.

There was a long pause here, and Joaquin seemed to be struggling to find a way to put his next question into words. Finally, he merely asked it as it had first come into his head.

"Marisita, are you in love with him?"

"Yes."

Daniel spared another drop of water. The tear fell to the dust. A pack rat raced out from the brush to grab it, certain it was a jewel because of its shine in the firelight. Daniel's sorrow had made it tangible enough to carry, and so the pack rat bore it back to its nest, only to later find that offspring raised on a bed of sadness fail to thrive.

Diablo Diablo said, "Marisita, there is a problem with your quest. We have a source here in the station who is telling me that if you are in love with him, you can't look for him. If you're in love with him, the family darkness will come on you, too, if you help him."

Marisita did not immediately answer.

"I think you better play another song," she finally said. "I need to cry some more."

Diablo Diablo did not immediately answer either. Daniel suspected (correctly) that this was because he was trying to find another thematic song in his prerecorded session. He put on Paul Anka's "It's Time to Cry." When it was through, he said, "Last question, Marisita: The Saint's darkness came to him because he helped you and interfered with your miracle. How did Daniel help you?"

Daniel curled on his side, the top of his head touching the radio so he could feel the vibration of the speaker against his skin. He closed his eyes, though his blind spiders' eyes stayed open to the night as they always did.

In a small voice, Marisita said, "I don't want to answer this one. I'm sorry— It just, it just makes me cry too much. I can't tell the story to someone else yet."

"That's all right," Diablo Diablo soothed. After a pause, he added, in a somewhat less Diablo Diablo voice, "Marisita, he'll be okay. He's too good not to fight it. Maybe we can have you on the show again?"

Marisita said, "I'd like that."

Daniel opened his eyes. But it was not very much brighter than it had been with them closed.

14

Being a pilgrim was a hard row to hoe. Nearly every person who came to Bicho Raro believed that the first miracle was the end point of their journey. They had only to make it to the point of receiving it and then their soul would rest easy. Things went pear-shaped for many when they understood it was the first of a two-step process, and as time passed, pilgrims began to fall into two increasingly disparate groups: those who performed the second miracle almost immediately after their first and those who, with every unsuccessful day following the first miracle, became increasingly unlikely to ever perform the second miracle.

Marisita Lopez was growing ever more frustrated with her status in the second group, although she was not surprised. She had a very poor opinion of herself. This was because Marisita believed in perfection, and held herself to that standard. If you're a wise person, you understand immediately that this is not a logical goal. The conception of perfection exists only so that we have something to strive toward: Impossibility is built into it, which is why we call it *perfect* instead of *extremely good*. The truth is that only a few things in history have ever been perfect. There was a perfect sunset in Nairobi in 1912. There was a bandoneon constructed in Cordoba that perfectly captured the drama of human existence in just a single note. Lauren Bacall's voice was unmatched perfection.

Marisita believed that a few people could reach perfection if only they tried hard enough. And as she had been trying, and had not reached it, she considered herself a failure at all times.

No one else counted Marisita as a failure. The number of things Marisita could do extremely well was a large one. She could do everything expected of a woman in the early 1960s: She could clean, and she could cook, and she could sew. But she could also play the foot pedal loom like Paganini played the violin, and it was said that the latter had sold his soul to the devil for his skill. She formed pots out of clay that were so striking that sometimes, when she went to gather clay for a new one, she discovered that the clay had eagerly already begun to shape itself for her. Her voice was so well trained that bulls would lie down when they heard her sing. She was so famed for her studied and just empathy that men and women would come for miles to solicit her as mediator in disputes. She could ride two horses at the same time, one leg on each horse, and still hold down her skirt to maintain her modesty, if she felt like it. Her segueza, developed from an ancient recipe, was so excellent that time itself stood still while you were eating it in order to savor the flavor along with you.

All of this was to say that Marisita was not perfect, but she came much closer to it than many people. But when you have set your sights on perfection, nothing less will satisfy.

The day after her radio interview, Marisita prepared for her next journey in search of Daniel. Although she had been frightened when she learned that her love for him made her vulnerable to his darkness, it hadn't changed her resolve to search for him. After all, it was no more and no less the risk he himself had taken when he'd offered his help to her.

However, the interview had given her the moment of introspection necessary to realize that her plan to search for him incessantly, without returning for supplies, was suspiciously close to her previous decision to walk out into the desert to die. When she examined her motive for searching constantly without replenishing her supplies or health, she was dissatisfied with the imperfection she found there. Marisita modified her plan to one that would circumvent any of her previous poisonous motivation: She would search for Daniel daily, but she would also spend enough time in Bicho Raro each day to stock up on food and water and to sleep.

Before, she had wanted to go out into the desert because of despair. She vowed that now she would go out into the desert only in the name of hope. She at least owed Daniel this new purity of purpose.

Now she cooked a new batch of tortillas to take with her that day. Although she was not a perfect cook, she was so much closer to perfection than anyone else had ever seen that she had been asked to be the official cook for the pilgrims. The food she prepared smelled and looked so wonderful that the Sorias were envious—though not envious enough to risk eating Marisita's food. (Rosa was the only Soria to cook now, as Antonia was too angry to cook and Judith had moved, and even she cooked listlessly, since Rosa herself dined only on gossip.) So her near-perfection was only for the pilgrims to enjoy. It was a difficult thing to prepare food when the sky was always raining on her, however, and so special accommodations had been prepared for her.

She already lived in a somewhat unusual home known as the Doctor's Cabin. It was the oldest surviving building in Bicho Raro and dated from the decade when the Sorias had arrived. It had never been occupied by a Soria, however. It had been built for and by the first pilgrim to come to them in Colorado, a doctor who'd received the first miracle and then remained with them until his death. He had never confessed to the Sorias why he had come to Bicho Raro—his darkness had built up inside him after he'd won a fatal duel with another doctor over forty years before. In many ways, the Doctor's Cabin was an appropriate home for Marisita to occupy, because the doctor worked tirelessly on healing others but never on healing himself.

It was old and crude enough that it still had a dirt floor, and after it was obvious that Marisita was not leaving anytime soon, Michael and Luis had dug a small drainage system through the cabin's three rooms in order to funnel water away from her bed and the kitchen. This prevented the cabin from filling with water and drowning her while she slept, and also kept the kitchen counters drained while she was preparing food. A previous pilgrim, now moved on, had used clear plastic and coat hangers to construct her a series of umbrellas in varied sizes. Marisita placed these over the various elements of meals that she was preparing in order to keep everything from becoming waterlogged. It had been difficult at first to see what she was doing through the rain-spattered plastic, but, as in most things, she eventually became extremely good at it.

"How are you today, Mr. Bunch?" Marisita asked. Theldon Bunch, the pilgrim with moss growing all over his body, had lurched to her doorway as she toasted chilies for a later meal.

"Mm," Theldon replied. He had his paperback novel folded inside out and stuffed in his armpit in a way that Marisita found painful to look at. "Is breakfast done?"

"Breakfast was hours ago," Marisita said. "You missed it. Sleep in?"

"Time got away from me," Theldon replied. Time was always getting away from him. "Is there any left, hon?"

"I can make you a plate." There were always beans simmering, and tomatoes didn't take long to heat, and a few eggs made the plate look full. Theldon slouched and read his book while he waited, scratching absently at the moss growing on his cheek as he did. While Marisita cooked for him, she thought about the radio show and what she would say about her past if she did agree to be on the show again. She wondered if Daniel could hear her, and if so, how he would feel about her telling the story of him helping her. It was a very strange development to be able to speak to the Sorias in any way, and she could not quite get over the shock of having a conversation with them yesterday after weeks and weeks of being told to not so much as whisper to any of them, after a day where she had seen Daniel Soria destroyed for that very thing.

"You're a treasure," Theldon said as she handed the plate to him. "If there's anything I can do." He said this every time she handed a plate to him.

"If you ever wanted to grind the corn for me, it's hard for me to do it without getting it wet," she told him. She told him this every time she handed a plate to him.

"Okay, that sounds good," he replied, and left with his plate. The exchange always ended the same way. Marisita always ground the corn herself. Time kept getting away from Theldon. Rain fell on Marisita; moss grew on Theldon.

A knock on the open door preceded the appearance of a solid-looking young man with considerable dust on his boots and white T-shirt. This was Pete, who had already been working that morning.

"Good morning," he said. "Am I in the right place?"

"That depends on what place you are looking for," Marisita replied.

"Antonia said that if I asked you, you might have something I could take with me to eat while I work."

Marisita disliked the delay but liked his gentle expression. "Then you are in the right place. Take a seat."

"Thank you, ma'am, but I'll stand. I don't want to get your furniture dirty—I'm a mess."

This gesture was difficult for Marisita. She appreciated that he did not want to get her stool dusty, but seeing him standing rather than sitting made her feel that she needed to hurry as she cooked, even if he didn't mean it that way at all. She could have asked him again to sit and could have explained that she did not mind the dust, but that seemed like it might make him feel bad about his decision to stand. So instead, she just asked him in her head and said nothing out loud. He kept standing there, making her feel urgent. She hurried.

Pete asked, "Can I do anything to help?"

"I'm going as fast as I can," she replied.

"Oh, I didn't mean that. I just feel strange watching you do all the work, is all."

Marisita was surprised by how he just said this out loud, freely, and also by how it made her feel better about his question. She wasn't sure which part startled her more: that he expressed his discomfort so easily, or that she was put at ease by the explanation. Of course, if she thought about it, she knew this was the way to do it. If a pair had come to her for advice back in Texas, she would have advised them to be free with each other no matter how foolish it seemed. She did not know why she found it difficult to take her own advice. Now, hesitantly, she tried it for herself. "I don't mind. But I feel the same way about you standing. It makes me feel strange that you are standing instead of sitting—like I should hurry."

It did not feel comfortable to say it out loud instead of in her head, but Pete let out a surprised laugh that was not at all put out. He clapped his hands against his dirty pants for a moment and then sat on the stool. She gave him a bowl of cherry tomatoes to eat and occupy his hands while she worked. In this way they spent a few minutes in easier quiet while Marisita finished the empanadas for Pete.

"I hope it's not rude to ask," Pete broke in, "but why don't they fly away?"

The butterflies on Marisita's dress opened and closed their wings, over and over, as water dripped over them.

"They are too wet," Marisita explained.

"One day the rain will stop, though?"

"Perhaps."

"Will you miss them?"

No one had asked Marisita this before, and she had to take a moment to consider the answer. It was difficult to imagine life without them. The butterflies were beautiful, but it was more that she had now been with them for so long that she could not picture what she would look like without them.

"I think I'd rather they flew away," Marisita said.

Pete was satisfied by this answer. "Good."

"Have you already performed the second miracle?" Marisita was surprised at herself for saying this out loud instead of simply in her head, but since she had already been forward once with Pete, it was easier the second time.

"Oh, I'm not here about a miracle," Pete said. "I'm just here about a truck. Oh, hey, that reminds me . . . I feel like a total heel for asking you to do more work, but I better ask 'cause I bet he hasn't been able to and even though we're not buddies, I'll feel bad if he starves. Do you know if Tony has gotten anything to eat?"

"The giant?"

"That's the one."

She was certain he had not eaten yesterday. In her distress, she had not cooked for anyone since Daniel's vanishing. The other pilgrims had fended for themselves; they had a kitchen of their own, after all, and leftovers. But Tony had not been given food and could not have fit into her kitchen to cook for himself.

"I'll make sure he gets something," Marisita said, feeling more impatient than she sounded. Time pressed heavily on her and her mouth felt dry when she imagined Daniel possibly without water. But when she remembered that Tony probably had not eaten since the day before, guilt won out over her impatience. She could be quick. "Here's your empanada."

"*Empanada*," Pete repeated. "Gosh, thanks. It looks great. See you later! Sorry about the dirt on the chair!"

After he had gone, Marisita hastily prepared Tony some food. She assembled a pile of crusty bolillos, a cantaloupe cut into a bright orange moon, a covered bowl of fried red beans, a thermos of creamy minguiche, two empanadas, three dark-red tomatoes from Nana's garden, and a fried bit of beef that had looked a little friendlier the night before. Although it would have been a tremendous amount of food for an ordinary man to eat, Marisita thought it nonetheless seemed insufficient to feed a giant. It was better than eating only memories, though.

Halfway through this process, she had a third visitor, although this one took her longer to spot. It was Jennie, the schoolteacher pilgrim who could only repeat what others said to her. She had been standing in the doorway for quite some time, trying to decide how long it would take Marisita to notice her, as of course she could not say anything original to get her attention.

"Oh, Jennie! I didn't notice you," Marisita said.

"Oh, Jennie!" Jennie replied. "I didn't notice you."

Marisita wanted to ask how long she had been there, but she knew from experience that it was pointless. She was sure Jennie wanted food, another delay that made Marisita want to snap, but she knew that she would only hear her ugly, short words echoed back at her in Jennie's voice. So Marisita just made her another empanada with the scraps of what she'd made Pete, and then she indicated the food she had just made for Tony. "Could you bring this tray to the giant? I need to go out."

"Could you bring this tray to the giant? I need to go out." Jennie echoed. But she held out her hands for the tray. She seemed to be trying to say something else to Marisita, but nothing else escaped her lips.

Marisita was quite suddenly overcome with frustration with all of them. Daniel's sacrifice hadn't healed her, because she was too tormented by her terrible past, and Jennie couldn't find an original word no matter how hard she tried, and Theldon kept growing moss, and they all seemed beyond hope. She missed Daniel, though she felt she had no right to. He had never been hers to miss, because she was a pilgrim, and he was a saint, and more importantly, because she would never stop being a pilgrim. She would always be Marisita and her butterflies. Tears were prickling in her eyes again, but no one would even know if she began crying once more, because this rain would never stop.

"We're a mess," she said.

"We're a mess," Jennie replied.

Marisita turned away, covering her face, and by the time she turned back around, Jennie had taken the tray of food away.

She collected her thoughts and she collected her supplies, and she went out to search for Daniel.

Tony had also been having a bad time as a pilgrim, although he'd had to endure it far fewer days than Marisita had. All he had wanted when he arrived at Bicho Raro was to find a solution to his hatred of feeling constantly watched. All he had gotten was a body that ensured that he would be constantly watched. His second morning as a giant, he had decided the best course of action was to leave.

"Hang it," he had said, to no one. "I'm blowing this Popsicle stand."

He currently stood an impressive twenty feet tall. Not tall as far as buildings went but very tall as far as men went, and too tall to fit into the Mercury (he tried). He would come back for the car, he decided, once he could fit into it again. He put his luggage in his pocket and looked around Bicho Raro to see if there was anyone watching him go. There was just that still, owl-eyed girl he had seen the first night (this was Beatriz). He saluted her. She waved. It was a small wave that seemed to say *Do what you want.*

So he left.

He limped off into the high desert on his one bare foot and one shod foot. The always-present sun painted sweat on his forehead. Dust billowed up with each step he took, but he was too tall for it to reach his face. Instead, it formed a whirling trail behind him, occasionally tossing up fitful dirt devils, before lying back obediently among the scrub. He did not look back. He only walked. Tony was not the first pilgrim to have done this—to have walked out without much of a plan other than to leave. There is something about the expanse around Bicho Raro that encourages this ill-advised wandering. Although the desert is not comforting and there are no landmarks within easy reach, something about the impossibility of it acts as a vacuum to those who don't know their way.

"Crazy fools," Tony muttered as he went.

He walked for the better part of the morning.

For most people, this wouldn't have gotten them very far, but Tony's giant footsteps took him all the way to the Great Sand Dunes near Mosca, forty or fifty miles away. The smoothly scalloped dunes were such an unexpected sight that he stopped short to evaluate them; they were a natural wonder scaled to his current size. The dunes cover more than one hundred thousand acres, the awesome offspring of an ancient extinct lake bed and fortuitous winds, and are known to produce a peculiar moaning sound under the correct circumstances. Twenty years before Tony stepped foot on the dunes, Bing Crosby with Dick McIntire and His Harmony Hawaiians had recorded a song about them called "The Singing Sands of Alamosa," and now Tony remembered with peculiar acuity the single time that he had spun that dulcet track on his show. As he recalled its not particularly remarkable melody, the oversized bare toes of his left foot wiggled and provoked a slow avalanche of sand.

As the grains of sand slid over one another, they sang the dunes' legendary song. It was a mournful, eerie wail, and the strangeness of it reminded Tony all at once that he had taken the craziest part of Bicho Raro—himself—with him on this walk. He stood there and cursed the unnamed woman who had approached him back in Juniata and all of her family and also his enormous Mercury, for taking him there in the first place.

The sun gleamed down upon him. He did not shrink. His stomach growled, frightening some cranes nearby. He hadn't eaten since before the miracle and was hungry enough to be twins.

He felt the crawling sensation of being watched. Sure enough, there were two tourists at the dunes that day, a man and a woman who were married, but not to each other. They were staring up at him. As they reached slowly for their cameras, it truly sank in that this walk had been a fool's errand. Until he found a way back to his ordinary size, there was only one option for him.

The sands slowly stopped singing.

Tony trudged back to Bicho Raro. The timing of his return was both fortunate and unfortunate, because just three moments before, Marisita had prepared food for him, and two moments before, Jennie had carried that tray of food out to where Tony had been spending his days, and just one moment before, Antonia's dogs knocked Jennie to the ground and ate all of the food and also the tray and also the blank journal that she had been trying to write in since her miracle.

And so the moment Tony arrived back in Bicho Raro was also the moment when he noticed Jennie, who had remained wordless throughout this experience since the dogs had not spoken out loud while they took her things. Jennie could not explain to Tony why she was empty-handed. She could only stand surrounded by torn notebook pages and clumps of dog hair.

Tony's soul was feeling bruised by the knowledge that there was no easy escape for him, so he sounded less humorous and more brusque than he ordinarily might have.

"What do you want?" he asked.

"What do you want?" Jennie demanded.

Tony was somewhat taken aback by the abusive tone in the young woman's voice; he did not yet realize that it was a reflection of his own.

"Nothing."

Jennie said, with the precise same tone, "Nothing."

Tony took this as disbelief. He stared her down for a moment, and when this failed to move her, he said, "You know what, who came over here?"

Helplessly, Jennie replied, "You know what, who came over here?"

Poor Jennie would have loved to explain herself, but of course she couldn't. Moreover, the more distressed she became, the more precisely she mimicked the tone of the original statement. So as Tony grew increasingly exasperated, so did she. Which meant the conversation may have grown more fraught if Padre Jiminez had not been making his loping way from the house to Marisita's kitchen to steal a bite to eat and a glance of her ankles. He saw what was happening with Jennie and swung to the rescue.

"Oh hello hello hello," Padre Jiminez said. "I've been looking for an excuse to introduce myself before now!"

Tony peered down at this newcomer to the conversation, saw that it was a man with a coyote's head, and said, "Oh, Jesus Christ, it never ends."

Padre Jiminez laughed in his high, yipping way, and then said, "I understand, I understand, but I'd thank you to not take the Lord's name in vain as I am a priest."

"You're *Lassie*," Tony said. This was an insult that had force in 1962, as the television show *Lassie*, starring a winning collie dog and the boy who loved her, had been running for eight years and was well known. Padre Jiminez's coyote head did not bear much resemblance to a rough collie, according to the American

Kennel Club rough collie breed standard at the time ("The head should be long, fairly narrow, and flat; ears small, set well back on the head, and carried semi-erect, but not pricked"), but the meaning was still clear.

"We don't judge here," Padre Jiminez intoned, which wasn't particularly true but in an ideal world would have been. "Everyone's darkness manifests differently! Jennie here, for instance. I was about to tell you that she can only repeat what someone else has said to her in a conversation."

"Is that true?" Tony asked.

"Is that true?" Jennie echoed.

"Well, Mary's nipples. How would I be able to tell if you were having me on?"

Jennie cast an apologetic glance at Padre Jiminez. "Well, Mary's nipples. How would I be able to tell if you were having me on?"

"So you see," Padre Jiminez demurred. Tony rudely whistled the theme song from *Lassie*. This might have troubled another man, but Padre Jiminez had been here long enough to see that all kinds of people had all kinds of coping mechanisms. And what was happening now was that despite being made into a giant, it had not properly struck Tony before how miraculous the Sorias and Bicho Raro really were. He had performed the common mistake that many do when confronted with the idea of the miraculous: He had assumed it meant *magical*. Miracles often look like magic, but a proper miracle is also awesome, sometimes fearful, and always vaguely difficult to truly wrap your mortal head around. Slowly, it was dawning upon Tony that he had not contemplated the full scope of the place, that he was but one of many recipients of peculiar miracles. Padre was patient enough to wait for him on the other side of this dawning.

Tony said, "This is a madhouse!"

"The world's a madhouse," Padre Jiminez corrected. "This is a place to heal it. What's your name, traveler?"

"Tony."

Tony eyed Jennie. "What, she's not gonna say that, too?"

"You were talking to me, not her, and the poor dear only has to repeat what's said to her, fortunately for her," said Padre Jiminez. "No last name to go with that Tony?"

"Nope. Just Tony."

"Well, all right. I'm Padre Alexandro Marin Jiminez, but you may call me whatever makes you comfortable. I'm here for your spiritual enrichment."

"From your head, it looks like you're supposed to be here for your own spiritual enrichment," Tony said. "I'll handle myself, thanks."

"Suit yourself," Padre Jiminez said. "But it can be lonesome to be out here and not talking to anybody. Jennie, what is all of this scattered on the ground here? Is this your notebook? Is that an edge of Marisita's flower tray? Were you bringing Tony food?"

Jennie repeated all of this back to him, but because she trusted Padre Jiminez and was a little calmer than before, she managed to make the final question mark sound like a period.

"Those dogs," Padre Jiminez said ("Those dogs," echoed Jennie). "We'll get you some food, Tony."

Tony *was* hungry. But he was also thinking about the thing he feared more than anything: being watched while he ate. He vowed to find a private location to feed himself when food did eventually show up. As he was quickly scouting for places that would make good view blocks, he spotted Joaquin Soria peering at him around the corner of a house. When he caught Tony looking, he vanished quickly.

Tony narrowed his eyes. "Who's that poking around?"

Padre Jiminez didn't turn his head; he just sniffed with his coyote nose. "Joaquin Soria. One of the younger boys."

Tony narrowed his eyes. "Why's he spying around?"

"Boys will be boys," Padre Jiminez said carelessly. "Might as well get used to the Sorias, Tony. They live here, too."

"Oh, hold it right there, *Padre*," Tony said. "I'm not intending on living here. I didn't drive all the way here to get a miracle just for the miracle to be that I'm living in someone's backyard. This desert's giving me a nosebleed and this sun's giving me a headache. I'm figuring out what the hell I have to do to get myself right and get myself out of here. Right, Jennie?"

"Right, Jennie?" Jennie echoed, startled. But after a pause, she nodded, too. Because other people's words had been the problem for so long, it had not occurred to her before that minute that sometimes, someone else's words might be exactly what she needed to say how she felt. Later, this new knowledge would come in handy, but for right now, she felt only a hint of the value it would have for her.

Padre Jiminez noted the complexity of this exchange. Priests are a bit like owls in that some of them also have a sense for when miracles are afoot, and he was having that suspicion now. Some priests fly like owls, too, like Padres Quintero, López, and Gonzalez, who all received the gift of slow-motion flight as a result of the first miracle when they arrived to Bicho Raro together in 1912, but Padre Jiminez was not one of them.

He said, "Sometimes it is good to be hungry."

15

Night fell, and the stars sauntered out.

Night fell, and the owls opened their eyes.

Night fell, and Beatriz had not yet cornered Pete.

This came as a shock to Beatriz, who had promised Joaquin that she would talk to him about the truck's fate. She kept glimpsing Pete and then losing him, which was not an easy thing to do in Bicho Raro. It seemed particularly impossible since Judith had assigned Pete to a single, specific task in a single, unmoving location: building a low wooden dance stage, ideal for staging a romantic birthday celebration, ideal for reminding Francisco and Antonia of the circumstances of their first fortuitous meeting. He worked diligently on that all day, setting legs into the ground and building a framework to rest upon the legs and scavenging boards from the side of a collapsed barn to be the stage itself. Even though he did not seem to ever take a break from this task, every time Beatriz tried to catch him at it, he vanished. She searched for him near the barn he'd picked over and she searched for him near the skeletal stage and she searched for him at all the places in between and was bemused to find him in none of these places. Then she would turn and find him back in the place she had just been. She could not understand it. Beatriz could not know that this was because of Pete's decision to avoid her at all costs.

He was so eager to keep from experiencing the jolt to his heart at the sight of her that every time he saw her heading across Bicho Raro, he did a quick about-face on his own journey. The closest brush yet came as night moved in. This was after stars had replaced the sun and the sunset was only three colors laid thin on top of each other at the horizon. He was headed back to his room when he saw Beatriz across the open space between the main buildings. First her shadow, cast long and dangerous by the porch light behind her, and then the rest of her.

Pete did a quick turn and marched back the way he had come, glancing quickly behind himself all the while. Beatriz was wearing a flowered dress that was made short by the way she was using it—she had gathered it up into a makeshift basket in front of her and filled it with a strange nest of wires and metal rods and limber twigs. She was not looking at him, but nonetheless, she was cleaving to his path so unerringly that it felt as if she was following him. He scuttled into the darkness between two cabins, tripping over something in the blackness (Antonia's dog bowls), and when he looked back, she had turned that way as well. He ducked around the back of the cabin, but she remained behind him. He hurried down the path past the goat pasture, but when he looked over his shoulder, he saw that he had come no closer to losing her than before.

Pete's heart was already thudding dangerously, but suddenly

he imagined that she might truly be following him with intention, that she might be trying to *speak* to him, and the idea of that became voluminous in his mind.

His heart lurched again.

With a gasp, and pressing his hand against the beleaguered organ in his chest, Pete broke into a run around the side of a barn, darted quickly across the yard on the opposite side, before vaulting a low set of scrubs. The night stretched up and covered his eyes, so he misjudged the jump. He crashed directly into something solid, which turned out to be the enormous toe of Tony's shoe.

"Hey, kid," Tony said. "Thanks for sparing me the trouble of kicking you."

Pete gasped, "Shucks," but couldn't get anything more out, draped as he was across the shoe, holding his chest and waiting for his heart to once more become invisible inside him.

"Where's the fire?" Tony asked.

"I—" Pete slithered down to sit in the dust. He peered up and up and up at Tony's face, barely visible in the dying light, lit only by the porch lights. "Fire?"

"It's an expression. Kid, you're so straight you make rulers look bad. I meant, why were you running?"

"I think I almost died!"

"Me, too," Tony said. "Of boredom."

But the two were not displeased to see each other, for no reason apart from familiarity. Tony sat down, arranging himself cross-legged in a scrubby field that cows and calves had eaten down to bare earth. Slouching, he hooked one elbow on the top of the tractor beside him. The bottom of his shoeless foot was quite filthy from all his walking around on it.

"Gosh." Pete looked all the way from Tony's dirty foot up to his face. "You really haven't shrunk at all."

"Neither have you," Tony said.

"I guess not. What's it like being . . . like that?"

"I can't smoke," Tony said. "Cigarettes are over before they begin."

Pete did not smoke, but he attempted to look sympathetic. "Well, is there anything I can do for you now?"

"Yeah, beat it," Tony said. But it was habit. Pete's company briefly took his mind off his restlessness. Ordinarily on nights like this, he would've put on the radio or taken the Mercury out across Sure-Kill Crawlway after all the traffic was gone. There were no highways here, though, and he was a long way off from fitting in the Mercury. "No, wait, kid. Take my Mercury to the closest town and get me a goddamn radio before I go insane. You've still got the keys, right?"

"Really?"

"Did I stutter? Here, take some——" Tony began to swear long and loud, because when he reached into his pocket to get some cash for Pete, he discovered that his money had become giant-size as well. He waved a dollar bill the size of a hand towel at Pete. Owls lifted off, startled by the movement. Tony railed, "Get a miracle, they said—here's your miracle! This isn't money—it's a magic carpet."

"I'll cover it," Pete said hurriedly. "Until you get normal again. I've got enough for a radio, I think."

"Look under the passenger seat," Tony said tragically. "Use that. Only the money. Leave the other stuff there."

Pete's mind filled with possibilities of what might be under the seat that he was not supposed to tamper with, but because he was an innocent sort, he was wrong about nearly all of them. "Any particular kind of radio?"

"A loud one," Tony said.

"I'll ask Antonia if I can take some time off tomorrow," Pete promised. "Where is your car, anyway?"

"Oh, yeah," Tony said, and moved slightly to reveal the Mercury behind him, the dry scrub flattened behind it.

Pete found that looking at the vehicle next to Tony produced an unusual vertigo. The Mercury, just a little too large to appear as an ordinary car. And Tony, rather too large to appear as an ordinary man. "How'd it get there?"

"I dragged it," Tony said.

"No way."

Tony gave the vehicle a little shove to demonstrate it, the contents of the interior rattling as he did, the car moving as easily as if three men had been pushing it. It was a magic trick that so delighted Pete that he covered a hand with his mouth and backed up several steps, kicking the ground to release some of his thrill.

"Gosh," he said.

"*Gosh*," mimicked Tony primly, but without malice. He was a performer, after all, and this small performance made him happy. He pushed the Mercury in a slow circle so that it came to rest in front of Pete. Dust swirled around the vehicle and the boy. "Some advantage to size. Hey. How's your work? Breaking your back yet?"

"It's good," Pete said. "Real good."

Tony waited, leaving a silence, as if testing the words for veracity, waiting for Pete to renege, but of course Pete had meant it. He had found the stage-building intensely satisfying, and he liked imagining the future celebrations that might make use of his day's work. Pete patted the Mercury appreciatively, still pleased at its previous journey under Tony's grip.

"God, kid. I can't decide if I hate or love what a square you are."

Pete grinned for the first time. "Better love it, because it's not changing, buddy."

This was the moment they became friends. They became even better friends after this, because time improves on these things, but this was the moment it began. Tony sensed it, because he rubbed the back of his neck and said, "Okay, now beat it."

"Beat it? Why?"

"Because I'm starting to think you're all right, and I don't want to give you a chance to say something that'll change my mind back again."

"Okay," said Pete, but he didn't go. Instead, he tapped on one of the Mercury's windows. "I wasn't looking through your stuff or anything, but when I was sleeping back there, I kept hitting my head on that box, so I looked in it to make sure I hadn't hurt anything in it. I've never seen that many records in my life!"

Tony had forgotten that he had the promotional records in the back of the Mercury, though, and now he felt a little bad about it. Not because he thought the station would miss them—he'd only taken ones that were duplicates or singles his producers would never play—but because it wasn't good for them to be subjected to direct sunlight. "That's because you haven't lived very long. You got a record player?"

"You saw everything I came here with. How'd you end up with all them, anyway?"

"Pass," Tony said. "Hard pass. Not answering."

"Pass? Why? Wait, did you *kill* someone over them?"

Tony burst out laughing. "Kid, you really have got more corners than a box full of boxes. I work in radio. Don't tell anyone."

"Why not?"

Tony was impatient with this question, as he felt it was the kind of question only asked by someone who had never experienced either fame or notoriety. "Because I said so."

"Sure, whatever you say. Like a DJ?"

Because Pete didn't seem too awed, Tony grudgingly answered, "Yeah."

"You'd think a DJ would be the last person to break the radio in their own car."

"Yeah, you'd think, wouldn't you? Now seriously, flake off before I regret telling you."

Tony had been watching Pete closely to see if this confession had changed anything, but Pete was less interested in Tony's past career than he was in his own future safety. "I oughta get some sleep anyway. Is the coast clear?"

"Of what? Those damn dogs?"

"No, a girl," Pete said. It had not occurred to Pete that he had actually weaponized Beatriz's appearance by avoiding her the way that he had; if only he had approached her calmly during the day, he would have been fine.

"You mean that girl?" Tony asked.

Pete turned.

"I need to talk to you," Beatriz said.

16

Not a lot of people know that there is a great salt lake and accompanying salt plain in Oklahoma; most folks are only familiar with the famous one in Utah. But the one in Oklahoma is no shoddy thing. Just a spit north of Jet, Oklahoma, the great salt flats start, the enormous and impressive remainder of a massive saline lake. Like the salt flats in Utah, they are white as snow and as flat as a board, but unlike the salt flats in Utah, Oklahoma's salt flats have treasure buried beneath them. Tiny crystals known as hourglass crystal grow here and nowhere else in the world, and if you are the sort to dig for treasure, you can bring your whole family to dig them up. Just make sure you hose your vehicle down afterward, because salt's not good for any set of wheels.

Pete's family had gone to dig up these rare selenite crystals one spring not long ago, and Pete remembered the unrelenting sun, the grit of salt and sand caught in his pants legs, the intimate joy of finding a crystal and holding it to the light to see the hourglass of time within it.

"Look, I told you, he's waking up," Tony said.

The image of Oklahoma's salt flats slowly became the starry sky over Bicho Raro.

"I need you to go," said a mild female voice. It was Beatriz, though Pete's gaze had not yet focused on her. "It's dangerous for us to speak."

"Fine, lady," Tony said. "My legs want to get out of here for a while anyway." The ground rumbled as he stepped over them both and walked into the night.

Pete and Beatriz were left alone.

Pete went to press his hand to his chest, only to discover that he had already done it, so he pressed a little harder. He was lying on his back in the gritty dirt, and from the vague ache on the back of his head, he guessed (correctly) that he had gotten there in an expedited way. Beatriz was crouched beside him, holding her skirt carefully to keep the wires she had collected inside the makeshift holder. The air smelled like roses for no reason that either of them could tell. This was because Luis had emptied a wheelbarrow of spent blossoms from Francisco's warehouse in this field, and Pete had made an accidental bed of them.

"You fainted," Beatriz told him.

He looked at her through slitted eyes, worried about his heart, but it seemed that now that the sight of her had knocked him on his back in the dirt, looking at her more didn't seem to cause any more hurt. You can only get shocked so many times by the same thing, after all. He said, "I've got a hole in my heart."

"Do you fall down a lot?"

"Only when I'm surprised."

"Do a lot of things surprise you?"

"Not really."

Because Pete was still dazed from striking his head on the rose-petal-strewn ground, he didn't offer his name nor ask hers, and he did not think to begin polite conversation. And because Beatriz was already uncomfortable about the truck and because she was not as empathetic as someone else might have been in the situation and because she was trying not to look at his elbows, she did not think to introduce herself or even allow Pete to stand up as she raised the sore subject of the truck's ownership. Instead, she merely explained that she had heard he was working for the truck but that her mother had not realized when she made the deal that Beatriz had resurrected it and gotten it running again and was using it for her own purposes. Only at the end of this monologue, when he was still looking at her dazedly, did she realize she had not solicited his thoughts.

"And so I'm open to your thoughts," she finished.

Pete said, "Antonia—your mother—told me it wasn't running." But even as he said it, he knew Beatriz's account was true, as the truck had been parked in multiple places since he'd arrived there, which was why he had not yet been able to examine it. Because he was a kind soul, this immediately triggered a conflict. He desperately wanted the truck, of course, and was unable to imagine what he might do without it. But he also could not imagine simply taking the truck out from underneath Beatriz if she had indeed invested so much work in it; it wasn't fair, and if Pete was anything, he was a fair person.

This dissonance distressed him so much that he thought he could feel his very core beginning to tremble. The ground seemed to be whispering softly against his spine with the movement of some deep and unwinnable debate.

In reality, this was because Salto, driven to madness by the lack of radio in the stable, had broken through the walls of his stall and had just rioted the previously sleeping cattle gathered near the barn. They now stampeded directly toward Pete and Beatriz, the stallion at their head. He was an enormous horse, nearly eighteen hands tall, and as chestnut as a violin. The cows were red as dirt with white faces and had horns for hanging men on. There were many of them.

Beatriz did not wait for Pete to move; she simply grabbed his leg and dragged him out of the animals' path just in time. The wire she'd gathered for her antenna scattered across the ground as she fell on her backside. Dust churned over them both, but all of their insides remained where they belonged. Pete sat up just in time to see the cattle slowly wind to a halt as they reached a fence line. Salto, on the other hand, sailed right over it.

Beatriz had no feelings for Salto either way, but she knew as well as any other Soria that his rare and pricey seed put food on their table.

She pushed up from the ground and ran.

"What are you doing?" Pete shouted.

"Getting that horse back!"

Pete leaped to his feet, stepping hard into his boot to put it back on, as Beatriz had nearly pulled it off in her hurry to drag him free of the stampede's path. Then he, too, broke into a run—only he ran for the Mercury.

This was the moment their love story began.

It may seem like madness for a young woman to chase a runaway horse, as a galloping horse travels at twenty-five miles an hour and a galloping woman travels at only fifteen. But runaway horses rarely have a purpose, and young women chasing them often do. When combined with the asset of a young man in a station wagon, the question of catching the horse becomes a matter of when, not if.

But *when* was still a long distance off.

The Mercury did not start straightaway—it turns out that it is not good for cars to be jostled by giants—and by the time Pete got the engine running and the headlights on, both Beatriz and Salto were out of sight.

"Sorry, Tony," he said, although Tony was still quite a distance away, having given them space as Beatriz had requested. Pete headed off in the direction the horse and the young woman had gone.

Several hundred yards away, Salto was pelting across the scrub with the enthusiasm of a horse that had been kept in a stall for too many years. Beatriz was not keeping up, but she still had him in her sights by the time Pete drove up alongside her. The station wagon scuffed to a halt and without pause Beatriz climbed into the passenger seat.

"We should try to cut him off," she said quite calmly, although she was out of breath. "Is there anything like a rope in here?"

"I don't know," Pete replied. "This isn't my car."

Beatriz squeezed between the seats to look in the back, striking her head on the roof as the Mercury experimented with gravity. Tony did not have a rope in the backseat of his car, nor in the cargo area, where Pete had spent a night. As she rummaged, Pete overtook Salto and skidded to a halt before him. The stallion, however, merely leaped over the station wagon like the cow over the moon.

"Gee," Pete said.

As he hit the gas again, Beatriz climbed back into the front seat. She was holding a revolver—an enormous Ruger Single-Six with a dark wood grip and a long, long barrel. It would have appeared at home in a very good Western movie and was large enough to have been purchased by a man who judged cars with a tape measure.

Pete was scandalized. "You're not going to shoot him?"

"This was in the back," Beatriz said. "It was cocked. That's very dangerous."

"It's not my gun!"

Beatriz closed it away in the glove box as Pete tried once more to block Salto with the station wagon. Again the horse sailed over them.

"Just follow him," Beatriz said. "He'll tire eventually."

"What will you lead him back with?"

Beatriz held up a silk tie that she had found under the passenger seat along with a large quantity of marijuana, a fifth of whiskey, and a small stack of cash. So Pete and Beatriz and Salto traipsed over the county as the stars moved slowly overhead and the mountains told stories to themselves. An hour into the night, Salto caught the scent of mares, and his journey took on a renewed focus. The stallion led the Mercury through the maze of abandoned stick buildings that used to be a mining camp, and the force of his passion caused already weak porches to collapse upon themselves. Then he careened through a muddy creek bed that sighed as it was galloped through and then driven through. Then past an abandoned general store and an empty house with a leaning, ghost-toothed picket fence out front. Then back into the desert hills.

Antelope joined them briefly, surrounding the car with hooved animals before they remembered their wildness and disappeared into the night. Far overhead, an upwardly mobile owl that had chased the whisper of a miracle far up into the atmosphere spotted the Mercury down below and dove after it. The owl was so far above the Earth that it had thought the station wagon was small enough to be prey; once it discovered its mistake, it peeled off just before hitting the windshield.

Beatriz watched it fly away. "You don't have darkness in you, do you?" she asked.

"Just the hole in my heart," Pete replied.

As the night cantered on, the stallion covered hundreds of acres to a ranch many miles away, only vaguely known by the occupants of Bicho Raro. The sign over the gate read DOUBLE D RANCH, and the gate was closed. Salto leaped it with aplomb and disappeared between the barns as mares sang winsomely from inside one of them.

Beatriz and Pete exchanged a glance. Pete knew nothing about this ranch, because he was from Oklahoma. Beatriz knew nothing about this ranch, because she did not own any roosters. In 1962, appearing at a ranch at night without warning was a good way to get shot. But in 1962, allowing a stallion to pillage another person's barn was also a good way to get shot. Pete and Beatriz weighed these options.

Pete stopped the vehicle.

"Lotta cars," he said. Because there were indeed a healthy number of vehicles parked in the drive on the other side of the gate.

"A lot of lights," Beatriz added, because each barn had a glowing orange light on it.

"Well, that's okay," Pete said, but doubtfully. "Because we're not doing anything criminal."

They clambered over the gate.

Double D Ranch was owned by a lady of some years named Darlene Purdey. She had run it for years with her lady friend Dorothy Lanks, and for decades, the two of them had done everything together: farmed, knitted, cooked, kissed, cleaned. But Dorothy had the nerve to die first, and since then, the ranch had fallen into disrepair. Either the changing weather or Darlene's grief turned the soil to ash, and nothing would grow. Pushed by desperation and cold with bitterness, Darlene now paid the bills by running an underground cockfighting ring. Her prize fighter, General MacArthur, was undefeated, and she used him to extort money from all of the locals who came with their own roosters and betting money.

Beatriz and Pete discovered this only when Salto made a grand entrance into the barn Darlene was currently using as a cockpit. She and another rancher crouched in the middle of a ring made of cardboard and scrap wood. Two dozen other men and women of varying ages watched from the outside of the ring. Staticky music played over a radio somewhere in the building. Wood shavings and blood and Salto hovered in the air over the fight.

Cockfighting is a very old blood sport. Typically, it involves animals bred for this purpose, a particular variety called a gamecock, as ordinary roosters will often give up the fight and turn away when they realize they are going to be bested. The gamecocks generally have their combs and wattles removed to prevent their opponent from gaining an advantage, and before the fight, their owners strap a blade to one of the creature's legs to allow it to draw blood more freely. It is illegal in many countries, including the one Pete and Beatriz were in at the moment, as it is considered cruel to encourage animals to fight to the death.

Darlene's rooster, General MacArthur, was unusual as he was an ordinary leghorn rooster still in full possession of his wattle and comb that fought bare-legged. Nonetheless he was undefeated and was preparing to defend this title in the moment Salto burst into the fight, Pete and Beatriz quick behind him.

One does not like to generalize, but the ranchers involved in illegal cockfighting at the time shared a certain personality type, which was how Pete and Beatriz came to find themselves facing a dozen drawn weapons.

"We're here for the horse," Beatriz said.

Darlene Purdey said, "This is by invitation only."

"We were just leaving, ma'am," Pete said. "Sorry for interrupting your night."

Salto, who had just completed a quick circuit of the barn in search of mares, now headed back for the door. Beatriz snagged his halter as he attempted to sweep past her. She maintained her composure as he dragged her a few feet.

"No one invited you or a horse," Darlene said. Before Dorothy had died, she wouldn't have spoken to anyone this way, nor tolerated guns pointed at even late-night visitors, but her heart had gone to salt along with her land. Now she found that bloodshed and suffering drowned out the sound of her grief, and although the past Darlene would have taken their side, the present Darlene was considering making these newcomers regret interrupting her fight.

"You want this, Dolly?" asked the man crouched in the ring with her, pulling out a revolver. This was Stanley Dunn, and his heart had been salt longer than it had been flesh.

He cocked his gun.

People had died for lesser infractions in this part of Colorado.

Outside the barn, an enormous commotion stole everyone's attention. The sound was multifaceted: roaring and squeaking and wailing and scratching. No one in the barn besides Beatriz knew what was causing it: dozens of owls suddenly attracted to the powerful sense of a miracle in the making. The darkness in Darlene alone would have been sufficient to gather them, and with Beatriz Soria in such close proximity, a miracle seemed imminent.

There would be no miracle. Firstly, Beatriz would not perform a miracle on the unwilling. Secondly, it was forbidden to perform a miracle where other people could get hurt, even if they were all the sort of people to stand around and watch chickens kill each other for fun. Thirdly, Beatriz didn't want to.

Pete used the distraction of the noise as an opportunity to snatch General MacArthur by his tail feathers. As the rooster pecked and kicked, Pete drew him close to his chest and took a step back toward the door.

"Don't shoot!" Darlene shouted. "Kid, you're going to be sorry."

"I'm already sorry," Pete said truthfully. "I said it before. We just want to go."

Beatriz was not sorry. She did not feel that their transgression warranted the threat of physical violence. When the guns didn't lower, she nudged Pete toward the night. She told the rest of them, "We're leaving. Nobody shoot or my friend strangles your rooster."

This was how Pete and Beatriz came to recover Salto and find themselves in possession of a fowl hostage. They escaped from the ranch and rode away with more horsepower than they'd arrived in: Beatriz riding Salto with a rein made of Tony's fine black tie, and Pete riding behind her in the Mercury with a rooster in the passenger seat.

It was not until they were miles away from Double D Ranch that the two slowed their pace. Pete drove the Mercury alongside Salto, who trotted far more demurely now that he had accomplished several years of galloping in just a few hours. Dawn glimmered. They had chased and escaped all through the night; they'd run clear around Alamosa and now had to go through it to get back to Bicho Raro. Every animal that had joined them in their chase was now sleeping, and every person who had been sleeping while they were away was now awake.

Beatriz looked at Pete through the driver's side window; he smiled.

He smiled is a good line for almost any kind of story. Beatriz found she liked the way he looked: sturdy and true, responsible and square. The night had left his white T-shirt dirtier than it had begun, and his neatly combed hair was no longer quite so neat—but it had only served to wear down the outer layer of kindness to reveal that there was only more kindness beneath. She smiled.

She smiled is a good line for almost any kind of a story, too. Pete found that he liked the way she looked: silent and apart, intentional and intelligent. The night had unparted her evenly parted black hair and she had a bit of chicken blood on her skin, but the disrepair of her appearance only served to reveal that her interior had remained cool and unruffled.

"I've never stolen anything," Pete confessed.

"You didn't steal that chicken," Beatriz replied. "You repurposed him. You did steal that car, though."

Pete was already falling in love, although he would have denied it if asked. Beatriz was, too, although she did not believe herself capable and would have denied it as well. The morning light looked good upon them both.

"We never decided what to do about the truck," Pete said, struck into memory by the trucks parked near Alamosa's small downtown.

Beatriz thought for a moment before saying, "I think you should come with us tomorrow night and see what we're doing with it."

"I reckon that sounds all right."

"Let's go back home now."

"Wait," Pete said. "I've gotta get Tony a radio."

17

Making new roses was a long process.

When it was spring, the first pollinating season, Francisco began work early, as soon as the sun appeared to give him light to work. He moved among his roses, finding the buds that were due to open that day, and then he removed every petal except the bottom five so that he would be able to find them again. Carefully, he detached the stamen from each bud and discarded it. These would be his seed parents, the mothers. They would dictate if the new roses would be bushes or climbers, dark-leaved or light-leaved. He would have already prepared the stud roses by cutting them a day or more before and leaving them to dry so he could shake the pollen from them onto a sleeve of white paper. The stud roses, the fathers, would tell his new roses what sort of blossom to have, lending their fragrance or shape or color.

Then, in the perfect silence of his greenhouse, he moved carefully with a small paintbrush and painted the pollen carefully on each of the rose mothers' stigmas. In the language Beatriz had invented, he marked the potential rose's father on a tag and attached it to the mother rose. And then he waited.

It took months for the roses to form rose hips full of seeds, and then those seeds had to be chilled and kept in the dark for nearly three more months. Those that he had not lost to fungus or poor spirits he carefully planted in pots marked with their origins. Then one leaf and two leaves and three leaves would appear, and Francisco carefully policed them for disease or pests that might have snuck into his greenhouse. Then, finally, six weeks later, each fragile rose plant would produce its first, hesitant flower.

If it was not the black bloom he was hoping for, he began all over again.

Sometimes, Francisco thought that people might be roses. It was not that he disbelieved Darwin and the classification of the species. It was only that every time he carefully applied the pollen, he thought about the process, how the pollen would work its way over the rose's stigma and then enter the egg cell and fertilize the egg nucleus, and how wondrous and strange it was that it was the same process by which we were made. Many of his days, particularly in these slow summer months, were spent engrossed in thought clouds triggered by small actions, and he lost weeks to thinking about what it might mean that so many creatures under the sun, from roses to birds to trees to sharks, came to life by the same, complex process. Even those whose process often looked quite different from the outside—like the meiosis, or cell splitting, of the sea urchin—still used much of the same raw stuff: cells, fertilizations, sharing of chromosomes. He mused on why it might be that evolution had not instead designed most of the world to share the simple asexual process sometimes used by plants such as pelargonium, a flower known commonly as storksbill. A cutting was taken from the original plant, dropped into moist soil, and left to make another plant. By the same process, to create Beatriz, he would have merely planted one of his fingers and she would have emerged later, fully formed and independent.

Why indeed, he wondered, did we need life to make more life? We took it for granted that two creatures met and mated and made another creature, when we would not expect a cloud or a fire or a cooking pot to be fashioned the same way. Yes, all of those processes required combining other ingredients as well, but without the cell, the egg—? If there was a great creator who had fashioned us in his own image, why, then, was more life not made in the same way, by merely breathing a word over a handful of dust? Instead, reproduction and love became a messy process, and messy processes meant there were many places where it could fail.

These were the thoughts that occupied Francisco's day.

An additional thought occupied the day following Beatriz and Pete's all-night chase, however, because late in the morning, Beatriz tapped on the glass before letting herself into his greenhouse.

"Good morning, Papa," she whistled in their language.

"Is it morning?" he replied in kind, not looking up from his notebook. He was not displeased that she'd come to visit. Francisco found it very difficult to work with certain forms of distraction, such as music or conversations with heightened emotions playing in the background, but he did well if people were reading to him in a fairly undramatic voice, or if the visitor had a quiet way about them. Beatriz generally had the latter, and had, upon occasion, read to him in the evenings when he had first moved out to the greenhouse.

"It is, though it doesn't feel like it. I need to ask you a favor, and I don't know if it is possible, so you can tell me now if it is not acceptable and I will be fine," Beatriz said.

It had been some time since someone had asked Francisco for something he was capable of giving, but that was mostly because they had only been asking him to move back in with Antonia. He dearly hoped that Beatriz, a highly intelligent young woman, was not here to request that.

"What is it?" he asked.

"I'd like for you to keep this chicken in your greenhouse for a while."

Beatriz was referring, of course, to General MacArthur, the fighting rooster they had repurposed just hours earlier. He was missing feathers in places from his fights, and had a wicked scar across his chest from another bird's blade, and still had a bit of blood streaked through the pale feathers around his head.

When Francisco turned to look, Beatriz added, "I didn't know if he will bother your plants."

Francisco divined immediately that there was an involved story to this rooster, but also that if his daughter had wanted to share it, she would have begun it already. He said merely, "I assume there is a reason why the rooster can't stay outside with the other chickens."

"He has a problem with aggression," Beatriz said. "And Rosa would not be happy if he killed her rooster."

Francisco considered the request. Chickens would eat rose petals, but he had plenty of discarded rose petals that could be fed to a chicken so it wouldn't bother the blooms still on the plant. Chicken manure was messy, but also very good for roses. He did not want to have to look after an animal, but he also felt his younger daughter never asked anything of him, and this was a small sacrifice to make for her.

"Leave him for the day," Francisco said, "and I will see how he does. What is his name?"

Naturally, Beatriz did not know the rooster was called General MacArthur, as they had stolen only the chicken and not his name. She held the bird out from her chest, his wings pinned to his body, as if he might somehow have his moniker somewhere about his person.

"I don't know," she finally admitted.

She set him down. There was nothing about the rooster that particularly encouraged sympathy. He had been angry the night before and he was still angry now. Francisco clucked at him, but he strutted away, looking this way and that at the roses. Both father and daughter watched the rooster for several minutes.

"Is there something else on your mind, Beatriz?" Francisco asked eventually.

There was nearly always something else on Beatriz's mind. She said the easiest of the options first. "Daniel."

Francisco, too, had been thinking about his nephew—really,

nearly his son. When Daniel had lost his parents, he had gained the combined parentage of the surviving adult Sorias at Bicho Raro. Francisco, Antonia, Michael, Rosa, and Nana had all pitched in to care for him, an unusual and excessive amount of love and ownership that led first to Daniel's extremely bad behavior and then to his extremely good behavior. Francisco had been thinking about it in particular that day because the year had just reached the point where the sun came in bright and multicolored through the window over his desk. This window was unlike any of the other windows in the greenhouse, because when Daniel was still in his hell-sent stage, Francisco had forbidden him to spend all night out joyriding in other people's cars. This might strike most people as a reasonable rule to make, but Daniel had found it both chafing and unfair, and to demonstrate his feelings, he had spent the night throwing rocks through every single pane in that particular window. The plants inside had perished in the night's frost. Daniel had been sentenced the task of repairing the window as punishment. Because even that could not be done without rebellion, Daniel had sourced glass from the closest junkyard. Instead of restoring the window to its previous transparent existence, each pane was instead replaced with four or five or even six tiny tinted ones—scrounged from bottles, jars, car windows, vases, flowerpots, pitchers. He had meant to be difficult, but he had not known that in the full sunlight, the ferocity of his rebellion would be dazzling.

Now Francisco nodded as he sat in the church-like light Daniel had inadvertently created all those years ago, and he thought about how Daniel was somewhere in the wilderness with his darkness.

"There must be a way to communicate safely with him," Beatriz said. Before Daniel had gone, she had been considering telling her father about the radio station, as she thought he would have found it an interesting thought exercise, too. But now that he had vehemently shared Antonia's feelings about connecting with Daniel, she didn't feel confident that he would allow them to keep doing it.

"If anyone can come up with a solution, I believe you can," Francisco said. He had great faith in his daughter's brain. "But I don't want you putting yourself in unnecessary danger."

"I don't want to put myself in unnecessary danger either," Beatriz reassured him. "But the doctor still treats the patient."

This kind of talk would have infuriated Antonia if she had heard it. Francisco often mused about the scientific points of the miracle, but to Antonia, this was not only blasphemy but dangerous blasphemy. To treat it as something contained by logic was to get comfortable around it, which not only made such a thing more dangerous but also made it less holy and thus less important. Antonia's kind of belief is not uncommon, but it has done both science and religion a disservice. By relegating the things we fear and don't understand to religion, and the things we understand and control to science, we rob science of its artistry and religion of its mutability.

"Do you have any thoughts on that in your notebook?" she asked.

Francisco sat back down at his desk, hands crossed over each other, back straight. He was a comely and poised version of his daughter when he sat like this, the same eyes, the same nose, the same obsession with the handsomeness of thought.

"Only that there must have been a better way at some point," he said. "Or the Sorias would have died out by now." He turned his cunning eyes upon his daughter. "And is there something else troubling you?"

There was, but Beatriz was less comfortable with sharing this one, as she could not quite sort out its shape. Part of it had to do with Pete and herself. And the other part of it had to do with Francisco and Antonia, and if there had ever been a possible future for them that did not drive Francisco to live in the greenhouse and her mother to live alone. Beatriz wanted to know if people like herself and her father—people supposedly without feelings—could be in love, or if they were not capable of producing the correct quantity of emotion to fill an emotional partner's glass for very long.

"Do you still love Mama?" she asked. This was a longer sentence in their language than it was in English or Spanish, as Francisco and Beatriz had developed several phrases to indicate all of the different forms of love they had identified in their study of humankind. The musical phrase that Beatriz used roughly translated to *need of the sort that can only be fulfilled by one thing*.

"Did Judith tell you to ask me?" Francisco inquired.

This was not an improbable question. In fact, through the window, Beatriz could see Pete at work on the stage that Judith had set him on. He was now creating upright pillars for hanging strings of decorations. While Beatriz appreciated Judith's attempt at strategy, she did not think that either of her parents were so straightforward that they could be tricked into falling back into each other's arms merely by re-creating the scene of their first moments together. "No. I'm not asking if you will move back in with Mama. I just want to understand why it doesn't work."

"Have you asked your mother this same question?"

"No."

"Would you?"

She imagined this scenario. Antonia, angry, and Beatriz, merely puzzled, both of these expressions feeding the other. It was exactly the kind of conversation that Beatriz spent much time avoiding.

"No."

"That is why it doesn't work," he said.

Beatriz took this information and put it into a projected future. In this projected future, she could not tell if she broke Pete Wyatt's heart merely by being herself. She could not tell if they would be unable to have conversations because they would both want something from the other that was impossible. She could not tell if it was safer to stop a love story before it ever truly got under way.

When she thought this, she experienced a physical sensation as profound as the surges that had struck Pete's weak heart. It felt like a blow, but it was actually a feeling. It was a feeling so sizable and so complicated that it would have been difficult even for someone with emotional practice to express, and for Beatriz, who was handicapped by her belief of not having them, it was impossible. The feeling was, in fact, a combination of relief that she might be able to use this conversation as an excuse to never speak to Pete again and thus protect herself from further complex emotions, and also the intense and heartrending disappointment that came from standing on the edge of something extraordinary and walking away from it. These seem like intractable opposites, but only if you are being logical about it.

Beatriz was being logical about it.

A tap came at the glass. This one made Francisco sigh heavily, as it was not someone who was a quiet soul. It was Joaquin, who did not wait for permission but pushed his way in instead.

"Beatriz," he said urgently.

"Shut the door," she said in her language, then, catching herself, again in English. "Don't let the rooster out."

Joaquin squeezed into the greenhouse. "Wyatt the Riot said Tony found something you need to see."

With some difficulty, Beatriz sorted her thoughts back into their proper places. Love, especially new love, is gifted at disordering them. "I'm coming."

"Beatriz," Francisco whistled. "The answer to your question, though, is yes."

18

What Tony had found was a message from Daniel. He had been out walking that morning, eating his breakfast on the move so that no one could see him at it, and discovered the message. The letters were sized large enough for him to spot from his impressive height. One of the *e*'s was written backward. Tony, who liked large things, approved, even if he didn't understand the meaning of it.

Now all of the Sorias stood three miles out from Bicho Raro, the various vehicles they'd used to arrive there scattered on the edge of the road some yards away. All work had halted for them to visit the site, as if any artifact of Daniel's was now a Shrine, and they were the pilgrims. It was a rarity to see all of them together at one time, particularly the middle generation. Michael, his work paused. Antonia, without scissors in hand. Francisco, far from his greenhouse. Rosa—well, Rosa was pretty much always Rosa. They had not been all together in one place since Judith's wedding, and before that, not for years.

"Why would he put it here?" asked Antonia. She looked accusingly at each of them, including Francisco, who stood on the opposite side of the circle. "No one would see it here."

"Maybe he misjudged," Michael said. "Meant to have it visible from the road."

Rosa adjusted the baby Lidia on her hip. "Who is Marisita?"

Spelled out in stones and dried branches torn from the scrub were the words:

Marisita

I'm listening

Daniel

Because as you have already guessed, Daniel's placement was no accident. His message was designed to be seen not by a vehicle on the road but rather by a vehicle that had left the road to secretly broadcast a radio station. And the message was deliberately cryptic as it was meant for no one but the cousins who spent time in that box truck each night, and for the young woman he loved.

Joaquin pressed one of his water bottles to his forehead as if the chill of it might steady him. Beatriz closed her eyes for one moment, and in that moment of darkness imagined Daniel returning to them safe and sound. When she opened her eyes, she and Joaquin found that they could not exchange looks as their secret hung between them and threatened to become visible if they both pointed their gaze directly at it.

But they both felt the same. It was one thing to be sending sounds out into the night with the hope that someone, anyone might be listening, and something else again to be sending sounds out into the night with the hope that someone in particular would be listening. And it is a third thing altogether to send sounds out into the night and *know* that you are being heard by the person you meant to reach.

"Isn't Marisita . . ." Judith began, "the rainy pilgrim who cooks?"

In a more dangerous note, Antonia said, "Why is he sending a message to a pilgrim?" But the tone in her voice told everyone there that she already knew why he would be doing such a thing.

"Love," Eduardo said reverentially, and Antonia flinched. Joaquin made a note of the way he said it, in order to have Diablo Diablo try it later. It was the round and splendid way that he pronounced the *o*, the gentle landing on the *v*. He did not realize that his face was soundlessly pronouncing the word until he saw both his parents frowning at him. He corrected his face, and they corrected theirs, but he was still contemplating the part of him that was Diablo Diablo, and even though they didn't know the name for it, so were they.

"What does it mean, Beatriz?" Judith asked. They all knew that Beatriz and Daniel were the closest of the cousins, and Judith assumed (correctly) that this also meant Beatriz knew what the message meant. Beatriz, however, said nothing. She said nothing for so long that most of them forgot Judith had asked Beatriz the question in the first place, including Judith. (People often forget the power of silence, but Beatriz rarely did.)

Francisco marked this absence of an answer, and put it away in his mind to think about later.

Nana said, "So he is still alive."

To this point, you have not seen anything of Nana besides a

few minutes of her picking tomatoes in her back garden. That was because Nana was old, and like many old people, she had arthritis. It was not bad enough to completely prevent her from moving, and in fact, she had precisely calculated the number of steps she could take each day without suffering for it that night or the following day (217). She had taken 15 steps to Eduardo's stepside pickup, and then he had lifted her in and twirled his mustache. Then she had taken 47 steps from the pickup truck to this message. That left her with 155 for the rest of the day's tasks. It was an expensive side trip, but one Nana felt she had to make.

"He could be close," Judith said. "Who knows when this message was left?"

"Don't get any ideas," Antonia warned. "It is still not a good idea to go looking for him."

But Judith had not said this as a message of hope. Rather, her old fear was beginning to creep up again, complicated by guilt. It was bad enough to be terrified that pilgrims might bring darkness on you; it was worse when the pilgrim was your own cousin whom you loved. She was torn in many directions. The easiest of these directions was *away*, and a huge part of her wanted to retreat to Colorado Springs with Eduardo. But that felt like giving up on Daniel. And even if she was willing to do that, a small part of her still thought that she might be able to convince her parents to reunite.

But it didn't seem very likely, looking at them now. Francisco and Antonia were closer physically than they had been in a very long time, but they appeared farther apart than ever.

Eduardo placed his hand upon the small of Judith's back, and she remembered the way he had said *love.* Her fear went back to sleep.

"I'm not an idiot," Judith retorted.

If Antonia and Francisco and Michael and Rosa had been paying attention, they would have marked that neither Beatriz nor Joaquin, the two most vocal supporters of actively helping Daniel, had spoken in favor of helping him now. As it was, only Nana noticed their quiet acceptance, and she took it for despair rather than secret collusion.

"I never said this wasn't terrible," Antonia said, feeling the silence of the group was castigating her for upholding their rules. "I don't know why you are always making me out to be the bad guy."

"I am in agreement with you, Antonia," Michael said.

"As am I," Francisco said.

There was a pause, and they looked sharply to Rosa, but it turned out that the gap in her agreement was only because she was removing her hair from the baby's mouth. "Yes, yes, we must be cautious."

The adults were soon discussing logistics in Spanish, which meant they were no longer actively soliciting the younger Sorias' thoughts. They could not leave water for him, because that was against the rules. But if he was this close, they mused, he could get water from any of the ranches if he was willing to drink with the cattle. And if he was sensible enough to leave this message, they reasoned, then he was sensible enough to be hunting down food for his body, perhaps. Which meant instead of the elements, maybe he was only having to fight the darkness.

They were desperately wrong about just one part, however, and that was the *only* in that phrase—*only having to fight the darkness.* Yes, Daniel was fighting the darkness, but there was nothing slight about it. They were not looking for the signs of how his darkness had manifested, nor could they have, but if they had, they might have noticed how uneven the letters were, how some of them were misshapen and only legible to the optimistic. They were words crafted by a young man with fast-failing vision.

But they needed this optimism to counteract their failure to act. Imagining that Daniel was still doing all right was the only way the adults could live with their abandonment of him.

"'Marisita, I'm listening,'" Rosa repeated, bouncing Lidia in time with the words, waiting for them to make more sense. "'Marisita, I'm listening.'"

Marisita, I'm listening.

Finally, Beatriz and Joaquin allowed their eyes to meet, and in that look, they saw that they were both thinking the same thing: If Daniel truly was listening, they needed to put on a show that felt like a miracle.

19

There used to be an enormous and fine barn at Bicho Raro, capable of housing two hundred bales of hay, twelve horses, a small tractor, and twenty-four barn swallows. The siding had been amber brown and the roof was gloriously red. It was, in fact, the very barn Pete was scavenging for the dance floor's boards. Shortly after it had been built, the wind nudged it, as it nudged all things in the San Luis Valley. Nothing happened, because the barn was very securely built. The wind nudged it for all that week, and still nothing happened. The wind nudged it for ninety-nine weeks in a row, and still nothing happened; the barn did not budge. But on the one hundredth week, the wind nudged the barn and the barn fell onto itself. It was not that the one hundredth week of nudging was any stronger than the previous weeks. It was not even that the one hundredth week of nudging was what had actually knocked the barn over. The ninety-nine weeks of nudging were what had truly done the job, but the one hundredth was the one around to take the credit.

We almost always can point to that hundredth blow, but we don't always mark the ninety-nine other things that happen before we change.

Things felt different in the box truck that night; things felt like change. Some of this was because their population had altered by one. Beatriz, Joaquin, and Pete were jammed together like crayons in a box as the truck lumbered slowly out into the dark. Beatriz wasn't much of a talker, and Joaquin wasn't feeling like being civil, and Pete wasn't one to start a fire in a room that didn't seem to be in the mood for smoke, so for quite a while the only sounds in the truck were the rumbling of the engine and the squeaking of the seats and the nearly inaudible thump of hearts when Beatriz's and Pete's fingers accidentally jostled together.

"Do you like music, Oklahoma?" Joaquin finally asked, more aggressively than one might have ordinarily, and more aggressively than one might have thought, considering the truck's cramped cab was pressing their shoulders together hard in a familiar sort of way.

Pete missed the tone. "I like Patsy Cline an awful lot."

"Patsy *Cline*," Joaquin echoed.

"Who's Patsy Cline?" Beatriz asked.

"Oh, you know who she is," Joaquin said dismissively. He threw a significant twang into his voice but otherwise did not attempt to make it musical. "*I'm always walkin' after midnight, searchin' for you.*"

Beatriz shook her head, no closer to recognition.

"*Craaaaaaazzy,*" Pete sang.

Technically, he was not a very good singer, wavery and low, but he was pleasantly heavy on the syllables in the way that Johnny Cash was, and Beatriz was charmed by it. Moreover, the tune was recognizable. Beatriz said, "I know that one."

Pete had a thing for crooners. He liked Patsy Cline, and he liked Loretta Lynn. Women with deep voices and a sense of history, singing in low, round tones over plucked and syrupy steel guitars. Once, one of his mother's brother's father-in-law's friends had stayed at their house in Oklahoma after blowing the engine of his new Impala on a cross-country trip, and while there, he'd told stories of meeting Patsy Cline back in Virginia. She'd been tough and funny. She'd called everybody Hoss, and drank like a man. Pete had taken an instant shine.

Joaquin was perfectly fine with Patsy Cline, in reality, but he was still angry about his father's admiring tone when speaking of Pete, so he couldn't find it in him to be kindly about his musical choice.

"We don't have Patsy Cline on the list for tonight," Joaquin said in an even ruder tone. He did not know that Pete hadn't been told yet what they were going into the desert to do, so his statement didn't make a lot of sense to Pete.

"That's quite okay, sir," Pete said with a smile. "I don't *only* like Patsy Cline."

Beatriz caught that *sir* in midair, like a bird, and studied it in her mind. For some, a *sir* in this situation might have been used for an equally rude effect, sarcastically spitting politeness at the party who had wronged them. For others, it might have been automatic, someone who said *sir* so often that it didn't mean anything at all. For Pete, it was launched with deference. *I'm no threat,* that *sir* declared, with a peacekeeping smile. *You're still king of the castle.* Antonia's dogs were always fighting among one another, and the battles ended when one rolled onto its back to show it had no fight in it. That was Pete's *sir* in this particular exchange. Beatriz found this unfair, as Pete had done nothing wrong, but also frustrating, as Pete would think Joaquin was always petulant, which was far from the truth.

The kindness made Joaquin crosser, because there's nothing like knowing that you were just a heel to a nice person to make you even madder at them.

"What is it you want this truck for anyway, Oklahoma?" Joaquin asked.

Pete once again explained the moving-truck business. He added, hesitantly, "I was going to go into the army, but I've got a hole in my heart."

There is a certain kind of wistfulness that spills out in our voices no matter how many dams we've put up, and only a real monster can hear it and not be moved. It came out in Pete's words there, and Joaquin felt all of his hostility shrivel.

He said, "Don't all men, Oklahoma?" and then he started to sing some Patsy Cline until Pete grinned. Beatriz smiled her private smile out the window, but Pete saw it in the reflection. Their fingers touched again, but this time it wasn't an accident.

Joaquin broke off singing. "Did Marisita tell you why she wouldn't do it tonight?"

"She just left a reply to my note that said 'not tonight,'" Beatriz said.

Joaquin did not say what he was thinking, and did not have

to. Beatriz was thinking it, too. No matter how good their show was tonight, it would not be what Daniel was truly hoping for.

"Maybe tomorrow," Joaquin said. "Hey, we could have Oklahoma ask her for us."

Just a few days ago, neither of them would have considered this a viable option. The unquestioning caution Antonia had expressed earlier had still run through their veins as well, back then, but things were different now. The true edges of the taboo were clearly more complex than they'd been taught. Both of them eyed Pete.

"Ask who what?" he replied.

"He doesn't know about . . ." Beatriz told Joaquin. She tilted her head toward the back of the truck.

Joaquin was delighted. Any remaining resentment vanished, replaced by the anticipation of the reveal. "*Oh.*"

His enthusiasm filled the truck for the final few minutes of the journey. When Beatriz brought the truck to a stop, Pete craned his neck, trying and failing to glimpse what made this particular patch of wilderness their destination. He was even more bemused when Beatriz and Joaquin climbed out, Beatriz with the flashlight and Joaquin with a bottle of water. The driver's side door hung open, and Pete looked out into that square of black night. He couldn't see anything, but he could smell the foxy, bright scent of the cold desert. It was a restless and wild smell, and it made him feel restless and wild as well.

"Come on, we need your help," Beatriz called.

Sliding from the truck, Pete felt his way around to the back, where the cousins were waiting.

Beatriz placed her hands upon the back of the truck. She was rarely boastful or excited, as the first required an interest in other people's esteem, which she did not often have (much to the frustration of her mother), and the second often required an element of pleasant surprise or perception of an event as extraordinary, which she also did not often have, as most events were predictable if you were paying close enough attention. But she found in this case she was feeling both boastful and excited; she was shocked to discover that she was proud of the box truck's contents, proud enough that instead of merely opening the door with a serene face, she had to think about keeping her face serene as she opened the door.

Beatriz drew open the back of the truck.

Pete was silent for a long moment.

"What do you think, Wyatt the Riot?" asked Joaquin.

Pete said, "Well, gosh."

Back in Bicho Raro, Tony had finally managed to operate the radio Pete had secured for him. The largeness of his hands and the smallness of the radio had presented considerable difficulty, but success had eventually presented itself. Although he had not yet managed to tune it to a clear station, he was shocked by how comforting even the sound of static was. It was not yet music, but it was about to be.

He had felt unhinged since leaving Philadelphia, a feeling

that had not improved with either a miracle or a good night's sleep. But now, as music strove through the static, he felt something like normalcy.

Suddenly, a voice sprang from the speaker.

"Hola, hola, hola, this is Diablo Diablo, roping some of those radio waves to pull my wagon tonight. We've got a great show for you coming up. We've got the Cascades and some Lloyd Price and that sweet little number by the Del Vikings, and we're also introducing two new features I think you're going to love. We've got the Weather Story, our local news told in the form of two abuelas talking about the weather, and we've also got the Teen Story, which is just me reading entries from the old journal I found under my cousin's mattress, one every night until he gets himself together and comes home to make me stop. Let's go, children. It's going to be a devil of a night."

Tony let out a breath that he hadn't realized he was holding. Below him, Jennie the schoolteacher also let out a breath.

"Oh, hang me," Tony said. "How long have you been there?"

"Oh, hang me," Jennie replied. "How long have you been there?"

She pointed at the radio, but it was impossible to tell what she meant by such a gesture. Then she lifted her other arm to show that she had brought a bag of snacks that the two of them could share.

Tony's mood shifted rapidly through annoyance at being interrupted to grudging acceptance of Jennie to hatred of eating in front of others.

"I'm not hungry," he said.

"I'm not hungry," Jennie said. So now it was two lies, since they were both hungry.

"Isn't it late?" Tony asked.

"Isn't it late?"

He relented. "Fine. Just sit down."

Her face cleared and she sat cross-legged beside the radio. "Fine. Just sit down." She shook some of the corn snacks out of the bag onto a napkin in front of her.

"Lady, you gotta fix that problem," Tony said. She echoed his words again and then nodded in rueful agreement. "How'd you get that way, anyway? Don't you have any words of your own?"

"How'd you get that way, anyway? Don't you have any words of your own?" Jennie repeated. With a sigh, she handed a corn snack up to Tony, who accepted it but left it sitting in his palm.

Diablo Diablo's program continued. His voice took on a more intimate tone. "Here's a thing Jack Kerouac said: 'What is that feeling when you're driving away from people and they recede on the plain till you see their specks dispersing?—it's the too-huge world vaulting us, and it's good-bye. But we lean forward to the next crazy venture beneath the skies.' If you're missing someone tonight, know that I, Diablo Diablo, am, too. It's an enormous sky out there with a lot of stars above it and a lot of folks underneath it, and all of us, stars and human, are missing someone in the dark. But I, Diablo Diablo, think that if we're all out there missing someone, that means that we're all really together on that one note, aren't we? So none of us are really alone as long as we're lonely."

It is difficult to convey how mesmerizing Joaquin was in this passage, how passionate and moving, because so much of the magic was in the swing and tug of his voice, which he practiced in places where others could not hear him. If you read his words out loud, you may get an idea, but nothing is quite the same as hearing it through the speakers of a radio.

"Now I'm gonna spin you a number from last year, Del Shannon's 'Runaway,'" Joaquin said.

The song began to play. Tony marveled that the music still worked on him, even as a giant. It seemed to him he should have needed more music, bigger music, louder music, to fill him up now that he was this size, but instead, he found that after all of his days away from it, the music was even more effective. Even though he had heard "Runaway" countless times before, tonight he felt it move him as strongly as it had the first time he'd heard it.

"What was that? That's Joaquin Soria!" Padre Jiminez said.

Tony and Jennie both jumped, as Padre Jiminez had approached soundlessly. Now his head was cocked intently toward the radio.

"Oh, why. What the hell are you doing here?" Tony asked.

"I heard his voice," Padre said. He had been clear over in his room, praying before sleep, but even with the window just cracked, he had recognized Joaquin's voice. He had excellent hearing because of his two large coyote ears. "That's our Joaquin!"

Tony raised an eyebrow. "Isn't he that kid in that shirt that barks?"

"Indeed indeed," Padre Jiminez said. "How I've watched that boy grow over the last few years! I would recognize his voice anywhere! But he didn't say that he was Joaquin on the radio, did he? What is he calling himself?"

"Diablo Diablo." Tony mimicked the way Joaquin said it, accidentally throwing in a bit of his Tony Triumph voice. It sounded impressive. Jennie's smile was full of delight.

"Oh dear," Padre Jiminez said. "I do wish that young people would realize there are better ways to appear edgy than invoking the great destroyer of men. Perhaps the station named him."

"No dice, Father Lassie," Tony said. "That's a pirate station."

Padre Jiminez craned his head back to peer at Tony. "I don't follow."

"It's an illegal station. He named himself."

"How do you know it's illegal?"

"No legit station has a kid DJ spinning Del Shannon at eleven p.m.," Tony said. Even from his great height, he saw Padre Jiminez's ears flag. "Don't get your pants twisted. He's getting his legs under him; it'll be good for him, as long as he doesn't get caught. I wonder if he built his gear himself."

"Joaquin?" Padre Jiminez said. "More likely Beatriz. Yes, Beatriz is much more likely to have built something."

Tony remembered Beatriz Soria felling Pete Wyatt at his feet just the day before. She'd been carrying a skirtful of wire, an odd nest that had puzzled him at the time but made sense now. Tony was provoked to interest despite himself.

"Is Beatriz into the radio?"

Padre Jiminez cocked his head. No one knew what Beatriz Soria was into. "She is a strange young woman."

"Don't get twisted, Padre," Tony said, "but coming from you, that's pretty rich."

The sound of conversation attracted Robbie and Betsy, the twins. They had been quarreling in their room out of boredom, and when they heard voices outside, they went to the window. When they saw a group gathered around a radio, they incorrectly assumed that it was a party. Some arguments are better than a party, but not theirs, and so they bundled up in sweaters and joined the others by Tony.

"Keep that snake away from me," Tony said, "or I'll step on all three of you."

As Diablo Diablo's voice came back onto the radio, the sound attracted Marisita's attention. She had just returned from yet another unsuccessful search for Daniel, and she was weary and disheartened. Because she had been out all day, she didn't know about the message Daniel had left for her, and she feared that he might be dead or too far away for her to ever find. Now she paused just inside the Doctor's Cabin, the door cracked. From there, she could hear the rise and fall of Joaquin's voice. It was too far away to make out what he was saying clearly, but she recognized the cadence from her time on the show. She could also see the other pilgrims from where she stood. Tony, looming, just his feet and knees in her sight, both barely lit by the porch lights. Jennie, sitting cross-legged by the radio. The twins and Padre, busily constructing a fire pit against the cool night.

Marisita imagined herself going to where they were all gathered, with delicacies in tow. In her head, she asked them, "Room for one more? I've made a few things for us to eat."

But in reality, she remained where she was, water dripping over her hands onto the floor.

She would have liked to attribute her hesitation to exhaustion, but she knew that it was more than that. If she thought about it, she could admit that if it had been a gathering of Sorias rather than pilgrims, she would have been inexorably attracted and, if not for the taboo, would have approached them at once. Marisita studied herself hard, trying to determine if it was judgment on her part. Was she biased against the pilgrims for being stuck halfway as she was? No, it was not that at all. What would be different about speaking to a Soria than a pilgrim? And then she hit upon it: It was the way the pilgrims spoke to one another. They were all aware that this was a temporary situation, and so they were cordial acquaintances, at best. Conversation skipped along the surface. She imagined the Sorias' gatherings were less chitchat and more *real*, the kind of intimacy that comes from knowing people for a long time and knowing you would know them for a long time in the future, too.

Then she realized that it was really that she just missed being part of a family.

It is entirely possible to have this kind of conversation with slight acquaintances, too, but none of this current crop of pilgrims had yet realized that.

Marisita would have left the pilgrims to their chitchat and gone to bed for some fitful and guilty sleep, if she had not just then recognized that what Jennie had brought to munch on was a bag of corn snacks. Marisita did not ordinarily require other people's things to be perfect, only herself, but corn snacks were so far from perfect that Marisita felt her own overall perfection draining.

She forgot her exhaustion and her guilt. *Corn snacks.*

She began to prepare food beneath her umbrellas, furiously, quickly, wanting to be able to deliver it before the radio show was over, before the others decided to go to bed. She heated up her skillet, and while she waited for that to be hot, she cut fat slices of watermelon and cucumbers and orange and squeezed lime on them, wiping the sprays of lime out of the corners of her eyes, and then she dashed chili powder and salt over them all. By then the skillet was hot enough for her to place as many fresh cobs of corn as she could fit into it. While the corn roasted, she cubed a fresh pineapple and added mint and sugar and more lime juice in the gaping mouth of the blender. While the blender ran in the background, she stirred together crema and guajillo chili pepper and mayonnaise and crumbled cotija cheese to make a thin sauce. She tore cilantro into fresh-scented shreds and added it to the bowl. Then, still waiting for the corn, she rapidly began to make colorful banderillas for those who didn't have a sweet tooth, spearing lip-puckering pickled gherkins, salty olives, and bright pickled red peppers. And finally, the corn was roasted and she transferred it to a platter and poured the crema and cheese over it.

It had been only ten minutes since she had decided to prepare refreshments and now she had some fruit with chili and some savory banderillas and some elotes and some eye-opening agua fresca to wash it all down with. It was not perfect, but it was closer than anyone else in Bicho Raro could come to it.

She piled it all up under umbrellas in her arms and walked briskly to where the others sat.

Padre Jiminez hurried over to relieve some of the platters from her arms. He licked his lips. "You're a miracle, Marisita Lopez."

Now the twins' previous assumption was correct: It *was* a party.

Even Theldon took part. He didn't come out of the house very far, but he at least put his chair outside the door instead of inside it. They ate Marisita's food and sang along to the songs, and the twins danced a little, as well as they could with the snake tangled around them. Tony veered dangerously close to Tony Triumph as he told the stories behind the music Joaquin played, but the truth was that Tony had always loved to tell people the story of music.

Padre Jiminez was the one who realized Marisita had probably not heard of the message Daniel had left for her. He gestured her close, which was a mostly unselfish impulse on his part, and told her of it as her miraculous rain sprinkled across his forehead.

"'Marisita, I'm listening,'" he repeated. "Did you know?"

Marisita's ears rang with shock, but her voice was quite calm. "No, Padre, I didn't."

"I didn't think so," he said with satisfaction. "Your elotes are perfection, by the way."

"Nearly," she whispered, but only in her head. Out loud, she said, "Thank you."

She sat with a pretty smile on her face, but inside, she was thinking about that message, and she was thinking about how Joaquin and Beatriz had asked her to be on the show again. Although none of the songs Joaquin played were particularly punitive, she nonetheless felt as if with every minute Joaquin spent trying to comfort his cousin, she was being reminded of how she was doing nothing. Yes, she was looking for Daniel, but that was what *she* wanted from her. What *he* wanted was for her to tell her story on air. She couldn't do it. He didn't realize that everyone would despise her. As the pilgrims warmed to one another, somehow united by Tony's irascible presence, she felt ever cooler. If they knew her real past, they would never call her a miracle.

In a pause in the programming, Jennie blurted out, "As I walk along, I wonder what went wrong."

All eyes landed on her. No one knew at first why the moment felt unusual, but slowly, they began to suspect that it was because no one had prompted Jennie with any words. She'd just said it. The pilgrims looked from one to another, replaying the conversation, trying to remember if any of the others had said that phrase.

Finally, Betsy asked, "Did you say that on your own?"

"Did you say that on your own?" Jennie echoed, but she nodded furiously.

After a long night of watching the other pilgrims being closer than they had ever been before, Jennie had wanted desperately to prompt Tony to talk about what had brought him here to Bicho Raro and how such a funny and loud person found himself stranded as a giant in the wilderness. Jennie had tried to string these words together from scratch, failing, as always, and then, finally, she had burst out with the rhyming couplet.

"How did you say that on your own?" Padre asked.

"How did you say that on your own?" Jennie asked. She looked helplessly to Tony, certain that he, of everyone here, would understand what had happened. Earlier in the evening, he would have merely responded to this appeal of hers with a snappy comeback of some kind, but now he looked at her hopeful expression made haunting by the porch lights, and he genuinely wanted her to have accomplished something that night.

Tony said, "Can you say it again, doll?"

"As I walk along, I wonder what went wrong," Jennie said.

This exchange astounded all of them. Not only had she not repeated what he'd said, but she had once again said something entirely different.

Things were changing.

"God moves!" Padre Jiminez cried, but Tony waved an impatient hand in his direction.

"Lyrics," Tony said. "It's lyrics from 'Runaway.'"

"Someone else's words," Marisita remarked, "but not when they say them! Can you do another one?"

"Can you do another one?" Jennie echoed. But then she struggled for a long moment, frowning, trying to think, trying to conjure words where there had not been any just a moment before. Then she said, "No matter how I try, I just can't turn the other way."

"Connie Francis," Tony said. "'My Heart Has a Mind of Its Own.'"

"Well done, Jennie, well done! This is progress!" Padre Jiminez said, clasping her hands in his. She repeated his words, but gladly.

"I reckon you could say almost anything you need to say with lyrics," Betsy said.

"I don't know about *that*," Robbie said.

"It's progress!" Padre Jiminez said again.

For a minute, no one spoke. There was no music, either, because the radio programming had come to an end. But nonetheless the air was noisy with optimism and cheer, every pilgrim buoyed by just one pilgrim's success. Then an owl hooted sleepily, woken briefly by the distant promise of Jennie's second miracle, and they all remembered how late it was.

Jennie peered up at Tony, and he realized he was, somehow, being consulted for wisdom. He said, simply, "You're gonna need to listen to the radio a lot more."

20

When Beatriz, Pete, and Joaquin arrived back at Bicho Raro, everything was quiet and dark except for the soft noises of owls that had begun to gather again. All of the pilgrims and the bonfire had burned out and quieted. Joaquin crept away to sneak back into the camper, a process that was possible only if he moved very slowly; it took an hour for him to accomplish it from beginning to end.

This left Beatriz and Pete standing in the cold night, gazing at Bicho Raro.

It is surprising how a strange place can change with just a little familiarity. When Pete had arrived in Bicho Raro not very long ago, the chilly night had felt full of eerie and unfriendly entities. The structures had seemed less like houses than outcroppings, none of it welcoming. But now it merely appeared to be a sleepy collection of homes, a friendly port in the vast dry sea of night. The whispers he heard were merely the owls on the rooflines; the shivers over his skin were merely from being so close to the desert and to Beatriz. He knew the bed waiting for him was only the floor beside Padre Jiminez's bed, but he didn't mind it.

It is surprising, too, how a familiar place can change with just a little strangeness. Beatriz had lived in Bicho Raro for her entire life and she could have navigated it in full dark. She knew all of the sounds and smells and shapes in it, and she knew how this invisible dark felt when it curled between the buildings to sleep. She knew that many people were frightened by Bicho Raro after dark, but night here had always been a comfortable time for her, a time when her thoughts could stretch into the quiet without anyone else's voice intruding. But tonight, her home seemed strange and awake, every board and every nail and every shingle sharply visible in the dim lights, all of it marvelously distinct like she had never seen it before. It was as if she was afraid. Her head wasn't frightened—her thoughts proceeded quite as usual. But her heart felt as if it was—it was racing.

But she did not think she minded it.

Pete said, "I'm nearly finished with the stage."

"I saw," Beatriz replied.

"Do you think you would like to test it with me?" Pete asked.

He held out his hand, and Beatriz thought for a moment before taking it. Together they climbed onto the amber-brown dance stage and walked across the boards into the very center. They stopped and faced each other.

"I don't know how to dance," Beatriz admitted.

"I don't either," Pete said. "I guess we'll figure it out."

Beatriz took his free hand and put it on her waist.

"It's cold," Beatriz said.

"It is," Pete said.

He stood a little closer to her so that they were warm together.

"There's no music," Beatriz said.

"We need the radio."

But the station had long since gone quiet, and Diablo Diablo had long since turned back into Joaquin.

Pete put his voice right by Beatriz's ear so that his breath warmed her skin, and he began to sing. It was nothing extravagant, just Patsy Cline sung in his low and uneven voice, and they began to dance. It was very quiet. No one else would have seen if not for the desert. But when the desert heard Pete Wyatt singing a love song, it took notice. The desert loved him, after all, and wanted him happy. So when it heard Pete singing, it rose a wind around them until the breeze sang gently like strings, and when it heard Pete singing, it provoked the air to heat and cool around every stone and plant so that each of these things sounded in harmony with his voice, and when it heard Pete singing, it roused Colorado's grasshoppers to action and they rubbed their legs together like a soft horn section, and when it heard Pete singing, it shifted the very ground beneath Bicho Raro so that the sand and the dirt pounded a beat that matched the sound of the incomplete heart that lived in Pete Wyatt.

The sound of this roused the Sorias from their sleep. Francisco looked out of his greenhouse and saw Pete and Beatriz dancing, and he missed Antonia. Antonia looked out the window of her house and saw Pete and Beatriz dancing, and she missed Francisco. Luis the one-handed took out his future love's box of gloves from beside his bed and counted them. Nana reached for the photograph of her long-dead husband. Michael had been sleeping rolled up in his own lengthy beard, but he woke up and returned to sleep rolled up with Rosa instead. Judith looked out her window and wept with happiness to see her sister happy, and Eduardo wept, too, because he always liked to dress to match his wife when he could.

As she danced with Pete, Beatriz was thinking that perhaps this was what performing the miracle felt like for Daniel. The sensation inside her felt like it came both from inside her and from someplace very much outside her, which was impossible and illogical and miraculous. If Daniel had been there, he would have told her that this was because holiness was love, but he was not, so she had to merely wonder if she finally understood her family a little better.

Pete was thinking that he liked Beatriz's quiet, watchful ways, and he was thinking that he liked the way that she felt, and he was thinking that he could feel his heart, but not in a bad way. He realized that he had been wrong to think that joining the army or starting a moving company would satisfy that hole in his heart. He had thought he had lived a happy life, but now he understood that he had only ever been content. *This* moment was his first moment of true happiness, and now he had to readjust every other expectation in his life to match it.

They both felt more solid than they had before, although neither had realized they had not felt solid enough before.

When they stopped dancing, Pete sweetly kissed Beatriz's cheek.

Beatriz took Pete's hand and held his arm still. Then she put her thumb right on the inside of his elbow. It was just as warm and soft as she had thought it would be when she first saw it. Her thumb fit perfectly.

"How about . . ." Pete started. "How about I don't take the truck until all this business with Daniel's darkness is over with?"

Beatriz considered. There were many ways that Daniel's darkness could end, some faster than others. If they didn't need to drive out into the desert to reach Daniel, they didn't need the truck. She could find another way to make Joaquin a radio that could be hidden in a hurry. It was very fair. Too fair. Because—

"That could be a long time."

"I know."

She put a hand on his gentle cheek. "I think you did a good job on this stage."

"Thank you," he replied.

21

You can hear a miracle a long way after dark, even when you are dying.

Daniel Lupe Soria curled in the blackness and listened to the slow but urgent movement of a far-off miracle slowly drawing closer. It was miles off, days off, maybe, but it was so quiet out here that there was nothing to interfere with his listening. He was so thoroughly a Saint that all of his body still responded to the call. His lips were already forming a prayer for whoever this pilgrim might be. He was halfway through a prayer to make himself more pure of mind and body before he remembered that he would not be performing this miracle. Daniel would not be anywhere near Bicho Raro when this pilgrim arrived. He didn't know what the pilgrim would find when she or he reached Bicho Raro. He didn't know if Beatriz would perform the miracle despite her misgivings, or if Michael might return to the position of Saint after nearly a decade away from it.

He didn't even know if it was still night.

His eyes were closed, but it didn't matter. It would look the same if he opened them.

Everything was darkness.

It had been nothing but darkness for many hours. After he had left the message for Marisita, he had begun to put distance between himself and the words, in case she or his cousins were tempted to find him. All the while, his vision had been narrowing, those black curtains closing on either side. He could not help blinking again and again, as if he would clear his eyes. But the darkness came on relentlessly. The creature that he had sensed before was still following him, too, although Daniel had not caught a glimpse of it. Now he could not shake the idea that the creature itself was taking his vision.

A few hours after Daniel left the message behind, his fortune had run out. By that time, his vision was gray and gritty, and so was his mouth. His limbs were heavy. When he found a barbed wire fence blocking his forward progress, he wasted uncountable minutes walking alongside it, hoping for a gate to pass through. But this was wild country and there was no need of gates, so the only way was through. This would not have been such an ordeal if he had been able to see, but with only starved light coming from the fast-setting sun and with only starved light coming to him through his eyes, it felt to him as if every inch of the wire was thorned. The spacing between the strands refused to make sense. His pack with its water and food in it snagged on one of the thorns as he tried to tug through, and when he retreated to ease the tension on it, the bag fell from his shoulders. It seemed impossible for it to have gone far, but his hands could not find it in the murk. His blind spider eyes brushed up against only grass, and more wire, and posts, and then again grass, and more wire, and posts. Knowing that he could be within inches of it without finding it made his search even more agonizing than it might have been.

It was gone.

Daniel did not have enough sight left to find a new source of water, so he instead felt his way to a large bush. He moved beneath it as slowly as he could to be sure he was not displacing an unseen snake, and then he curled there. It was not much, but it would be some shelter from the sun when it came out next. It would at least keep him from dehydrating as quickly, and after he died, it would take longer for the birds and foxes to find him.

Now that he was no longer trying to move, he had enough energy left to be surprised that this was how the darkness would kill him. It seemed mundane and inappropriate for a Saint to die from lack of water rather than from an epic battle for his soul. Daniel had expected that the Soria darkness would be virulent and hellish, not ordinary and wasting. As he lay in the dry scrub, he began to doubt that he had been a good Saint after all. Perhaps, he thought, he had been doing a disservice to the pilgrims. Perhaps another Soria could have freed them from their darkness faster or better. Perhaps he had been just a man playing at God.

"Forgive me," he prayed, and his heart felt a little lighter.

As the stars had come out that night, he had turned on the radio, waiting—hoping—for Marisita's voice to come out.

"Forgive yourself," he told the air.

But Marisita had not forgiven herself and so she had not come onto the radio to tell her story. He'd had to settle for

Diablo Diablo, which was still a comfort. He laughed and winced as Joaquin read one of Daniel's old journal entries about his time as a hell-raiser, and he sang and sighed as Joaquin played some of his favorite songs. Around the time that Jennie was realizing she could speak using lyrics, Daniel had cast his eyes up to the sky and realized the stars had vanished for him.

The radio fell into dull static as Joaquin and Beatriz stopped transmitting.

The creature clucked. Daniel was now entirely in darkness. He curled more tightly around himself and hooked his finger into the divot in his skin where the hailstone had marked him a sinner.

When things are dark, we cannot stop our minds from running wild, and so it was with Daniel. He could not prevent his thoughts from galloping to a future where Joaquin was the one to find his body. And then his mind advanced even further to when Antonia and Francisco and Rosa and Michael would be forced to see another Soria who had fallen prey to his own darkness. Daniel was no fool: He knew he was loved, and he knew how love can become a blunt and relentless weapon at death. They didn't deserve this pain a generation later. And Marisita! Hadn't she suffered enough? She was already doubled up with guilt, and she would easily take the blame for his death, even though it was all on Daniel.

And of course Beatriz. She would be made the Saint; he knew it was true—Michael would never be persuaded to take on that role again. She would do it, and she would not complain, but it would be a prison for her.

The idea of his family's suffering tormented him, drowning out the dryness in his mouth and the blackness in front of his eyes. Instead of praying for himself, his cracked lips formed words for them instead. *"Mother—"*

But it was not a mother who answered.

Pebbles skittered against pebbles, and the smell of crushed sage came to Daniel. Something large was moving toward him. He heard the cluck of that creature again, and then a flap—he guessed correctly that whatever it was had wings. It was flapping farther from him, driven away by whatever approached. But not too far away.

He heard breathing. Creaking.

Daniel sat up then, but he was too dizzy to defend himself, even if he had been able to see. Something clasped his throat. Rough hair strayed across his cheek. Breath panted across his face. Daniel imagined a horse-haired monster, a devil's plaything finally come to finish him.

Another hand clasped over his jaw. Daniel gasped.

Water poured over his lips and into his ears. He was so shocked that he coughed on it at first. It trickled over his cracked lips and down his throat and onto his chest and it felt so good to be wet after being so dry that he could not believe he was not dreaming it, except no dream can feel as good as a drink of water when you are dying of thirst.

His relief melted, though, as he revived enough to worry that he had been found by a Soria.

"Who are you?" he asked.

Damp fingers pressed his useless eyes and smeared water and grease on his chapped lips and poured more water into his mouth. Three different voices muttered in three different languages. He could have never guessed who had come in answer to his prayer, and he may not have been able to guess it even if he had been able to see, because it was a form of miracle of the kind that even a Soria did not normally experience. The spirits of the wild men of Colorado—Felipe Soria, who had killed the sheriff for his femurs; Beatriz's financier, who had hung himself with his own beard; and the German, who was a fox as of the time of his death—had come to him.

Who knew why they came to him then and not before or after. Perhaps they were atoning for the sins of their lives. Perhaps Daniel's prayer was fervent enough to call them from wherever spirits lingered. Perhaps they were just passing through on their way to another traveler in distress and stopped to aid Daniel along the way. For whatever reason, they let him drink until he was full.

The financier found Daniel's canteen and the German filled it and Felipe Soria put it in blind Daniel's hand.

"Zwei Tage Wasser," the German said.

"Two days of water," translated the financier, who had once spent a year in Frankfurt chasing success.

Felipe Soria leaned close.

"Fight, my cousin," he whispered in Daniel's ear. "Quien quiere celeste, que le cueste." No one had to translate this for Daniel: He who wants heaven must pay. He pressed his thumb into Daniel's other shoulder, and Daniel cried out. When Felipe removed his hand, he had left a divot that matched the one the hailstorm had left him with.

Then they were gone, and Daniel was left alone, in the dark, but alive, for now.

22

Pete worked.

He got up at first light because Padre Jiminez yipped and paddled his legs in his sleep and because the floor beside Padre Jiminez's bed was hard and cold and also because Pete's mind kept returning to Beatriz and also because Pete was good at working and liked doing it.

As no one else was around to direct him otherwise, Pete decided to simply continue work on the stage. He had barely stepped out into the cold, thin air, however, when Antonia appeared before him. She had not been sleeping either. After seeing her daughter and Pete dancing on the stage the night before, she had stayed awake all night long feverishly cutting paper flowers to occupy her mind. When the sun rose, she looked down and realized that she had constructed piles of black paper roses, all but one of them marred by tears. She had stormed out to meet Pete the moment she saw him get up. Now she stood before him in the early blue light and raged at him for several minutes while he mutely accepted it. Finally, as the sun began to cast long morning shadows behind the buildings, she spat on the ground and gave him his task: Finish the small house that he had begun to construct the first day he had arrived.

"Padre Jiminez can live there when you're done," she said. "And then you can have his room."

Pete was bruised by her raging, but he recognized this small kindness and was surprised by it. Tentatively, he admitted, "I thought you were angry at me."

"Angry? At *you*?"

"For dancing with Beatriz."

It had not even occurred to Antonia that he might take ownership of her undirected anger. Her surprise over this passed swiftly away from shock, took an inexplicable side trip through grief over Daniel, and finally arrived at yet more anger. She snapped, "I'm not angry at you or Beatriz!"

"Ma'am, do you mind me asking who you're angry at, then?"

As Antonia Soria opened her mouth, dozens of names filled the space behind her teeth, waiting to be said. But in that moment, as she saw Pete's guileless face and, behind him, the outline of Francisco's greenhouse and, in it, its sleepless occupant looking back at her, she realized that the only name that was true in that space was her own.

"Just get to work, Wyatt," Antonia said. "I'm going back to sleep."

But Pete did not just get to work. He meant to, but as he crossed the early-morning quiet of Bicho Raro, his attention was snagged by the sight of Tony rummaging in the back of the box truck.

He changed course immediately.

Tony had gotten up even earlier than Pete and Antonia. The moment it was light enough to see, the very first thing he had done was seek out the source of the radio program he had heard the night before. He had several clues. For starters, he knew it had to be someplace that Joaquin Soria, a sixteen-year-old boy, was capable of reaching each night. He knew it had to have some kind of antenna apparatus, and that an antenna of the size required for such a sound would be difficult to hide in a small space. And most importantly, he had been dozing only lightly the night before when Joaquin and Beatriz and Pete came back, and so he had seen them climb out of the truck. There were some advantages to being a giant.

When Pete found him, Tony had the back of the truck wide open and was in it up to his shoulders. He was thrilling over what he found inside. All of the things that frustrated Beatriz about the makeshift station—the ingenious work-arounds, the repurposed equipment—delighted Tony. As a radio personality, he didn't touch anything like this. The station he worked at was vast and polished, with two friendly Serbians to make sure it was all performing well as he did his show. It had been a very long time since he had been near the guts and organs of radio. Now he reached his oversized arm in the truck and gently prised out components to examine.

"Did your mother raise you to be a sneak and a thief?" Pete asked.

Tony removed his arm from the truck and turned to Pete. "Did your mother raise you to be a Boy Scout?"

"Yes," said Pete.

"Look, kid, untwist yourself, I'm not hurting anything. You're absolutely lousy when you lose your sense of humor. I was just looking."

"Why?"

Tony turned back to the truck. "Why not?"

Pete was ready to launch into an explanation of how the truck belonged to someone else and it was considered rude to rummage through other people's property, but before he even said it, he realized that Tony already knew these things quite well.

"I need you to give my box of records to that kid, if they haven't melted to pancake batter," Tony said. His voice was muffled inside the truck. "Diablo Diablo. They're new, new stuff. Tell him he better listen to them all, because he needs some fresher music."

"Shhh. I think his identity's a secret."

"Kid, nothing's a secret when you broadcast it on AM radio. Tell him—tell him I want to help him."

"Are you sure?" Pete asked. "That sounds suspiciously like a nice thing to do, which doesn't sound like you."

"Look, there's your funny bone; I thought you'd lost it. Tell him I want to see his script for tonight. Tell him who I am."

"I thought *that* was a secret. Like Diablo Diablo."

Tony pulled his head out of the truck to face Pete with all of his height. Pete could not know it, because he had never known him before he had gotten burned out at the radio station, but Tony currently looked more like his normal self than he had in years, even at twenty feet tall. The life had returned to his eyes. "Are you going to do it, or not?"

Of course Pete was going to do it. He agreed under the condition that Tony cease and desist his trespassing, and then he returned to work.

By then, the rest of Bicho Raro had woken. Everyone, pilgrims and Sorias alike, heard Jennie enthusiastically practicing her new skill. As the radio blared from her bedroom, she spoke loudly and independently in fragments of lyrics heard minutes before.

"Oh, what a beautiful morning!" she greeted Padre Jiminez.

"Life is sweet! It may sound silly, but I don't care!" she told Robbie.

"I'm gonna fix this world today," she told Pete as she marched past the little house.

"I'm glad to hear it," Pete replied, and she merely grinned instead of repeating what he said.

Her enthusiasm was catching, and no one caught it harder than Joaquin. By midday, both he and Beatriz had found their way to Pete's worksite and kept him company in their own way. Beatriz sat silently out of the way, constructing a dipole cage antenna, admiring how Pete had stripped off his T-shirt as the work grew harder. Joaquin paced on top of a beam, prattling endlessly with increasingly grandiose ideas. He was in bright spirits. For the first time in his young life, he felt he was doing what he was truly meant to do. He was proud of last night's broadcast and hoped that Daniel really had been able to hear it. He was also more than willing to take credit for Jennie's improvement. He was full of pride, too, that his audience had widened to include the pilgrims.

"Our broadcast could heal them all," he said.

This was such a boastful statement that Beatriz finally broke her silence. "It may have been coincidence. She may have been just about to make a breakthrough anyway." When Joaquin pouted, she added, "I'm not saying the radio wasn't part of it. I'm merely saying it requires another trial."

"What kind of trial would satisfy you?"

"Something very specifically directed with the intent of helping, so we could measure the results and know it was from us."

"I don't know what that means."

Beatriz put down her antenna. "For instance, if you prepared a program specifically for the twins, highlighting what they needed to heal themselves. Then, if they improved quickly, that would be a result."

Joaquin shivered where he sat, both with the thrill of having such a direct effect and with the residual fear of breaking a long-held taboo in such a dramatic way. "But with the purpose of it hidden," he said. "No names mentioned. So no one would realize it was someone from Bicho Raro."

Pete spoke from inside the half-finished house. "Also, if you don't use any names, everyone who has a problem sort of like theirs will think you were talking straight to them."

Joaquin was so overcome with the idea of it that he had to drink two of his bottles of water in a row to cure the sudden dryness of his mouth. This felt like the future to him. This felt like real radio.

"Show me the inside of the house," Beatriz told Pete. She did not really want to see the interior, but she had been thinking hard as Joaquin spoke, and wanted to speak to Pete alone about these thoughts. As she suspected, Joaquin did not notice this strategy. He continued pacing on the beam, contemplating his grand show, as Pete joined Beatriz inside the little house.

The structure was more impressive than Beatriz had expected, considering its humble origins. Now that Pete knew the little house was going to be completed instead of torn down, he took its construction more seriously. It had to earn its place among all the other buildings here if it was going to stand for any length of time. He liked the sense of Soria history and memories he had heard so far, so he had begun to build as many Soria memories and feelings into it as he could manage. He used some of the optimism from the already scavenged barn to support the floorboards, and he tinted the windows with some of the handsomeness of thought from Francisco's greenhouse, and he took some of the warm sentiment from Nana's garden for the grout between the stones. He had not meant to add his own steadfastness, nor any of his new love, but those traits had also nonetheless joined the others. This is the way of our work: We cannot help but color it with the paint of our feelings, both good and bad.

Beatriz felt all of this inside the house. Her feet stood on memories and light streamed through memories onto her and dust drifted down from the memories in the roof supports. In a low voice, she said to him, "I have an idea and I'm afraid if I don't say it to you, I might say it to Joaquin, and I think that would be very unwise."

She was a little surprised at herself for even telling Pete, but she knew that to give words to Pete was to give them to a vault.

"Okay," said Pete.

"I don't think Joaquin is wrong that the radio can help the pilgrims. I think what they have always needed is someone to guide them through, even though we are not allowed. We've seen so many pilgrims come through and we've learned how they solve their problems, but we can't share any of this knowledge with them. I don't think this was the way it always was, but I don't have any way of knowing that. Anyway, if it is true—if Joaquin's program helped Jennie last night, and if it helps the twins tonight as I think it might, then"—Beatriz lowered her voice even further, and Pete leaned into her so that she could barely speak the words into his ear—"then we might also be able to reach Daniel and help him heal himself."

Because while Joaquin had been discussing the radio show, he had been pacing beside the pilgrims' lodge site and thus thinking about the pilgrims currently overflowing Bicho Raro. But Beatriz had been thinking about a different pilgrim: Daniel.

Pete straightened. "It's all right to be upset," he told her.

This frustrated Beatriz, who could not understand why he would say such a thing. "I'm not upset. I am telling you the facts."

She did not realize that both of these things could be true.

"All right," Pete said.

"I'm not."

"I said, all right," Pete repeated. He didn't want to annoy her, so he hurried on. "Here's what I think. I think you should tell Joaquin what you just told me."

"And if I'm wrong? Then it's false hope."

Pete wasn't much for speeches, but he'd been thinking on one sort of like this since Antonia had given him an earful before the sun had even come up. So he laid it out for her. "Well, I reckon that's what you just told me the problem was with the pilgrims, right? There's an awful lot of things that go on here that don't get said. A lot of shut doors and closed eyes, just to be on the safe side. Maybe if you want things to change, you should start in yourself. Tell him what you're thinking. You might just find that it's already occurred to him, too. Everybody's thinking about Daniel, aren't they?"

Beatriz was quiet for a long moment, processing his words. In that quiet, she could feel the prickle of an oncoming miracle, but she couldn't tell if it was a Soria miracle or merely the potential miracle of a life-changing radio station in a box truck.

"I think," she said, finally, "I think you might be right."

In this way Beatriz left the house a slightly different person than she had entered it. This was to become a hallmark of this house once it was finished, although Pete did not know it yet. She signaled for Joaquin to leave off his pacing on the beam, and when he did, she quietly shared her hopes for the radio's potential. Joaquin drank a bottle of water, and then he drank another one. He would have drank a fifth one, but he didn't have one.

Eventually, he muttered, "I feel like I need to write a really good show for tonight."

Pete said, "I know someone who wants to give you a hand."

23

Francisco was of two minds about Dorothy's rooster. One of those minds hated the rooster, and the other loved it. Francisco was accustomed to working on his own by now, and he was surprised to find how pleasing it was to have the rooster as a companion. Just the presence of another living creature puttering around, living its own life alongside him, was intensely grounding in a way that he had not expected. This was only when the rooster was in a good mood, however. The rooster was also of two minds, as much as a chicken can be, because of its fighting past. It had not been bred to be a fighting rooster; it had just become one as it took on its mistress's bitterness, and so the chicken was torn between its more placid self and the furious creature it had become. It would sink into the former quiet for hours at a time, pleasing Francisco, but then the light would change in the greenhouse, and the windows would become mirrors. Ragefully, the rooster would hurl itself at its own reflection with such vigor that it threatened to crack it. Blood would smear the glass, but it was only its own.

Francisco had tried many things the first day: calling to the rooster, tossing pencils at the rooster, and ignoring the rooster.

Francisco, after all, preferred to remain a nonparticipant in most wars, including this one. Eventually, however, he decided that he could not sit by and watch the rooster bloody itself on the glass. He felt it was cruel for an animal to harm itself in this way, and also, it was going to be a lot of work to clean all of the glass. So when the light changed as the sun set and the low windows became mirrors and the rooster began to attack itself again, Francisco climbed from his chair, pulled on the long gloves that he wore to protect himself from the roses' thorns, and went to the rooster. The rooster was engaged in clawing the glass and did not think to run away.

Francisco wrapped his hands around the rooster's body, pinning its wings to it, and merely held the rooster still before the glass. The rooster was forced to stare at this other impudent bird without attacking it. The bird struggled in Francisco's firm grip, and for several minutes, Francisco worried that the bird might actually harm itself in its fervor to escape. It clawed the air and jerked its head. Its wings were miniature earthquakes beneath Francisco's palms as the rooster tried to free them.

Finally, the bird stilled, panting, and gazed at itself. The rooster in the glass peered back as well, full of loathing. Francisco sighed and sat cross-legged, allowed the rooster to do nothing but look at the reflection. He remained as calm as he possibly could, so calm that the rooster would be able to feel this serenity and adopt it for itself, or at the very least, to prevent anger from turning to fear. Minutes became hours, but eventually, the rooster's expression changed as it realized that the image in the glass was only itself. Its body sagged. Its eye turned wistful. The anger had gone from its body.

Francisco released the bird, but the rooster merely slumped to the ground, still peering at itself. Dorothy would not be pleased, but Francisco was. Her rooster would never fight again.

Francisco found, however, that he had become the opposite of calm. As he had been sitting there, holding the rooster still, he had been reminded of Daniel as a baby. Although it was not usual for men at that time to involve themselves in the care of an infant, Francisco had been given the lion's share of dealing with young Daniel's nightmares as Rosa, Antonia, Michael, and Nana could not soothe Daniel during them. It was impossible to say what the infant Daniel was dreaming so terribly about—possibly the memory of being hacked from his mother's body—but one night out of every ten, he would wake in an inconsolable terror. Francisco would hold the infant, saying nothing, merely breathing, for as long as it took. Five minutes, five hours. Once, while Daniel was teething, five days. Eventually, this stillness would transfer to Daniel and the baby Daniel's breathing would grow long and match Francisco's. Finally, he would fall back into an unfrightened slumber.

As Francisco held the rooster, he remembered all of the nights he had spent doing such a thing, and by the time the anger had drained from General MacArthur, Francisco found he could not bear the thought of Daniel in the desert any longer. He could contemplate nothing else. Leaving the rooster pensive on the floor, he fled through the night to the place that held more of Daniel than any other place in Bicho Raro: the Shrine.

When he entered the Shrine, he found Antonia already there. His wife kneeled before the sculpture of Mary and her owls, all of the votive candles burning. She, too, had finally been overcome by the horror of Daniel's plight and there was nothing she could do to avoid thinking of him, not even cutting paper flowers at her kitchen table. Wordlessly, he joined her, falling to his knees in the rut Daniel had worn in his years of praying as the Saint.

Francisco said nothing, growing ever quieter in his distress, and Antonia said nothing, growing ever angrier in her own. They were both destroyed imagining the young man who had occupied this Shrine only a few days before.

Antonia, too, began to recall Daniel as a child. As a baby, Daniel had been as much a hellion as he had been in his teen years. He would chomp on Antonia's breast and feed dirt to himself and tip over his cradle with himself in it and eat the hair off the barn cats if they got into the house. In many ways, though, Daniel's terribleness had been a blessing. If he had been a sweet baby, Antonia's grief would have never allowed her to look at him, imagining only what it would have been like for her sister-in-law to raise him for herself. But since he was awful, Antonia would say, "It was lucky Loyola died so that she never had to suckle a demon at her breast," and spend all her moments with him and love him ferociously.

Now these memories of Daniel choked Antonia, and she began to rage in the Shrine. Ordinarily, Francisco would have said nothing or would have removed himself, which only would have increased her anger. For years he had been saying nothing or removing himself. But now, he recalled General MacArthur and Daniel and, in the same way, put his arms firmly around his wife. He turned her to the mirror that was opposite the sculpture of Mary and held her there. She looked at herself, at her twisted face, and at Francisco's tear-lined face, and at Mary and her owls behind them both, reminding her what the Sorias were really meant to do. Minutes passed like this, with Francisco still and Antonia rigid.

Antonia's anger died inside her. She collapsed against Francisco and for several minutes they wept together.

"Look at us, Francisco," Antonia said. "Look what we've become."

Francisco pressed his lips together. "I don't want to. I'm too ashamed."

Daniel's presence in the Shrine was so potent that they found themselves speaking English, as they would have if he'd really been there with them. They realized it at the same moment and shed more tears.

"What can we do?"

"I don't know. I just don't know."

They clung to each other still. Judith had thought that if she convinced them to dance on the stage as they had when they first met, her mother and her father would fall back into each other's arms, and she was not quite wrong. But it was not the hundredth blow of wind to knock the barn over, merely the ninety-ninth. This place, the Shrine, reminded them of who the Sorias really were. To turn away from this calling was to ruin themselves. Francisco and Antonia were both so choked up with unperformed miracles and their own darkness that they had nearly destroyed themselves.

In this way, losing Daniel's parents had begun to tear them apart, and in this way, losing Daniel brought them back together.

Outside the Shrine, they could hear owls shuffling and calling, sensing the presence of a looming miracle—in this case, the untended darkness inside both Francisco and Antonia resonating against the unused saintliness inside Francisco. But they were not pilgrims, they were Sorias, and they had both seen for themselves that Soria darkness was a harder thing. Both thought of the wooden Soria family housed in another shed nearby. Of Daniel, lost in the wilderness.

"We cannot orphan our daughters," Antonia said wildly.

The door to the Shrine flew open.

Both Antonia and Francisco jumped in guilt and shame.

"Rosa," Antonia said. "Rosa, I can explain."

But Rosa Soria, her round and beautiful form lit by headlights behind her, was there neither about the owls on the roof nor Daniel in the desert.

"Come to Eduardo's truck and listen to the radio," Rosa said. "Tell me who it sounds like to you."

It was inevitable that the other Sorias would hear the radio station eventually. In past years, when the family had stayed up late enjoying one another's company, it would have taken no time at all, because the assembled members would have noticed the cousins' absence. But because the Sorias had slowly parted, falling into their individual sadness, it took a late-night trip to uncover the secret.

Eduardo and Luis had gone to Alamosa to play cards and on returning had seen the pilgrims gathered close together. It looked like a witch's gathering, with Tony the giant at their center, a fire pit at his feet. Although he was married to Judith Soria, Eduardo Costa had an outsiders' understanding of the pilgrims. This meant he usually did not think of them at all, and when he did, he thought about how they were uncanny, he thought about his wife's family's legendary history in Mexico, and he thought probably this proved that God was real, and if not God, at least the devil. Up close, they made him uneasy, and so it was with suspicion that he drew his beloved stepside truck close to them.

When he exited, he realized the pilgrims weren't truly gathered around Tony or the fire—the real focal point was a radio.

"Hola hola hola, it is Diablo Diablo again, tiptoeing through the night with just fifteen volts and a dream. We've got a great show for you tonight. Our theme is gonna be love. I know what you're saying—'The theme for every night on this show is love, Diablo Diablo!'—but I don't mean love like that. Not a-kissing and a-hugging, my friends. We're talking love like for your mother, for your brother, for your sister, for your auntie. So what

have we got, what have we got coming up? I've got some love letters—not love like that! Not love like that! You wait—that
listeners have written for me to read on air. I've got another entry
from my cousin's journal. And I've got some fresh new music
shipped in from a friend back east who's got an ear for what's
hot. I know it's late, but stay tuned and stay awake, because here
we go. Let's get under way with a classic from Trío Los Panchos."

Eduardo instantly recognized Diablo Diablo's voice. *Joaquin!*
he thought. His fancy and useless sixteen-year-old cousin by
marriage, a disc jockey! Eduardo was no fool, and he had heard
some pirate radio in this time, and he knew at once that that was
what he was listening to. Because Eduardo was a proper macho
of the kind who was much prized at the time and because a
pirate radio carried an element of risk to it, this raised Joaquin's
esteem in Eduardo's eyes by several degrees. Before Joaquin had
been merely ridiculous to him, but now Eduardo revised all of
the memories he had of him to include his role as a pirate DJ.
Now his strange sense of fashion seemed like a coy nod to
Joaquin's secret life. His hair was a wink. Eduardo was an old-
fashioned cowboy; Joaquin was a radio cowboy. This was to
change their relationship for the rest of their lives.

"Where is Joaquin broadcasting from?" Judith asked.

"*Shhhh,*" Nana hushed.

All of the adult Sorias listened to the broadcast. Because the
cousins had taken every other radio in Bicho Raro, this meant
they were assembled in and around Eduardo's pickup truck. Rosa
and Antonia and Judith and Nana were crushed inside the cab,

huddled together for warmth. They did not want to turn on the heater in case the blower would drown out any of the broadcast. Francisco and Michael and Luis perched in the truck bed. They were cold, too, but they suffered it alone. Eduardo sat on the hood and smoked a cigarette. He did not believe in suffering, so he felt plenty warm.

Diablo Diablo said, "Here's a letter from an anonymous listener. He says, 'People always said I was lazy, a do-nothing who just took up space. My sister always thought the best of me and I feel a little bad for letting her down. She always thought I was going to turn out to be something and she used to cuss at anyone who said otherwise, and it's too bad that I didn't turn out to be something because I feel like all her cussing was for nothing. Of course maybe she would have cussed anyway.'"

The pilgrims had written the letters. This was one of the ideas Tony had suggested to Joaquin during the course of the afternoon. Tony, after all, had firsthand experience with how well listener participation could boost a radio station's success. The two of them had gotten along as well as two folks could when all communication had to go through a young man from Oklahoma, particularly when they discovered they both loved the same part of radio: the intersection of music and stories.

Diablo Diablo continued, "'If she were listening, I'd tell her that I really needed her cussing. I guess it didn't make me do anything, but it made me happier while I wasn't doing anything. Maybe one day I still will be somebody. Maybe.' Sounds to me like this anonymous listener needs some gas in his engine.

Luckily, I've got just the thing, I just heard it today and I haven't been able to stop listening to it since: Here's the brand-new 'Loco-motion' by Little Eva. Let's get moving."

A mixture of emotions filled the space around the radio in Eduardo's truck: shock, anger, delight, pride, and finally, as owls began to circle the pilgrims, anxiety. Unperformed miracles hung thick in the air and the birds were going mad with it, swooping and calling, feathers drifting all around. There were second miracles choked up in the pilgrims and first miracles in the Sorias.

"Let's have another pair of letters from two more anonymous listeners. Remember, those of you pricking your ears to us from home, the theme for tonight is love, and these are love letters, letters about all the strange kinds of love we feel for our family and friends. While you're listening to these words, friends, think about what you would tell these anonymous writers. Would you give them comfort? Advice? Agreement? Or maybe just a swell little song from the Shirelles. Ah, you know what, I'm gonna spin that and we'll be back to read the letter on the other side."

The Sorias said nothing for the two minutes and thirty-eight seconds it took the Shirelles to ask if they would still love them tomorrow. They waited with rapt attention until Diablo Diablo returned with the letter he had promised.

"'I don't know if I love my sister or if I *have* to love her because we're basically the same person. People are always saying we look alike; it's the first thing they say. Then everything else is measured by comparison. *You're actually a little taller than your sister* or *She ate more than you* or *You read longer books than her.* Nothing ever happens that's just about me. I guess that makes me selfish, so that's stupid. I'm glad these are anonymous.' Have you ever felt like that, listeners, like you only exist in relation to someone else in your life? It's a terrible feeling. People are like sweet, sweet chords—we love them when they're playing all together nicely, like in the pretty number I'm going to spin next, but it would be a crying shame to forget what a lovely little noise a D major makes strummed on a single guitar."

All of the Sorias in Eduardo's truck imagined themselves first as part of the Soria song, and then as individual chords. All considered that the song they had been playing collectively was not a very harmonious one.

Diablo Diablo continued. "Hold that thought . . . I'm gonna read this second letter now, because it's also from a sister to a sister. 'I love my sister, but I also hate my sister. We fight all the time. She knows everything about me and I know everything about her, so we don't really have anything to talk about. We just fight. Sometimes, I pretend that I have gone out and gotten myself a very exciting life with exciting friends, and at the end of the day I'll come back to her and be able to tell her all about it and it will be nice again, but I'm too afraid to do that, actually. She likes me because she has to like me. What if nobody else does?'"

Nearer to the fire, Robbie and Betsy were squirming a little. They were the authors of these twinned letters, of course, and it was hard to look each other in the eye, hearing them read out loud. It is often easier to be truthful with yourself and others in writing, and that was the case here.

Diablo Diablo said, "I've got a song for these two sisters, but I've also got a piece of advice. I know what you're saying: 'Nobody asked you or your mama for advice.' I know it, I know it, but it's not from me or your mama, it's from Frida Kahlo, offering some truth to everyone out there who can't let go. Here's what she said: 'Nothing is absolute. Everything changes, everything moves, everything revolves, everything flies and goes away.' Sisters, I want you to think about that while I sing you a song that's a lot about love but also just a little about liberation. Here's Brenda Lee's 'Break It to Me Gently.'"

As Brenda Lee began to croon through the speakers, Francisco suddenly put it all together. The radio, the letters, the owls swooping overhead.

He said, "The pilgrims are the listeners. They wrote the letters."

And now, for the first time, the Sorias were directly answering their questions.

24

Because Beatriz's mind was a busy and practical thing, she had played over the possibility of her family discovering the radio many dozens of times. She had considered all sorts of possible outcomes, both positive and negative. She had prepared herself for Joaquin's unbearable smugness if he received a compliment from any of the family. She had developed persuasive arguments for why the radio was probably not truly a bait to the FCC here in the wilds of southern Colorado, where the radio waves were not worth enough to send city folk out to take them back from young pirates. She had decided how she would describe the building of the radio to her father so that he would be delighted by the process. She had considered how to defend the use of the otherwise pointless box truck in this way.

But she had not ever, before that night, thought about how she might defend herself after breaking the most serious rule the family had. She had not thought about it because before Marisita, Joaquin and Beatriz had not ever used the truck in such a way, and before Jennie, they hadn't realized they were going to do it again. Beatriz was not particularly a rule breaker, as she didn't mind following a rule as long as it didn't get in her way, and she didn't get into arguments, as she never raised her voice, and she didn't interfere with other people's lives, as she herself didn't like to be interfered with, so she was not used to being in trouble. The last time she had gotten in serious trouble had been when she'd been born because she was supposed to have been a boy. (Alexandro Luis Soria was the name both Francisco and Antonia had chosen for her, and Antonia had imagined her to be a garrulous and dashing man like Antonia's father had been before he'd died early in a freak airship accident. Francisco had imagined her as a clever and intelligent scientist, assuming thoughtlessly at the time that only a man could be so rational.) Everything else since the shock of her femaleness at birth had been minor dispute in comparison, so it was not a consequence that readily occurred to her when predicting the future.

But now she was in trouble.

As soon as the truck pulled back into Bicho Raro and parked, its lights turned off for secrecy, figures appeared in front of the truck like spirits. All of the Sorias had turned out to confront Beatriz and Joaquin and Pete. Beatriz had never seen their faces the way they looked tonight, not even when they were looking at Daniel's message to Marisita. She understood now that this was not going to be about the disobedience of a pirate radio station. There was a taboo, and it came with real consequences, and Joaquin and Beatriz were experimenting on the ragged edge of it.

"Do you hate us?" Rosa said. She had believed that Joaquin had broken the taboo the moment he read the letters out loud from the sisters, and now was crying from fear and relief on seeing that he was unchanged. Merely disobedient, not lost to darkness. "Why would you play with this, Joaquin, like it is nothing, when Daniel has lost everything for the same price?"

Joaquin stood frozen. He had been suspended in the high of the show. He had thought it was good while he was writing it, and he had thought it was even better with Tony's notes, and he had thought it was very good when he recorded it, but when he heard it broadcasting from the radio, he had thought that it was great, and he was not wrong. He was still suffused with the powerful sensation of doing exactly what he had been designed to do. This was *his* miracle and he was drunk with this electric holiness. For the entire drive back to Bicho Raro, the thrill and correctness of it had left him unable to contemplate anything else.

So when he found himself confronted, he could not think of what to say. It was too opposite to how he had just been feeling.

"And *you!*" Antonia said to Pete. "I trusted you and thought that you respected my family. Instead, you're throwing us into danger like we are nothing."

This struck Pete hard, as everything she said was true, both the good and the bad. He had passed messages between Tony and Joaquin all day. He had coordinated the pilgrims' letter writing. He had come along and pounded ground stakes into the ground and helped Beatriz to erect the ever taller antenna and then hurriedly packed it all back up again when they were done. He had known from the beginning of his time here that the Sorias were not to interfere with the pilgrims, and yet he had let himself be used—joyfully, gladly!—as a conduit between them. He was as guilty as the cousins.

"I want you gone at first light," Antonia said. "This is unacceptable. How could I trust you again?"

Beatriz could bear neither Joaquin's expression nor Pete's expulsion. She said, "It was my idea."

"But *why*, Beatriz?" Judith asked.

"It was a calculated risk," Beatriz went on, already knowing how these words would sound to her family before she said them. Daniel's decision had been a calculated risk as well, and now he was gone. "We thought there had to be a better way."

"And what if it had come for you, Beatriz?" said Francisco, and she knew he was angry because he spoke this instead of whistled it. "What if the darkness had come upon you while you were out in the desert performing this secret experiment, this calculated risk? What if Judith came to look for you and also fell prey to it, and then your mother came to look for you and fell prey to it, and so on and so forth? Did you calculate that?"

Beatriz did not say anything. She had thought about the possible consequences, but not in that way. That first night with Marisita, she had offered to send Joaquin away if he was afraid, because she knew the risks. If she had brought darkness on herself, she would have done exactly the same thing as Daniel and exiled herself in the desert and made sure she was not found. She was very good at puzzles, and she had been certain she could make one out of her location if it had come to it; Judith would never have found her. Beatriz weighed the benefit of saying all of this out loud and did not see any value to it, so she said nothing.

"How can you not believe in the taboo after what happened to Daniel?" Antonia asked.

The true answer was that Beatriz believed in the danger, but she didn't believe in the taboo. She weighed the value of saying this and found this also useless to say out loud. She thought that by so doing she was improving the situation, but anyone who has held an argument with a silent participant will realize that silence sometimes can be more frustrating than a defense.

This was the case with the Sorias and Beatriz. They grew more upset and said more things to both cousins while Beatriz merely listened. The more she listened, the more distressed they became, and the more distressed they became, the more she was certain she could not truly make them feel at ease with her decisions. She did not know how to apologize for a rule that she had broken after considering the risks, because although she understood why they were angry, she still was not sorry that she had done it. She understood only that she could not tell them this truth or they would be even more upset.

"Don't you want things to be different?" Joaquin said finally. He was only sixteen, but in this moment, he was the Joaquin he would become instead of the Joaquin he was. He was the man who would be Diablo Diablo in a bigger city, a voice to pilgrims in the night. "We spend all of our time hiding in our houses when we see a pilgrim walking by! We see them suffering and we say nothing! We smell Marisita's cooking and we are too afraid to even tell her that it smells delicious! We starve! We starve of—of *everything* because we are too afraid to eat! Look at us, all standing here, because we're afraid of them. That's why you're here, right? Fear!"

"And where is your cousin Daniel, Joaquin?" Rosa demanded. She had not called him anything but Quino since he was a child and now he recoiled from his true name, although any other time he would have welcomed it. "We are not afraid because we are cowards."

Antonia said, "Do you think we love him less than you? He is our son. He is our Saint."

The grief in her voice was no greater than the grief any of them were feeling.

"We thought," Joaquin said, and stopped. He could not be logical and even-tempered. "Beatriz, you tell them."

Beatriz said, "We think the radio is making a difference. Jennie made progress yesterday after listening to the radio; she can speak in lyrics. Tonight's program was for the twins. If they are changed by the radio, and we are still safe after broadcasting, then we've found a way to help heal them without causing danger to ourselves. We could help pilgrims move on so that they would not fill Bicho Raro for so long."

"We're building a lodge," Michael said.

"We would rather have a lodge than our children turned to darkness from stupid risks," Antonia added.

Beatriz persisted with the most important part. "We thought

if we found a way to help pilgrims, we could find a way to help Daniel."

Now everyone was as silent as Beatriz ordinarily was.

"Beatriz," Francisco whistled, sadly, finally—but she didn't want his pity; she had merely been stating the truth.

"Daniel wanted us to think harder about this," she said. "He wanted us to think about why we do the things we do.

"Hand me the keys," Michael said. "To the truck."

"But *Daniel*!" Joaquin protested. "He's listening. Remember the message?"

They all remembered the message. Now it was agonizing to all of them.

"Please," Joaquin went on. "We can't stop or he won't have us to listen to. He'll be alone."

Judith began to cry softly, over the impossibility of it.

Michael held out his hand. "I'm thinking about my family who are not yet lost and that includes you, my son. Now give me those keys and do not make me take them."

"Please," Joaquin said again, and he, too, was near to tears.

The sound of his voice and indeed all of their conversation was nearly drowned out, however, by the commotion of owls. Every Soria there knew what the birds' carrying on meant: They were whipped to wildness by a miracle. The family searched the sky and the ground for the source of the owls' enthusiasm, but they saw nothing but darkness.

"Joaquin," said Michael. He did not want to carry out his threat of taking the keys by force, but Joaquin had not moved to give them, so he started toward him. At the last moment, Beatriz stepped in front of Joaquin and relinquished the keys.

No one felt particularly victorious. There is no joy to be had in defending inaction and fear.

The owls soared over the family into the night and Bicho Raro fell into an unusual quiet. A feather floated past Beatriz. She could have caught this one, but she did not stretch out her hand.

Out of the quiet darkness, two figures approached. They were silhouetted by the bold light of the truck headlights. Every Soria ceased what they were doing to watch them approach, because a process of elimination proved that they must be pilgrims, and they were.

"Stay back," Antonia warned them. "You know better."

But the pilgrims kept approaching. It was the twins, Robbie and Betsy. All of the adult Sorias recoiled. The night felt dangerous and unusual, and it seemed like anything could happen, even pilgrims attacking them with their very presence, intentionally violating the taboo.

"Don't worry," Robbie said.

"We're just going," Betsy said.

"Going where?" demanded Antonia.

"Home," Betsy replied.

Because they were no longer pilgrims.

Days before, when Pete had arrived, the girls had been tangled together by a snake that wouldn't allow them to live separate lives. Now the snake was gone. Instead, they were merely girls standing side by side, close, but not close.

"You killed the snake," Joaquin said.

"No," Robbie replied. "Well, kinda. We decided to, together, but as soon as we decided to, it just . . ."

"Disappeared," Betsy said. "While the owls went crazy."

Their decision to work together to be apart had set them free.

"It worked," Joaquin said. "Beatriz, it *worked*."

And this was yet another miracle the Sorias had not witnessed for a very long time: hope. All of the Sorias, Beatriz and Joaquin included, immediately found their eyes drawn to the Shrine where Daniel used to be. Where Daniel *should have been.*

Michael handed the keys back to Beatriz.

25

Buildings are not very good at remembering the people who once occupied them.

The high alpine desert around Bicho Raro had more than its fair share of abandoned buildings, and Marisita was slowly working her way through them. Every time she thought she had searched all of the buildings within easy distance of Bicho Raro, she found another one. They came in all shapes. There were collapsed barns, of course, like the one the Sorias scavenged wood from, and old mining towns like the ones Pete and Beatriz had chased Salto through. There were equipment sheds and well houses. But there were also real houses, scattered homesteads, substantial cabins with porches and forgotten histories. Marisita was always shocked by how little she could learn about the people who had lived in them, even though some of them had been neglected only for a few years. Fabrics and rugs faded to colorlessness, glassware and knickknacks got smashed, and scents disappeared. She had heard that houses like these used to be lived in by families who were bought off by logging companies or terrorized into leaving by white ranchers, but she had no way of knowing for sure. She found it depressing, how fast memories were replaced by rumors. Tragedy left behind such subtle artifacts.

Marisita climbed through yet another empty house the day after the radio station had stopped being secret. This one had a front door (sometimes they didn't), but it was missing the knob. Scavengers, both human and animal, had already had their way with the interior, so only a few featureless chairs remained, knocked on their sides. There was no bed, but it would have been a good place to seek shelter from the cold overnight.

"Daniel?" Marisita called.

There was no reply. There was never a reply. Marisita checked all four of the rooms anyway, in case Daniel couldn't speak or was dead. When she returned to the dim entry room, she carefully righted all of the chairs, attempting to return the room to as close to perfection as it was capable of. She looked at them for a long moment, trying to imagine what kind of family would have sat in them, and then she sank into one of the chairs and cried. Water pooled around her feet and slipped between the gapped old floorboards.

"Please be alive," Marisita said, but only in her head.

After a few minutes, she rose and took up her bag from beside the front door and left the house behind. She wanted to be back in time for the radio program. Tonight was different than all the other nights, because now that the Sorias knew Beatriz and Joaquin were running a station, they insisted that the cousins broadcast live from Bicho Raro. The single-minded goal was to reach Daniel, and the whole family wanted to be there to watch.

Marisita had a letter in her pocket from Beatriz. It was probably soaked through, but she remembered what it said, as it was so brief: *Marisita, I hope you will consider completing your interview tonight. Beatriz.*

But Marisita's heart had not changed. She still did not want to tell her story. The thought of saying it out loud made her feel as ill as the days when her past had unfolded, and every time she relived the memories, her tears came fresh, and the rain fell harder on her and her butterflies. She thought the Sorias already probably despised her for luring their Saint into darkness. How much more would they despise her, she thought, if they knew what kind of person she was?

She thought about the last thing Daniel Soria had told her, and remembering it reddened her eyes again, as it always did. She loved him and missed him, and she scanned the bright horizon for signs of him.

There was no sign of Daniel, only another small house, a twin to the one she had just searched. There was a story that linked those two houses together, but it had disintegrated with the curtains. The front door fell off as Marisita opened it, startling a thread snake, also known as the blind snake, from beneath it. The dust that rose in the air reacted with the storm over Marisita so that electricity crackled. Marisita waited for it to calm, then she stepped inside. There was no furniture in the main room. There was only a shrine to the Virgin of Guadalupe in the corner. Marisita crouched before the statue. Mary, her eyes softly downcast, as gentle as Daniel's, stood upon a crudely sculpted pile of yellow roses. The words *¿No estoy yo aquí que soy tu madre?* were painted among the blossoms. The rain from Marisita's miracle speckled the ceramic, giving the appearance that the Virgin wept.

Marisita closed her eyes and meant to pray, but instead of a prayer, she thought about the lost stories of these abandoned houses, and about Daniel, and about the struggling Soria family. She thought about how a careless or foolhardy Saint could all too easily reduce Bicho Raro to yet another one of these abandoned homesteads, a badly placed conversation sending deadly darkness through an entire family. Daniel had put them all in danger despite his best efforts to separate himself, because he had somehow forgotten how tenacious love was, even in the face of fear. She had seen it before she left that morning. His family was still afraid, and yet they rallied around hope.

She removed Beatriz's letter from her pocket. It was soaked, but the ink had not bled. Beatriz's request remained intently bold.

Marisita knew that her fear of sharing her story was selfish. She had seen how music had helped Jennie, and she'd seen how Diablo Diablo's subtle exploration of the truth had helped Robbie and Betsy defeat their darkness. It was entirely possible that telling her story could help Daniel. They didn't know what he *needed* to hear to defeat his darkness, but they knew what he *wanted* to hear: Marisita. And yet she was here, because it was easier for her—she had been fleeing her past for months and she knew in her heart that this had become just another way of fleeing.

The sculpture of the Virgin had ceased praying and was instead holding her ceramic hands out toward Marisita. With a sigh, Marisita folded Beatriz's damp letter before draping it over the Virgin's hands.

Marisita made a vow: If she did not find Daniel that afternoon, she would return to Bicho Raro, and she would tell her story on the radio.

Only a few minutes later, she discovered Daniel's lost pack of supplies. It was hung up on a strand of barbed wire, just a few threads tangled around one of the barbs. Marisita ran to it as if it might run away, and she caught it up in her arms. It still smelled like him, like the candles of the Shrine, and she held it to her face until she could feel the fabric growing saturated by the rain over her. Then she opened it and searched its contents. To her distress, she found it was full. She guessed, correctly, that this meant that he had not meant to leave it behind.

"Daniel!" she called out. "Daniel, can you hear me?"

Marisita found a hand-sized stone, which she set on the top of the fence post closest to her so that she would have a marker of where she had found it. Slinging the pack across her shoulders in addition to her own bag, she began to walk the fence line, looking for evidence that a young man had squeezed through. Back and forth she went, in ever-widening circles. Her mouth had not been overly dry before she found his supplies, but now, all she could think about was lowering her bag from her shoulder and taking a drink. She refused to, however, imagining how dry he must be, feeling selfish for knowing that she could take a drink at any time.

She knew he might already be dead. She knew he might have sent out that message to her in vain.

She called his name again.

She did not know that he could hear her.

Daniel was perhaps one hundred feet away from her, still curled by the brush that he had sheltered under before. When he heard her voice, his heart leaped and then fell. He longed to let her find him, to hold him, to drive away the creature that still accompanied him. He imagined her pressing her fingers to his eyelids, as if his blindness was a pain that she could ease through touch. He could hear the rain falling around her still and the sound of that water nearly drove him to weakness. But instead, he mustered his strength. Slowly, he crawled around the opposite side of the plant in order to remain hidden.

Marisita came closer, calling. Although Daniel did not want to be found, his heart cried for her so strongly and her heart cried for him so strongly that she was pulled inexorably in his direction.

Only feet from him, her pulse pounded so strongly that it was as if she had already found him.

"Daniel," she said, "I'm not afraid."

This was not true, but she wanted it to be true badly enough that the difference did not matter.

There are many kinds of bravery. The one Marisita displayed right then was one of them, and the kind that Daniel displayed was another. Everything in him wanted to call to her, but nothing in him gave in to the impulse. He had risked everything in order that she might live without her darkness, and he would not give that up just because he did not want to die alone.

Marisita hesitated. She believed that her desire to find him had invented the feeling of certainty inside her.

"Daniel?"

The Saint remained hidden.

Marisita returned to Bicho Raro to tell her story.

26

ightning and love are created in very similar ways. There is some debate over how both lightning and love form, but most experts agree that both require the presence of complementary opposites. A towering thundercloud is full of opposites: ice and positive charge at its uppermost point, water and negative charge at its base. In electricity and in love, opposites attract, and so as these opposites begin to interact, an electrical field develops. In a cloud, this field eventually grows so powerful that it must burst from the cloud in the form of lightning, visible from miles away. It is essentially the same in a love affair.

The night that Marisita agreed to finish her interview, the air felt remarkably charged, prepared for either lightning or love. The wind was full of words not yet said, miracles not yet performed, and electricity not yet discharged. All of this interfered with the station's signal. A test signal from their new broadcasting site—Bicho Raro—had traveled poorly, and even when they retried it closer to where they ordinarily broadcast, the signal remained weak. The atmosphere was simply too uncertain.

Beatriz sat in the back of the box truck, the doors open wide, looking out at the familiar sight of Bicho Raro at sundown. The truck was parked beside the stage Pete had built. Wires snaked to the ground poles and to the antenna fixed to the truck's roof. Another cable led to where a microphone sat in the middle of the stage. Beatriz could see several Sorias from where she sat, and well beyond them, several pilgrims, including Tony's towering form. Very few people enjoy trying to solve a problem with an audience, and Beatriz was no exception. Moreover, the instability of the atmosphere seemed to be mirrored inside her. This was because her self-inflicted puzzles had previously had no time limit and no stakes, and this puzzle had both in spades. It was also because she had seen Marisita return with Daniel's bag, and she knew as well as Marisita what the loss of it meant for her cousin.

Her thoughts were as turbulent as the air. Ideas refused to come.

"There's no point broadcasting into a void," Joaquin said. He sounded dramatic, but it felt warranted. There seemed little reason to encourage Marisita's confession if Daniel had no chance of intercepting it.

Pete, as ever the willing go-between, told Joaquin, "Tony said that you need height. For your antenna."

"Height!" Joaquin said. "Yeah!"

But this information was not useful to Beatriz. She had known from the beginning of the radio project that she needed height; it was the simplest way to improve reception. This is why professional radio antennae soar hundreds of feet in the air and require blinking lights to prevent aircraft from having unexpected trysts with them. Their antenna had never posed any such threat to aviation. Beatriz explained to Pete that she had reached the extent of her antenna-building capacity and did not know how to improve it, although she was willing to hear suggestions.

"Hold tight," Pete replied, and jogged back to where the pilgrims loitered. The mood there, gathered around the radio and fire pit, leaned closer to anticipatory than fearful. With the twins healed and Jennie well on her way, it felt as if the spiritual weather was finally breaking. Theldon had not picked up a paperback novel all day, and Jennie had listened to the radio and cooked in Marisita's kitchen while she was out. The resulting casserole was unimpressive in comparison to Marisita's elegant creations, but the enthusiasm in it tasted plenty savory for the pilgrims, and Jennie had added several new songs to her repertoire.

For his part, Tony found himself filled with the satisfaction that comes from seeing someone else do well—or, in this case, hearing them do well. Joaquin had done far more with his suggestions than he had hoped, and now Tony's vicarious ambition ran ahead of him. He imagined inviting Joaquin back east, getting him in front of microphones, watching his star rise. In this bright future, Tony imagined Diablo Diablo doing well enough that Tony could quietly retreat from the public eye and produce for him instead. It was an appealing image.

So it was a Tony Triumph full of philanthropy who told Pete, "I can hold the antenna. I'll stand on that dish and hold it like Lady Liberty."

This might not have been such a relevant suggestion if Tony hadn't been a giant, but he was, making him fourteen feet more useful than anyone else in Bicho Raro.

"That'll do it?" Pete asked.

"Kid, me plus that dish will get that station heard through this whole valley," Tony said. "That saint of theirs won't be able to avoid us unless he got in a car."

Or died, thought Marisita, but she did not say it out loud.

Since she had returned, she had watched the occupants of Bicho Raro prepare for the broadcast that night with growing anxiety. She attempted to pray in the Shrine, but it only made her more overwhelmed. She tried to cook some dessert to follow Jennie's casserole, thinking the routine would settle her, but her hands would not cease shaking enough to hold the instruments of cooking.

"Marisita," Padre Jiminez said as the sky turned full black. "Come with me."

She followed the coyote-headed priest. She expected him to give her priestly wisdom, something about believing in herself because our father and savior did. Instead, he led her silently to the edge of Bicho Raro and there, in the dark, he simply embraced her. Marisita had been held only once in recent memory, and before then, not for months, and so the force of simply being held was enormous. She stood quivering in Padre Jiminez's arms until she stilled, and Padre Jiminez tried unsuccessfully to not enjoy the embrace as much as he did. Perhaps that does not take away from the original intention of the embrace, as Marisita accepted the offering as first presented.

"Gracias, Padre," she said.

"Of course, Marisita," he said, and licked his lips over his sharp teeth as he said her name. "Are you ready?"

Marisita looked to the stage. It was decorated as if for a birthday celebration, with flags and lights strung between the upright stands. A small umbrella protected the microphone from her stormy presence. It would have been a fine setting for the beginning of a love affair, or for the reunion of a couple long separated. But she supposed it was also a fine setting for a night supplying comfort to a dying young man. She smoothed her hair, cast her eyes over the watching owls, and tried not to think about all the saints who were listening.

"Yes," she said.

27

It was 1955, and Texas was drying out.

It had started drying out in 1950 and would keep it up until 1957, but in 1955, they didn't know that it would have an end. It just seemed like it would go on forever. Dust drifted over driveways and highways and filled swimming pools and elementary schools. Crops turned to black ash like a biblical punishment. The dry-eyed sky stared down as farmers burned the needles off cactuses so the cattle could eat them. Students held hands with each other on the way from the school to the bus so they would not lose each other in the dust storms. If you were the sort who liked to sing sad songs, you sang sad songs. If you were the sort who liked to stay alive, you moved to the city.

Marisita's parents were the sort who liked to stay alive, and so, when she was nine, they moved the Lopez family to San Antonio from the ranch they had worked on for Marisita's whole life. There were six of them: Marisita's mother, Maria; and her father, Edgar; three younger sisters; and Marisita. There was also Max, the oldest brother, but he was sometimes not quite like family. They traded the house on the ranch for an apartment in an old hotel. Even though it was still dry out there in Texas, in the city, it was a different picture entirely. San Antonio was a modern city of half a million people. There were shopping malls, racecourses, subdivisions, highways bustling with cars. There was *water*—in the river, in the old gravel quarry, and in ponds in the cemetery Marisita passed on the way to school each morning. On her way home, she'd sometimes see boys fishing in the cemetery.

"What are you trying to catch?" she had shouted once.

"You, baby!" one of them shouted back, and Marisita didn't ask after that.

There was less drought to be found in San Antonio, but there was less money, too. It was expensive to live in the city, and Maria and Edgar both worked two jobs to afford the apartment. Max was probably old enough to work, but he couldn't—he got angry very easily, and Maria and Edgar told Marisita and her sisters that Max was working it out with God. God didn't seem to be working through it very quickly, however, and so the Lopezes had to do without Max's income. They managed, though, and Marisita made friends and taught herself how to be as perfect as she could.

In 1956, Elvis Presley came to San Antonio.

He was scheduled to play at the San Antonio Municipal Auditorium, the building where Edgar Lopez worked as a maintenance man. It was not as rewarding as working on the ranch, and Edgar was a lesser version of himself than he had been, but it was a paycheck. Or at least that was what Edgar told himself as he moved ever more slowly in both his body and thoughts, worn to ordinariness by the slow-motion tragedy of life. Edgar didn't complain about his fate, but the truth was, years of doing what needed to be done and nothing else was getting to him; he was getting old.

In 1956, the King of Rock and Roll was pretty near the beginning of his career, quite a bit further away from the slow-motion tragic end of his own life, and San Antonio was unprepared for the newfound force of his fans. The plan had been for Elvis to play two shows and then sign autographs for any interested listeners. This plan was trampled by the six thousand girls who queued up hours before the show and then refused to leave after. "We want Elvis!" they chanted, as Elvis fled into his dressing room. "We want Elvis!" they chanted, lining the halls until forced to leave. "We want Elvis!" they chanted outside, as Elvis waited them out in the now-empty arena. He played a few tunes on the pipe organ while reporters and Edgar Lopez listened.

No one had seen anything like Elvis before Elvis—especially an older man like Edgar Lopez, a man who never went to concerts, a man who worked two jobs at an ever slower pace. The show was nonstop action—Elvis sang, danced, played the guitar wildly, and gyrated his hips in a way that made Edgar avert his eyes and some mothers cover their children's eyes. Elvis was tireless. No wonder the girls screamed, Edgar thought, because they were witnessing a rock-and-roll saint.

But if Edgar had only experienced the show, nothing would have changed for Edgar himself. The show was memorable, yes, but not life changing. But that combination of events, which led to Edgar and Elvis being together in the performance hall once everyone else was gone, was life changing. Because Elvis was trapped in the San Antonio Municipal Auditorium long after his show, Edgar got to see him while not performing. While waiting for the girls to leave, Elvis sat at the organ, picking out "Silent Night" without any particular craft.

It was this that moved Edgar. He would not have been prompted to action by Elvis performing, because Edgar could tell himself that Elvis wasn't real. But seeing Elvis afterward proved that this was indeed the work of a man. Perhaps an extraordinary man, but nonetheless a mortal like Edgar. Edgar decided he would no longer live his life in his diminished state; he would become, like Elvis, the loudest version of himself.

And so that night, after Elvis had finally gone and Edgar was cleaning up after the horde, he sang a bit of "Blue Suede Shoes" and jogged up the stairs of the municipal building with renewed vigor. He was much older than Elvis, and much less practiced at vigor, so he caught his foot sideways on one of the steps and fell all the way to the bottom, breaking his leg.

This was the beginning of the failure of the Lopezes' fortunes. Edgar's leg never healed correctly, and so his job prospects shrank. He spent many days in the apartment with his leg propped up. The weight of earning fell upon Maria Lopez's shoulders. Many women would have been crushed under this newfound responsibility, but Maria Lopez became an enraged lioness in the face of bad luck. She got a third job. She bought

Edgar a radio to listen to on his leg's bad days. She joined the newly founded PASSO (Political Association of Spanish-Speaking Organizations) and campaigned fervently for better governmental representation, better health care, and labor rights. Years passed. The Lopez family scraped by.

Then the 1961 San Antonio Stock Show and Rodeo happened. Each year, the show opened with a Western parade, and every year, the parade grew grander as the show aged. That year, the stock show, already large, gained new fame when Roy Rogers and Dale Evans—the King of the Cowboys and Queen of the West—starred in a nationwide NBC telecast featuring the rodeo. Hundreds of cowboys trotted through San Antonio, the horses wearing fancy bridles and turquoise-crusted breastplates and elaborately tooled saddles with metal-plated horns, and the riders wearing white cowboy hats and fringed shirts and beautiful boots. Convertible cars followed them with local and national celebrities waving from inside.

Marisita, who by then had grown into an elegant and near-perfect teen, took her three younger sisters to see the parade; Edgar and Maria had been planning on going, but Edgar's leg was having one of its bad days. Max had initially come with Marisita and the girls, but anger took him before they got there, and he stormed away into the crowd.

Maria stayed with Edgar in the apartment, listening to the sounds of the music and the horses and the applause outside. Although Edgar did not complain, Maria finally could not take it.

"Let us see the parade," she told him.

"Ah," he replied, "I can't go down five flights of stairs."

"No," she said. "But I can carry you up one."

It was one flight to the roof, and even though Edgar was not a small man, Maria had been carrying him in all of the other ways for half a decade. She put her arms around him, chair and all, and she carried him from the apartment and up the stairs. As the revelry grew louder outside, Maria climbed faster, fearing that she would not get to the top before the parade was over. Filled with passion by the sensation of being carried by his wife, Edgar told Maria that she needn't hurry on his behalf; this two-person parade in the stairwell was far better than anything he might see outside. It was not that Edgar had stopped loving Maria at any point during that fraught decade of their marriage, but he had stopped saying that he loved her. Maria was so overcome by these words of his that she placed her foot wrong on the top stair.

The two of them pitched backward, and surely Maria would have died from the fall if Edgar had not broken her fall somewhat. As it was, she only broke her leg, the opposite leg from her husband, and he only got a bruise on his chest where she had landed.

Maria could not work now either, and the Lopez household suddenly became all dependents and no laborers. They came to the end of their money. They promised the rent, and promised the rent, and then they came to the end of their promises. They should have been thrown out on the street, but the landlord was kindly, and the Lopezes had been good tenants for years until now. Moreover, he noted, he had a shy son with no luck in the lady department, and he had noticed that Marisita had become a clever and lovely young woman. He suggested—if Marisita was agreeable with it, of course—that the two of them might meet. Possibly love would bloom.

The rest was left unspoken; of course, if love bloomed and a marriage came of it, he would not throw his in-laws into the street.

Marisita agreed to meet the landlord's son. She had been, she remembered, both nervous and excited. Their landlord was a kind man, and there were many reasons why in San Antonio in 1961 he would not have been excited to introduce his son to the daughter of his Spanish-speaking tenants, and he did it anyway, without condescension. Either his son would be obviously unsuitable or he might be marvelous, and save them all.

But the problem was that he was neither.

His name was Homer, and he was neither handsome nor ugly. He was neither terrible nor wonderful. He was shy and awkward, a little shorter than Marisita, a little sweatier than Marisita. He fell madly in love with her straightaway.

Marisita did not fall in love with him, neither straightaway nor after several weeks of courting.

Now, this was no arranged marriage. No one was forcing the two together. She could have walked away. But every evening, she would return from cruising with Homer and find Edgar in his chair with his leg elevated, and Maria in the chair opposite with her leg still in its cast, holding hands across the space between them, and she would see her sisters sleeping sweetly in their beds in the next room, and they would ask her how it went, and she would have to say, "Wonderfully."

She could not let them down.

And so the wedding was set. Marisita tried to fall in love with Homer, and then she tried to convince herself that she did not need true love to be happy, and finally she dreamed that she might not live to be very old and perhaps in the next life she could have her life for herself.

She cried when no one could see her and smiled and laughed when they all could.

The wedding was to be held in the Cathedral of San Fernando, a location made possible only by the landlord's connections. It was a grand old building, constructed in the early eighteenth century. White pillars held up the roof, and white beams arched down the ceiling like a whale's rib cage. Any bride would have been happy to be married in such an awe-inspiring space. It was a place for an epic love story.

But Marisita was not in an epic love story.

Homer stood at the altar and waited for her with the priest. Marisita stood at the doorway. Edgar was on her arm; he could not walk well, but he would limp down the aisle to give his daughter away if he did nothing else. Marisita could see her mother's face at the very front of the church, and she heard her little sisters laughing around her as they waited to follow her with flower petals. Max was not sitting as he had thrown a fit over his suit and was waiting outside for someone to fetch him and tell him that he had been right all along and please would he come inside.

Marisita looked at her family, and she told herself that she was saving them all. Her tears welled inside her, but she held them back and reached for a smile.

She could not find it.

And so she ran.

She ran out of the church, and her father couldn't follow her because of his bad leg, and her sisters were too shocked to realize that she didn't mean to stop, and Max let her go because he never chased anything but his anger. So Marisita ran and ran and ran. She ran all through her wedding day and all through her wedding night and another day and another night, over and over, holding up her wedding dress in both hands, crying over how she had betrayed them.

Then she found herself in Bicho Raro, and the miracle rose up inside her.

28

T hat is when you received the miracle," Joaquin said. He was using his Diablo Diablo manner with great effort, because he, like everyone else listening, was quite affected by Marisita's tale. He and Pete and Beatriz gazed at the closed doors of the box truck, imagining Marisita standing on the stage outside it.

"Yes," Marisita confirmed. She was crying again now, but she spoke through the tears. One cannot always hear tears on the radio, but they were audible in this instance. Not the ones that fell, because those were still drowned out by the rain always falling on her, but the ones that choked in her throat.

Joaquin wished that Marisita's family could have heard her tell her version of the story, just as Robbie and Betsy had heard each other's letters the night before. But they were hundreds of miles away, so he simply continued. "And it was sometime after this Daniel helped you?"

Marisita whispered, "I knew he was risking himself."

She felt sure that the Sorias would despise her in the next few minutes, if they didn't already hate her after hearing how she'd betrayed her own family. But she pressed on. "We knew we weren't allowed to speak. But sometimes . . . he would come to my kitchen and just sit while I cooked. I didn't cook for him—I knew that wasn't allowed. But sometimes, after he left, I would realize that there were a few biscochitos or churros missing, and then I just started to make them for him and leave them where he could steal as many as he liked. And—I knew we were not supposed to speak, but sometimes I would go to the Shrine and pray in the garden with him. He was not supposed to give me anything, but sometimes he would leave little things there for me to pick up. Just thread for my sewing, or a little harmonica, or a bird's nest that he had found. We didn't speak. We knew we weren't supposed to speak. We knew we weren't supposed to be together at all. But finally . . . we began to walk into the desert together. We didn't speak. We knew we shouldn't. We knew . . . we shouldn't."

"That crazy fool!" Joaquin said.

"That crazy fool," Marisita agreed. "And we broke that rule, too, eventually. We spoke. Just a few words here and there, more every time that nothing terrible happened when we did. I know we were fools. I know how it sounds. I'm so sorry."

This apology meant nothing to Diablo Diablo and everything to Joaquin and the rest of the Sorias—but not for the reason Marisita thought. Contrary to what Marisita feared, none of them were angry with her, and none of them hated her. They did not need this apology to make her actions right. But it still meant something to them that she cared enough about them to offer it.

Generously, Joaquin said, "It was him as well as you, Marisita. Always take blame for your own actions but never take blame for someone else's. Was this when his darkness fell?"

"No," Marisita said.

"Well, I don't understand why not."

"Because he hadn't helped me yet," Marisita said. "He hadn't interfered. I wasn't any closer to the second miracle just because I fell in love with him. In fact, I only felt worse. Daniel is so good, and he loved his family so much, it only made me think about how I hadn't heard from my own family—how could I have? I assume they have been thrown in the streets. They—they must hate me. I've put them through so much humiliation. I failed them. I didn't even save myself, and so all I have is this guilt."

"But this is an outrage," Joaquin said. Beatriz and Pete furiously wrote messages to Joaquin and held them up for him to read them. "What about this brother of yours—Max! He should be carrying the guilt! Yes, all of us in the studio agree that he's the villain."

"He was just so angry," Marisita said.

"So am I!" Joaquin said. "At Max!"

"If you'd met him—"

"I'd be angrier! Tell us what happened that night, the night Daniel came to you."

On that night, Marisita had decided to walk into the desert until she could no longer walk. She had been contemplating it for weeks, and it was not an easy decision to make. It was the ultimate in failure. The ultimate imperfection. But it was made—or it had been, until Tony and Pete arrived, interrupting her. Now she could not go until the dogs had settled and Bicho Raro had fallen back to sleep. Even this small delay destroyed her, and she curled on the floor of her home and sobbed. Deep down, she knew that walking out into the desert still did nothing for her family; it was merely another selfish act. In the end, she still thought only of herself. If she wanted to truly cure her family's woes, she would return to them and beg for Homer's forgiveness. Even in this moment of despair, she could not make herself do that. Self-hatred and rain poured around her. She had not been dry or warm in months.

Slowly, the commotion outside died down. The dogs' barking vanished into the night. Engines were silenced. Voices rose and fell. Owls screamed and called and finally fell silent.

The night was quiet.

A knock came on Marisita's door. She did not get off the floor, nor did she answer. A moment later, the door cracked open and footsteps came to her. They stopped beside her, and the owner of the feet stood there for a very long time. This was because it was Daniel, and he was still wrestling with himself over what he wanted to do and what he was supposed to do.

With a heavy sigh, he curled himself around her.

This was not allowed, to embrace her like this, but he did it anyway. The rain fell on her, and the rain fell on him, and they were both soaked to the skin. In this moment the scent of rain mingled sweetly with the scent of the Shrine's incense, and Marisita remembered what it was to be warm and safe.

Then Daniel did what he would do for her if she had not been a pilgrim, as if he was not afraid. Still holding her tightly, he spoke into her ear. He told her that she could not hold herself responsible for all of her family's financial woes, and that it was not her place to be the sacrificial lamb. There were other solutions, but her family had settled on the easiest and ignored the signs of her unhappiness. Moreover, she was honorable for not giving herself to a man who she couldn't love; Homer didn't deserve to live a lie.

"But they didn't make me," Marisita had told Daniel. "They were not cruel. I was at fault for not going through with it, or not telling them sooner that I couldn't."

"You can forgive yourself," Daniel had insisted.

"I don't think I can," she'd replied.

He continued to hold her. "I know everything feels wrong, but you can be right again, Marisita, if you try as hard at it as you try with everything else."

This was when the black rose of his darkness had bloomed. Neither Daniel nor Marisita knew what part of that visit triggered it, but the truth was that it was not Daniel coming to comfort her, nor the sensible council he gave. It was not his arms around her or the warmth of his words in her ear. It was, in fact, the way that he said *Marisita* to her in this last sentence. The way he said her name conveyed all of his sympathy, and it confirmed all of the truth of his advice, and it promised her that she was worthwhile and redeemable, and it indicated that he treasured the way he had seen her selflessly interact with the other pilgrims, and it hinted that if any single thing was different about their circumstances, he would marry her immediately and live with her for decades until they died on the same day just as in love as they were in that moment. This may seem like a lot to be contained in the single word that is a given name, but this is why in more conservative times, cultures took great care to refer to each other by Mr. and Mrs.

"And then he left," Marisita said.

Joaquin was too overcome by his cousin's bravery to immediately answer. Right then, he was so ferociously proud and scared for Daniel that love and hope and fear choked his Diablo Diablo voice from him. With great effort, he managed to say only, "We're going to take a brief musical break. Here's Elvis with 'Can't Help Falling in Love.'"

While Elvis crooned, Joaquin held himself and wiped away a tear, and Pete and Beatriz looked steadily at each other because stories about lovers always hit other lovers hard.

Joaquin pulled himself together as the song drew to a close. "Now we're back. Thank you, Elvis, for singing the words we were all thinking. And the darkness?"

"I don't know when it came upon him. It must have been soon after he left, because he returned only a few minutes later with the letter for Beatriz. He slid it under the door and gave me the instructions for the letter. Then he was gone, and I never got to tell him myself that I love him."

There was silence.

Joaquin said, "If he is listening tonight, you just did."

Marisita said nothing.

Joaquin said, "Marisita?"

"It's just—" Marisita started.

"Yes?"

Marisita held out her hands to the sky and examined them again. "It's just that the rain has stopped."

29

Of all the Sorias there, only Luis the one-handed had ever been in Michoacán at the time of the great monarch butterfly migration. Millions of butterflies travel to Mexico each fall, sheltering in the forests there as winter punishes the land farther north. It was a sight he would not soon forget, the air shimmering with drifting color, the butterflies floating on wings that looked like Antonia Soria had cut them at her kitchen table. Some people said that these butterflies were the souls of the dead returning to earth in time for Día de Los Muertos, but Luis had thought he had never seen anything so alive.

He hadn't believed he would see anything like it again, but on that charged night, the Sorias found themselves gazing at a sky that rivaled that enchanted one. Once the storm had ceased over Marisita, it took only a few moments for the butterflies on Marisita's dress to dry. Now they took off all around her, hundreds of them, swirling up and around into the sky. They mingled with the miracle-crazed owls who circled and dove, driven to excitement by Marisita's miracle.

It was an awesome sight, but a charged one. Miracles are a strange thing in that sometimes a miracle will trigger another one, or sometimes trigger a disaster, and sometimes both of these are the same thing. So when the butterflies swelled upward, dots of orange and yellow, they flew right into that atmosphere that had begun the night so charged with anticipation and fear and hope. Those molecules vibrated and agitated as hundreds of wings brushed against them again and again, and in the black sky, an electrical charge mounted. The Sorias could hear it down below—their ears momentarily went dull and dead in anticipation—and then there was a mighty crack, as though the sky itself was ripping open.

A massive lightning bolt flew from the dark.

Lightning hunts the largest prey, which in this case was the antenna on top of the radio telescope, with Tony as its human base.

There was an explosion of light.

The antenna and the dish and Tony were all obscured by it. Everyone down below was forced to avert their eyes lest they be blinded. In less than a second, the electric pulse raced white-hot down the wires that ran from the antenna to the truck, and every ground wire exploded from the soil with a sizzle and pop. A thunderous crash shook the ground they stood on.

When the air cleared, there was no sign of the antenna. The telescope dish was blackened. Tony was stretched out in the dust at the base of the dish, the remains of the antenna blasted in copper bits around him.

He was no longer a giant.

He was not currently breathing.

Before the lightning strike, as Tony had listened to Marisita's confession, he had been looking down from this very great height onto Bicho Raro and he had been thinking about the enormity of what they were doing tonight and how this entire family had come together to do it. He was thinking about Joaquin's incredible promise. And finally he was thinking that it wasn't all bad being a radio giant, as long as you looked for the things you could do as a giant that you couldn't do as anything else, like hold up someone else's voice so it was just a little louder.

The second miracle had come easily.

"Tony, gosh, Tony!" Pete said. "What do I do?"

Joaquin, who had torn off his headset to jump from the truck, put his ear on Tony's chest, trying to hear his heart or check for breathing. This is a terrible way to check for evidence of life. Beatriz, who had leaped out with Pete and Joaquin, did it in a less terrible way. She lifted Tony's hand, noticing the branched and peculiar lightning flowers that covered his arm, ending at his fingers.

"There's a pulse," she said. "He's alive."

It's a difficult thing to be struck by lightning. It's also a difficult thing to fall dozens of feet from the top of a radio telescope. Tony's breath had been knocked all the way out to the highway, and it took a full minute for it to make its panting way back to him.

"He's breathing!" Joaquin announced for the benefit of the other Sorias.

But they were not paying attention to him. They were shouting and pointing at something completely different: the box truck. Because Pete, Beatriz, and Joaquin had jumped out of the box truck so swiftly to attend to Tony, they had not realized that the truck had become extremely warm immediately following the strike. The lightning had raced down the wires so hot and ferocious that it had lit everything it touched on fire.

The box truck had been quietly and furiously burning to the ground in the minutes they were distracted by Tony.

Beatriz said, "Save the transmitter!"

"I'll get buckets from the barn," Pete said.

"I'll help," said Antonia.

"Yes," agreed Michael.

Anyone who has fought a fire of any size knows that there are some fires you can kill and some fires that will die only on their own. This was the latter. The interior of the truck was an inferno. The smell of melting electronics filled the night as clouds of dark smoke blocked out the stars. As buckets were passed from hand to hand and precious water poured out on the sand, the fire popped and groaned and hissed like the living thing it was. The egg Beatriz had hung in a hairnet nest began to agitate and scream. It had never grown warm enough to incubate and hatch but now, finally, in this miraculous, destructive fire, it cracked open. A strange dark owl of a breed none of them had ever seen burst from the fire. It circled around their heads once, and when it looked down, for a moment, its paler face looked like a woman's—a little like Loyola Soria, and a little like the face of the sculpture in the Shrine.

Then the owl was gone, and the truck was, too, singed to smoldering ashes.

It is difficult to give up hope, particularly when you have just been filled with a lot of it, particularly when you have gone without for so long. Humans are as drawn to hope as owls are to miracles. It only takes the suggestion of it to stir them up, and the eagerness lingers for a while even when all traces of it are gone. And the Sorias were riled up over more than just a suggestion. Marisita's second miracle had happened right before their eyes, and then Tony's had, too. They finally truly believed what Beatriz and Joaquin had posited: For years they had been doing it wrong. The danger had been real, but the taboo had not. Now they imagined a generation of pilgrims coming and learning from previous pilgrims and from Sorias and from the indefinable wisdom that comes from music, even if the words don't always sink in.

So when the box truck burned to the ground, they did not immediately realize that something had died with it.

It occurred to Beatriz first.

"No," she said, just one word.

To communicate with Daniel, they would need another radio, and she could build one, but it would require new parts. New parts would require a trip to Alamosa at best, ordering them from elsewhere at worst. It would mean she had to build a new antenna. Even with all the help of everyone here in Bicho Raro, it could not be done in a day, or even two days.

She had seen Marisita return home that day with Daniel's bag. He didn't have two days. He didn't have one day. He might not even have had this day. Now that the owls and butterflies had dispersed, there was only one species left soaring overhead: vultures.

"Where is Marisita?" asked Judith.

Marisita was gone. Now that she was healed, her shame and guilt gone with the rain, she found that her desire to find Daniel remained. She was determined to find him and offer the same comfort that he had given her.

This struck Beatriz as the ultimate folly. It seemed obvious to her that if Marisita had not found Daniel before now, there was no reason why she could hope to find him in the midst of an ashy black night.

And so, in this moment of terrible loss and hardship, Pete and Beatriz did what lovers often do when things are the worst for the other: They fought. It was made worse by neither of them realizing that they were fighting. Instead, they thought they were being quite reasonable.

"I can't believe it's gone," Pete said.

Beatriz said, "It will take me weeks to rebuild it."

"Oh. I just meant the truck."

Pete felt blindsided by the sudden loss of his future, a loss that Beatriz pointed out was only a loss in his mind, as he did not need a moving truck to be a whole person, and in fact only required a sense of worth, which was something that came separate from a job title or being shipped off to another country to shoot at people like your father or father's father had been before. This did not, as you might imagine, make Pete feel any better, as very few people are ever healed by being told a truth instead of feeling the truth for themselves.

"You don't have to be cruel about it," Pete said. "I know you're upset."

"I'm not upset. Please stop saying that I am!"

She sounded so certain that Pete regarded her fresh, trying to understand if he was reading her wrong. Her expression was complicated by the ash on it, and she did not wear her feelings like anyone else he had met, but he felt strongly enough about it to press on, with sympathy. "Look, you're allowed to be upset. All this—the fire, Daniel—you're allowed."

"I don't have feelings like that."

"Don't have feelings like that?" Pete echoed. "You're not a doll. You're not a robot."

"I'm trying to tell you something about myself," Beatriz said. "You're wrong."

But Pete was not wrong. He had not been wrong before when he'd said it, and he wasn't wrong now. If only Beatriz believed her strangely shaped feelings existed, she would have seen it, too. Instead, she found herself impatient with him, thinking about how Francisco and Antonia's relationship had fallen apart because they were too dissimilar. Pete, she thought, was merely proving how he was an emotional being and unable to see her for how she truly was, unable to understand what she was unable to give him. She believed that this conversation was exactly why people like her father and Beatriz ended up alone in greenhouses with their work.

She didn't realize that she was being torn to shreds inside.

"I don't need to be made into something that I'm not," she said, "something easier, with feelings, something more like you. I am trying to think of what to do next and it's taking all of my mind and I don't need you to imagine me as something softer to make you feel better about who I am!"

Pete stared at her, but she didn't soften these words, because she fully believed them. And because she fully believed them, he thought that he must have been wrong. She knew herself better than he did.

As her eyes glittered coldly at him, he waited just a moment longer to see if there was any feeling or kindness in them, but she believed herself the girl without feelings too much for that. Behind him, the box truck he had wanted so badly smoldered. His heart lurched dangerously, a pit inside him, the hole enormous and irreparable.

He turned without another word and he left Bicho Raro.

30

Francisco Soria had begun work on his marvelous green-house directly after an early fight with Antonia. She had been shouting at him as she had shouted at him each day for months, and he had realized all at once that he had nothing to say to her in response. Not only for this current argument, but for all of them. Rather than wait for her to finish so he could explain this truth to her, he had merely walked out of their house into the bright day and begun construction. Antonia had found this impossibly cruel, but Francisco had not left to hurt her. He had left to ease his own mind. Too much noise and too much anger acted like a flue on his thoughts, and as Antonia's grief overtook her, his ideas had been choked down to only a tiny flame—and what was he, if not made purely of ideas? In those early months, he had worked on the greenhouse's construction entirely after dark, when every other Soria was asleep, because he found that, having lived with so much noise for so long, he hungered for absolute silence. It was only after many days of quiet that his prized fluidity of thought had slowly built back up again. Once he had finished the greenhouse and begun work on his roses, he finally returned his schedule to a diurnal one.

In this way, he lived a small and solitary life in a small and controlled world. It was not his best life. But it was an acceptable one.

In the ruins left behind after the truck had burned down, Beatriz found that her small and controlled world was denied her. The radio dish was still smoking hot, and the truck had burned to ashes. There was no private place she could climb on or under. Beatriz's mind refused to settle, though, and eventually, she went to the only sanctuary she could think of: the little house Pete had built.

There she sat inside the dark. There was only a little porch light coming through the windows, the glass still filtering the handsomeness of thought from her father's greenhouse. She curled her arms around her knees and struggled to piece together a solution to reach Daniel, but her thoughts would not order. She tried to cast them up above her, outside of her head and into the sky, so that she could study them from all directions, but they refused to leave her body. She kept testing her thoughts on branches of logic and finding the logic would not hold.

She had been sitting there for countless moments when she heard a whistle.

"Beatriz?" whistled her father gently.

She did not respond, but he ducked his head and entered anyway. He had already, through process of elimination, decided that she must be in the house. He drew close enough that she came into view, still and owl-like in the corner. Father and daughter did not embrace or touch, but he sat close to her, facing her, mirroring her posture.

"What are you doing?" he whistled to her.

"Thinking of how to reach Daniel before it is too late." It was not so much a whistle as it could have been, but he understood her.

"There was no way to save the truck," he said.

"I know."

"Pete has gone," he said.

"I know."

There was a long moment of quiet. Because they were both good about being quiet, it is difficult to say just how long this moment actually lasted. It was shorter than the night, but not by a lot.

Finally, Francisco said very softly, in words, not whistles, "I believe that we have been wrong about many things." When Beatriz didn't answer, he said, "I'm moving back into our house."

Then he patted her knee and stood up and left her there.

Beatriz began to cry.

She had not known that she could cry, and she did not know why she was crying, and she did not realize that this in many cases is just how crying goes. She cried for a very long time and then she thought about how she had told Pete she was not upset when she had been the most upset she had ever been in her life. And then she thought about the vultures and Marisita and she cried even more. Finally, she thought of how they had been wrong about the taboo for so long and it was probably going to cost Daniel's life.

When she was done crying, she wiped her cheeks—the dry air took away all the tears she had missed—and the girl with strange feelings saddled up Salto and rode into the desert to find her cousin.

31

Riding astride Salto, Beatriz followed the buzzards, and soon she caught up with the owl she had seen hatch from the egg in the fire. It coasted overhead with unshakable certainty, and Beatriz felt positive no owl would travel with such surety unless it was headed toward a miracle or a disaster. And what other miracle or disaster could be taking place in this valley tonight but something having to do with the former Saint of Bicho Raro?

As she rode, she wondered what she would do when she found Daniel. She had water, and a little bit of food, but she did not know what to expect.

The stars stopped their laughing to watch her gallop beneath them, and the moon covered its face with a cloud, and then, as she grew close, the stars scrambled down below the horizon so that they would not have to watch. The sun delayed its rising, too, so as to not bear witness, hesitating just at the edge of the earth, so the early morning hung in an eerie half-light.

The buzzards and pale-faced owl all gathered in the same place, a low flat area of scrub with a dune pressed up against an overgrown barbed wire fence. In this place, Beatriz caught sight of a figure and pulled Salto up sharply, meaning to be cautious. But then she recognized Marisita's familiar dress, crumpled into a lopsided monument as she kneeled. She had Daniel's head and shoulders in her lap. Her arms circled him.

"Do you have his darkness?" Beatriz called.

"No," Marisita said.

This seemed impossible, as Daniel had broken the taboo by holding Marisita in her distress, and now Marisita was doing the same for him. And there was no doubt that she loved him—she was there, after all, and so she should have been an heir to his darkness. Beatriz began to wonder if they had been wrong about the savagery of the Soria darkness along with everything else, and dangerously, hope trembled in her. "How is that possible?"

"I cannot interfere with his miracle," Marisita said with a little sob in her voice, "because it's too late. He's dead."

Now Beatriz scrambled down from Salto so quickly that she terrified even Salto. The animal leaped back from her as she hurried to Marisita's side and crouched in the scrubby grass beside her. Here was Daniel Lupe Soria, the Saint of Bicho Raro, worn to a frayed thread in Marisita's arms. He looked like all of the icons Beatriz had ever seen. The martyred Saint, gaunt and frail, long hair hanging. Marisita was the Madonna, holding him close.

Beatriz thought she knew then what Pete felt like with the hole in his heart.

Movement to her right startled her.

"What's that?" she demanded.

"His darkness," Marisita wept.

It was a dark, pale-faced owl, standing nearly as tall as Beatriz. It was not the same owl that had hatched from the egg in the truck, but it was the same species. It was no natural owl, but rather an uncanny creature bred of miracles and darkness. Like the one Beatriz had seen hatch, its face was not quite an owl face. In fact, as Beatriz studied it in the pale light, she realized it had Daniel's eyes painted on it. Daniel's mouth, too. And Daniel's ears, painted on the side of its head, as if it was made of both owl and wood.

"It took his eyes," Marisita said, "and just when I got here, it stole his breath. I tried to catch it."

This, at least, made sense to Beatriz. She had been told her entire life that Soria darkness was a terrible and fearful thing, far stranger and more difficult than an ordinary pilgrim's darkness. And this owl with its stolen eyes and mouth and ears was a terrible and fearful thing. At least one of the stories Beatriz had been told was true.

She did not want to get closer to the creature, but she took an experimental step toward it anyway. With a little cluck, it pranced backward. Not far. Just a few steps, its wings flapping, its expression perhaps jeering.

Marisita gazed at it with loathing. "I just can't believe he's dead."

"Until his darkness leaves, he is not dead," Beatriz said. She studied the bird. It skipped from foot to foot like a boxer, as if preparing for her to make a leap for it. "The miracle dies with the pilgrim."

"Why is there another one?" Marisita asked.

Beatriz tilted her head back to look at the other owl, the one she had hatched. Her thoughts flew up into the air to join it.

The problem was that she needed to know where Daniel's darkness originated in order to know how to solve it. What was he supposed to learn from this owl, this lechuza, that had his eyes and his ears and his mouth and his breath? It could not be easy, or he would have solved it himself already. Beatriz took another step toward it. It took another step back. Again with the hectic, hateful, almost playful skips. She took another step. It took several more back, getting a little farther away. That was the wrong tactic, then, Beatriz decided. She would drive it away if she continued to chase it. Beatriz wondered if she could strike it, but she did not understand the rules of its theft. She didn't want to risk injuring Daniel's eyes or his breath. She didn't think the owl was supposed to be defeated through violence, anyway, as there was nothing to learn there—Daniel had never lacked for fight or bravery.

Beatriz thought about what she had learned from the events of the week before. When she made assumptions, she came to faulty conclusions. She looked at the owl again, brand-new, as if she knew nothing about it. She looked at Daniel, as if she did not know him. She removed all her fear of the darkness and all her grief at her cousin's lifeless body. Then she asked herself what this scene could mean if she had drawn no previous conclusions about it. She struggled to school her impressions to be free of fear or rumor.

"Marisita," she said, "what if it is not wickedly taking his breath, his eyes, or his face? What if it is just keeping them for him?"

"Why?" Marisita's voice did not sound interested. She was losing hope.

"What if it's only there to help him?" Beatriz said. "A teacher instead of a predator?"

Marisita threaded her fingers through Daniel's spider-eyed ones. "My teachers never took my eyes."

Beatriz stared down the owl, and the owl gazed back at her with Daniel's gentle expression. It was not so terrifying when she imagined it as a teacher, something positive, something trying to tell Daniel something about himself. She took a step toward it, but again, it pranced back away from her, even farther.

"It will never come to you," Marisita said.

But Beatriz thought she knew what Daniel's darkness stood for now. She did not like the conclusion she had come to, which is how she knew it was free of her personal bias. The lesson Daniel was meant to learn was that miracles were made to be interfered with. He was never supposed to be able to banish this darkness alone. His darkness was a puzzle that was meant to be solvable only by another Saint.

"I think it will," Beatriz said in a smaller voice. "Because owls are very attracted to miracles."

Marisita said, "Who are you going to perform the miracle on?"

Beatriz said, "Myself."

32

This was Beatriz's thesis: The Sorias must have once upon a time confronted their own darkness in the same way that all pilgrims were asked to confront their darkness. Somewhere along the way, a Soria must have lost the taste for facing their demons, however, and either died before performing the second miracle, creating a legend, or merely stopped the practice in its tracks, proclaiming Soria darkness too difficult to tackle. And so Sorias forgot how to solve their darkness, and they let it build up inside them until it became too treacherous, with a handful of Sorias being struck down each generation, falling prey to years of backed-up darkness.

The only way Beatriz had to prove this theory, however, was by testing it on herself. And if there was any other explanation— if Soria darkness was truly impossible, or if it had become impossible—Beatriz might become wood like Daniel's parents or blind and breathless like Daniel himself.

"Take Salto and go," she told Marisita. "I don't know what will happen."

"I won't go," Marisita said. "I endured my own darkness and I will endure this, too."

"Then take Salto and at least ride a little ways off so you can watch safely."

She waited until Marisita had retreated just a little with Salto, and then she went to her cousin. She tied her bootstrap to his wrist so that nothing could carry her away from him before she could give him back his eyes and breath. She called her thoughts back down from where they were soaring with the buzzards and the other lechuza, the one with the woman's face, the one who had hatched from the fire. Then she peered at the strange owl still on the ground, the one with Daniel's face.

Do you have darkness inside you?

Beatriz thought of how Marisita had just overcome her darkness, and the twins, and Tony.

Do I have darkness inside me?

She remembered those owls sitting on the edge of the radio telescope, watching her hopefully, and she knew that she did.

The miracle swelled inside her.

The lady-faced owl dipped down low from above, finding the promise of the miracle irresistible, but that was not the owl she needed. She let her pending miracle rise even farther, huge and terrifying. It was such an enormous, backed-up miracle that it began to call to owls as far away as Bicho Raro, and beyond. She heard their distant cries as they began to flap toward this scrub as fast as they could, hoping to get to her before it was over.

The miracle grew so much that now, finally, the owl with Daniel's face could not resist its call. It hopped slowly toward her, as she had hoped it would. All of its evasion was gone: It simply wanted to be as close to this oncoming miracle as possible.

She let the miracle out.

Immediately, she felt darkness surge up behind it. If you have never had a miracle performed on you, you cannot quite imagine what it feels like to have your invisible darkness suddenly given flesh. It is a little like reaching for a step and finding there is no ground beyond it. The sudden weightlessness and vertigo make it seem for a brief moment like you have no body, but you realize a second after that you will be given this body back just in time for it to be dashed to the ground. It is not fear, but it is something people are often fearful of, so it is easy to see how the two are confused.

Beatriz's vision began to narrow. She was going blind, like Daniel.

Doubt widened.

Doubt was not truth, though; it was opinion. She pushed past it to a fact: She needed to get ahold of the owl with Daniel's face before her miracle left her completely blind.

As black curtains pressed on either side of her line of sight, she seized the owl. It was not a real animal after all; it was only fear and darkness under her fingers, which seem solid only until you have them in your grasp. She tore Daniel's face from it and sucked his breath into her mouth. She saw his eyes appear on her own hands, painted lightly, like his spider eye tattoos, and she knew that she had taken his vision from the owl merely by touching it. It no longer wore his face or ears, so she knew she carried them too. The owl nodded to her, and Beatriz saw that it had wanted her to figure out this puzzle all along.

She couldn't thank it for the lesson because she still held Daniel's life breath in her mouth, and she couldn't let it escape until she reached him. So she simply nodded back.

The owl vanished at once with a sound like a wind kicking up in the distance.

Above her, the other, lady-faced lechuza swept low, right over Beatriz. The owl's wings brushed her face and she just had time to catch a glimpse of how it was now wearing Beatriz's eyes.

Then everything went completely black.

She did not have much time. Now that Daniel's darkness was gone, the only breath he had was in Beatriz's mouth, and it was useless there. Lost in darkness as complete as night, she hurriedly felt along her bootlace to Daniel's wrist, and then from his arm to his chest to his face. Leaning swiftly, she breathed his breath back into his nostrils first, so that he would not die, and then she pressed his eyes back onto his eyelids and his hearing back into his ears.

She did not think she could bear it if it was too late.

Because Beatriz existed mostly in her own head, she was never generally overcome with wanting for anything that she didn't have. The things that made her happiest didn't have concrete forms, which made them extremely hardy. Ideas couldn't die.

Cousins could die.

She wanted Daniel to be alive, and the ferocity of that wanting hit her harder than anything she had felt so far. She could not believe she had told Pete Wyatt that she didn't have feelings, that *anyone* would have told her that she didn't have feelings, because even if the force of her fear for Daniel's fate hadn't convinced her of their existence earlier, the force of her wanting him to be alive now would have.

Daniel gasped.

She gave herself only half a second of relief before she hastily untied herself from him. His darkness was cured. Hers was not. That meant that her second miracle could be interfered with, and even though Daniel's lesson was that Sorias could interfere with miracles didn't mean that he was in a state to help her.

"Give him water," Beatriz said to Marisita, though she had no idea if Marisita was still close. "Don't come close to me!"

"What should I do?" Marisita called.

"Don't talk to me!"

Beatriz kept backing away, hands outstretched in the blackness. Above her, the lechuza's wings batted air at her, out of her reach. There were no more miracles for her to perform to draw it close, however. And in any case, she didn't think that she was supposed to solve her darkness in the same way that she'd solved Daniel's. This was about her, somehow—a lesson, not a fearful punishment. She asked herself what she had learned, and what she still needed to learn. Casting her thoughts up again, out of herself, into the dark air above her, wherever her eyes were, she imagined looking down at the pilgrims. From that height, she considered how they had healed themselves. She mused on how the Sorias' real collective darkness was that they would not let themselves help others because they were too afraid of losing themselves, that they were so afraid of being open and true about their own fears and darkness that they put it in a box and refused to even accept that they, too, might need healing. And the longer they blocked it up, the more the pilgrims also blocked up, and the worse everything got, until husbands and wives parted and siblings fought and everything was terrible.

But this was not the puzzle Beatriz had to solve, because Beatriz had broken the taboo against helping the moment she suggested interviewing Marisita. So her darkness must be something else. Now, for the first time, she truly realized how difficult it was to be a pilgrim, a realization Daniel had just come to days before—a realization that all budding Saints should be led to. It was often so easy to identify the darkness from the outside. But from the inside, your darkness was indistinguishable from your other thoughts.

It could take forever to learn yourself.

Something touched Beatriz's hands. She flinched back, but the touch pursued her and she realized it was another set of hands, gripping hers. She tried to pull back from them, but they hung on.

"Beatriz," Pete said.

"You left," she said.

"I did."

He'd tried to, anyway. He had walked out to the main road

and he had even convinced a trucker to pick him up so that he could hitchhike back to Oklahoma. But as he thought about leaving the desert, he realized he didn't think he could actually survive it. He'd already broken his heart once that night, and he thought that if it happened again, it really would kill him. In fact, it was only love that had kept him dying from the first heartbreak. It has a way of plugging holes in the heart even as it punches new ones. But he knew there wasn't enough love in the world to help him survive leaving the desert so soon after leaving Beatriz, and so he asked the trucker to let him out. The desert was so moved by this act of love for it that it cast a wind that rose the sand and dust, and this amorous breeze rolled Pete head over heels over scrub and fence and through dry riverbed, tumbling him through the night like one of its weeds, until it brought him here to Beatriz.

Once he saw her, he knew what he needed to do.

"You can't be here," Beatriz said. "You'll get my darkness."

"I know," Pete whispered. "It's already here."

"What?"

Dread seeped through her, and he held her fingers more tightly.

"Don't let go of my hands," he said. "I can't see anything."

Faith is a funny thing, and Beatriz, as only a reluctant Saint, had never truly accepted it. But now Pete was relying on her to be able to cure herself so that she could cure him.

"How do you know I can do this?" she asked.

"I reckon I don't know," he admitted. "I don't know much of

anything about what's gonna happen. I don't know what I'm going to do now that the truck's gone. I don't know if I'm ever going to see again. But I guess I do know this: I want to be with you."

In her head, Beatriz heard all of the arguments she had mounted against the possibility of a relationship with him, a young man so kind and so soft, and her, the girl without feelings.

And then, of course, just like that, she had it.

"I was upset," she told him.

"I know," he replied.

"I was upset every time you said it," she said.

"I know."

"I don't show feelings like other people."

"I know that, too."

She hesitated. It felt very peculiar to express this out loud, but she suspected that meant she was supposed to. "But that doesn't mean I don't have them. I think—I think I have a lot of them."

Pete wrapped his arms around her. He was covered in all the dust the desert had rolled him through, but she didn't mind.

"I *know* I have a lot of them," she said.

The sun rose, and they both saw it.

EPILOGUE

Miracles and happiness are a lot like each other in many ways. It is difficult to predict what will trigger a miracle. Some people go their entire lives full of persistent darkness and never feel the need to seek out a miracle. Others find they can exist with darkness only for a single night before they go hunting for a miracle to remove it. Some need only one miracle; others might have two or three or four or five over the course of their lives. Happiness is the same way. One can never tell what will make one person happy and leave another untouched. Often even the person involved will be surprised by what makes them happy.

And it turns out that owls find both miracles and happiness irresistible.

There was plenty of happiness to be found the night the Sorias finally celebrated Antonia's and Francisco's birthdays the following year. Marisita and Daniel danced on the stage that Pete had built, lights twinkling over their heads and rose petals swirling under their feet. Marisita wore a blue dress she had never worn before. After having to wear a wedding dress every day for over a year, she had vowed that she would never again wear the same clothing two days in a row. That night after the dancing was done, she would sit at the kitchen table with Antonia as she had every night before, tear the seams out of the blue dress, and sew herself a new one. Daniel held her fondly as they danced, and his hands bore eight more tattoos: eight closed half-moon eyes just below his open spiders' eyes, to remind him of what he had learned during the hours that he could not see.

Antonia and Francisco had just finished dancing, and now they exchanged gifts while Judith looked on with joy. Antonia presented Francisco with a small box. When he opened it, he discovered a shapely, night-black rose. It was not quite as perfect as the one he had been hoping to breed, but that was because she had fashioned it out of the ashes of the box truck. Francisco kissed his wife in delight, and then he retrieved a large box from the table behind him. When Antonia opened it, she discovered a black-and-white collie puppy. It was not exactly the same as the one he had owned when he met her all those years ago, but this one had a bigger smile. Antonia said, "I love dogs."

Pete and Beatriz had yet to dance. Currently, they both sat on the blackened wire mesh platform of the radio telescope, looking down at the festivities from above. From here they could see Marisita's family joyfully chattering near the stage (Max had remained in Texas with his anger for company), and they could also see Joaquin demonstrating the use of the turntable and speakers to one of Marisita's younger sisters. His bag was already packed beside him; he was headed to Philadelphia that summer, but he'd promised to stay for the party. He was on his way to becoming Diablo Diablo even during the daytime, and the Sorias couldn't have been more proud.

"I'm happy," Beatriz told Pete. It was a sentence she wouldn't have thought to say out loud only a few months before.

"Me, too," Pete whistled back.

Above them and below them, owls began to cry out. They lifted from the rooftops and soared off the edge of the radio telescope, and Beatriz and Pete hurriedly descended to discover the source of the commotion. All of the Sorias watched as a pair of headlights slowly pulled up beside Eduardo Costa's beloved stepside truck. Owls careened toward the newcomer, some of them landing on the vehicle itself. Owl talon on metal is not a fortunate combination, and the sound is equally unpleasant.

The lights turned off. It was a large farm truck with the words DOUBLE D RANCH painted on the side of it.

This was Darlene Purdey, the owner of the rooster Pete had repurposed the previous summer. Deprived of her prize fighter, she had shifted her focus from hosting cockfights to searching for the two young people who had taken him from her. After all this time, she had finally tracked them to Bicho Raro by means of a classified ad—the Sorias had listed Salto for sale in the newspaper, and Darlene had recognized him from his description alone.

Now she climbed out of the truck, a shotgun hooked over her elbow. She was no less bitter than she had been the night that Pete and Beatriz had burst onto her ranch. Darkness had only continued to layer on top of her existing grief until now she could barely move for it. All she did was sleep, and look for General MacArthur.

"I'm here about a rooster," she snarled. She swept her free hand over herself, attempting to clear the chaos of owls away from her. Some of the smaller birds had settled around her feet, flapping and trilling. They barely moved when she nudged the toe of her boot at them.

"Lady," Eduardo said, "you look like you need a miracle."

Darlene snapped, "Yeah, have you got any of those lying around?"

The Sorias faced her.

"Yes," Daniel said. "We do."

ACKNOWLEDGMENTS

There are quite a few crooked saints I'd like to thank for the making of this book. The team at Scholastic has been a ceaseless champion for years and continues to be, but for this novel, I must particularly point fingers at my editor, David Levithan. He could tell what I wanted this book to be long before it had become the book I wanted it to be, and worked joyfully to close the difference.

Thanks to José de Jesús Salazar Bello, for advice before I began; to Francisco X. Stork, for advice while I was writing; and also to my two sensitivity readers, for their advice after I had finished. They were all incredibly generous with their language and stories; all inconsistences and errors are entirely mine.

A tip of my hat, as ever, to Brenna Yovanoff, Sarah Batista-Pereira, and Court Stevens for hours of wordplay.

Thanks to Ed for holding my hands in the darkness.

And thanks to my old Camaro, which hurtled and lurched its failing way into a small Colorado town years ago. I was looking for a miracle, but I got a story instead, and sometimes those are the same thing.